THE PHANTOM SONGBIRD OF NEW YORK

ALSO BY STEVE ZOUSMER

"Famous" with Richard Liebmann-Smith

TV News Off-Camera

Galapagos: Discovery in Darwin's Islands, with Dr. David Steadman

You Don't Have To Be Famous: How To Write Your Life Story

How To Write For The Big Guy

Falling Into The Mob

THE PHANTOM SONGBIRD OF NEW YORK

a Novel

STEVE ZOUSMER

ZOUSMER
BOOKS

NEW YORK, NEW YORK

Library of Congress Control Number: 2020912491

   Steve Zousmer, author
      The Phantom Songbird of New York / Steve Zousmer
      New York, New York; Zousmer Books
      ISBN: 978-0-578-72322-8 (paperback)
      ISBN: 978-0-578-72323-5 (ebook)

Cover Design, Lon Kirschner: www.kirschnerdesign.com

Printed in the United States of America

For Ginger

CHAPTER 1

The whole thing started the day Sinatra phoned to call me an asshole. Frank's call came at almost the same moment I was being called an asshole by my boss, Sid Lepanzer. Either one of them calling me an asshole wouldn't be a shocker but what are the odds that *both* would decide at virtually the same moment that despite my status as one of New York's premier gossip columnists, I needed a tongue-lashing?

Who else wanted to join the Dump On Chick Lopritz Club?

Would Ike give me a snarly buzz from the White House?

Would Elvis kick mud on my blue suede shoes?

Let me explain how I got into two doghouses on the same day and then got into much bigger trouble later.

First, Sid.

Sid was steamed because a rival columnist aced me on a gossip item. It was a tasty tidbit about Salvador Dali setting fire to a menu at Sardi's after a rich lady saw him doodling on it. She figured a doodle and signature by a world-famous artist like Dali would make that menu a high-value collector's item, so she offered him all the cash in her purse for it, said to be about two hundred dollars.

I guess Dali was insulted by two hundred dollars. Or maybe he was just doing his temperamental artist shtick. I didn't know because I'd missed the story completely. My tipsters had been asleep at the switch. (Like my distinguished rivals, I've got a network of spies—maître d's, bartenders, waiters, cigarette girls, and hang-around guys. They see things and they call me and I toss them a sawbuck or more for usable items. Someone should have buzzed me on the Dali thing. Somebody let me down. Somebody would get a punitive punt in the papayas.)

I didn't even know about the Dali screw-up till noon when my assistant, Dawn, rang in with my daily wake-up call. I put her on the story and before I was shaved, showered, and suited up for another shift on the Broadway gossip beat, she called back saying the story was a half-and-half, meaning half true and half bogus.

I relayed this to Sid who was momentarily soothed. If the story was even half bogus he was glad we'd missed it. Sid has scruples. He's not at ease with what passes for accuracy in the gossip trade. It's not that we lie, it's just that our readers give us leeway to play up the entertainment value of stories as long as we maintain a foundation of truth and stop short of full-fledged fabrication.

In medieval times mapmakers gave the label "Here be dragons" to unexplored and therefore horrifying territories on their globes; to gossip scribes, outright fabrication is "here be dragons" territory. A reporter entering this territory finds himself outside the walls of journalistic protection. He finds himself wandering in a wilderness where he has no friends, no defenders, and no way back. He has violated readers' trust in the printed word and before long the dragons will catch him, breathe fire on him until he's medium rare, and chew him up like a New York steak.

As I write this, I can tell you I know how it feels because I've been there. I've been up to my chin in it. Because in a moment of craziness I did something that amounted to a sin against my profession. My motive wasn't evil but I wasn't innocent because I did it and kept doing it even when I could have weaseled out and avoided deceiving lots of people, *millions* of people. And this wayward path led me into even bigger complications, including a female angle the likes of which (as a guy with a down-to-earth romantic background) I'd never experienced. I'm not even sure how many women were involved. One, two, or three? Or just the same woman in three different forms?

I know that sounds psycho. I'll try to explain but first you need a quick fill-in on the state of my job—and my soul—when this thing got off the ground.

Much of my crazy moment reflected the titanic turmoil in the tabloid business. Nasty competition was putting the squeeze on the rules of yore. Standards were slipping through the cracks. Editors were increasingly willing to glance the other way if it meant a whammo story. Truth be told, they wanted the whammo story far more than they wanted integrity. The pressure to top yourself every day with something bigger and better (but still within the limits) led to fear and frayed tempers. There was lots of blaming and backbiting, lots of bellowing and blowing up. A day at the office was like getting a ten-round beating from Rocky Marciano.

At my paper there'd been firings and constant rumors of firings. We worried that the paper itself was on the brink of going belly up, not just because of slumping advertising in a bad recession but also because a new generation of the McAdoo family had taken the helm and didn't know its tits from its toenails.

The new co-publishers were the callow thirty-one-year-old McAdoo twins, Duffy and Kingsley. We called them the Anus Brothers. Their father, Chester, who'd lost his marbles and been put out to pasture in a luxurious retirement lodging, was a larger-than-life ruffian and entrepreneur who delighted and terrified everyone with his swashbuckling but brilliant ways. But for all his faults, Chester loved the paper, treasured it as a family trust, and would be a lion in its defense, unlike his midget-minded progeny who were assholes (hence their nickname), spineless and embarrassing twerps who, if the ship went under, would simply skim the leftover assets and grab the next Bentley to horse country.

In the war I'd served in the army under brave officers who didn't let their fears spread to the troops but the Anus Brothers never took Leadership 101: They let panic flow into every nook and cranny, into the elevators and air shafts and down the stairways in never-ending threats and warnings and rash decisions that accomplished nothing but creating ulcers and ugliness and beaucoup de bad thinking by everybody including me.

This turbulence was eating Sid alive. Prowling the newsroom in shirtsleeves with his tie unknotted, a substantial spare tire drooping over his belt and a pained expression on his face, he had the look of a man with a perpetual bowel obstruction. His tantrum about the Dali story was not so much anger at me—hey, everybody misses an item now and then—but a foretaste of what would come down from upstairs. The Anus Brothers rarely gave a hint that they read any of the paper's better journalism but they *studied* the gossip columns. They would spot my Dali screw-up and a hurricane of horseshit would come splattering down upon the balding pate of poor Sidney Lepanzer, and from there it would slide downhill to the likes of me.

This sort of thing made for unrelenting tension and there was only one emotional release from it: yelling. Guys in the news biz lived to yell. It's part of the newsroom tradition, compensating for bad pay, no future, and a low standing in the community. I called it "fuck-yelling" because it sounds like "Fuck, fuck, fuck you, fuck me, fuck this, fuck that." Then you hurled a pencil or kicked a wastebasket. You topped it off with a big loud final

FUCK! and felt momentarily manly instead of emasculated. You forgot that we in the news racket were just a chorus of chipmunks jabbering in the background while the real actors did whatever it was that made a difference.

The cynicism I'm expressing here is fairly new to me. It replaces the opposite view that carried me through my idealistic youthful days in news-papering. It puts me at an ever-expanding distance from fellow scribes who still think of themselves as ink-stained knights in the truth crusade.

Three things set this separation in motion for me.

One was an accumulation of disgust with the crap I saw as a gossip columnist: egomania, preening and pretending, money-grubbing, groveling, malice and mud fights, pathetic greed, lust and envy and colossal smallness of character and spirit—all of which would be a big yawning ho-hum *except* when it involved people who'd been tapped by the magic wand of celebrity and therefore seemed to merit slavering attention.

I'm not looking down on the gullible masses who ate this stuff up like Alpo. I'm not calling anyone a sucker or dimwit. I was just as bad. Once I caught the fever of gossip writing, no one was more magnetically attracted than me to Celebrosaurus Rex. I used to love hobnobbing with the stars and chasing them around and I'm not saying they're all bad because some of them are quite okay. But I was starting to get sick of it.

This was a fairly recent development. I hadn't really confronted it yet but it was coming on like the flu.

A second thing pushing me away from the gossip racket was the contrast with truly important things. I was in the war in Europe and saw nightmare stuff that hugely dwarfed scenes like a half-sloshed movie star flinging a baked (or mashed) potato at a rival star at another table. But in the past few years I'd had a close-up view of something more personal, namely my wife's horrible decline and the wreckage of our married life. What happened to her really opened the drain on my enthusiasm for sleaze. She had been my partner in gossip-gathering and she made it fun and enjoying it made me good at it. We wanted it to go on forever but when she couldn't hack it anymore, the carousel stopped and my heart was never in it again. The whole thing started being an insult to things that really mattered.

A third cause of my changing attitude was the shocking discovery I'd made on my recent birthday: I was forty-two years old. How the hell did this happen? I was no longer a kid. No longer an eager beaver. Forty-two is when you look in the mirror and reality looks back at you with a big snicker on its face. You see who you are and what you're never going to be. Chick Lopritz would never be ranked among the likes of Humphrey Bogart or

Edward R. Murrow or Mickey Mantle or Jonas Salk or Pablo Picasso. Not even close, not even honorable mention. The future was no longer a joyous destiny waiting to embrace me and shower me with opportunities. The odds of a leap to a new and wonderful level of life were about as unimaginable as getting all the way through *Ulysses*.

At forty-two and beyond, hanging on is all you can hope for. Anything more earthshaking than that would require a stunning but highly unlikely turn of fate.

And luck.

* * *

I was confident that my increasingly sour attitude had not visibly seeped into my professional performance. Let no man try to pin the newspaper's troubles on me. In fact, I was something of a star attraction. I'd penned a must-read celebrity column in New York for eight years. My jottings were syndicated nationwide to ninety-one papers. At one point ninety-eight papers around the country ran my column but instead of cresting the hump at a hundred I've been in a mild backslide, which was pointed out to me in every fuck-yelling office encounter. But I don't suffer like Sid. He's a devoted tabloid newsman and his world is past its peak or soon will be, and he's grieving. I feel for him. And I take it as a tender sign of friendship that he prefers yelling at me to going into a newsroom full of shrieking crybabies and yelling at *them*.

Sid was soaring toward the zenith of his Dali-related chew-out when Dawn stuck her face in the door to say Sinatra was on the line waiting to talk to me.

That silenced Sidney. Personally, I figured it was fake, a clever dodge by Dawn to get Sid off my back and maybe even impress him that I routinely received direct calls from the gods of show biz. It couldn't be for real: Frank Sinatra seldom called reporters because he equated members of the Fourth Estate with blind disgusting little worms that slithered across the ocean floor. He'd only phoned me once before.

"Chick," Sinatra said, and one syllable was all it took to identify his golden pipes. For a few words he was mock-friendly but you could hear the blast building up. "Oh, and did I forget to mention that you're a complete asshole, you shithead? An utter asshole? And what else?"

What else? What did that mean?

A familiar voice in the background said, "A parasite" and another called out, "A rancid piece of ordure," and there was an explosion of uproarious manly laughter. Frank, chuckling, said, "You're a parasite and a rancid piece of—"

"Ordure," came a voice.

"What the hell is ordure? Give me another."

"Incompetent dung flea on a Mesopotamian sleaze dog."

He threw that one at me too, laughing now.

I got the picture: Frank was sitting around having P.M. cocktails while entertaining his amigos with sadistic abuse of the lowly Yours Truly. It was the whole exalted Rat Pack in the background heaping scorn on me. Dean. Sammy. Joey Bishop. Maybe Peter Lawford, though Lawford had class but on the other hand he was desperate to be in Frank's club.

Frank paused. I didn't know why—to freshen his drink?, to await more suggestions?, to give me an opening to jump in with a groveling apology? I was willing to do the groveling apology bit—it was part of the game when you deal with the kings and queens of the fame world—but I wasn't sure what I'd be groveling *about*. My most recent Sinatra item reported that he'd left a club in the wee hours with a glamorous actress who'd suffered an acute bout of loneliness caused by her husband leaving a few hours earlier for a movie shoot in Morocco. I hadn't personally witnessed Frank's arm-in-arm exit with the actress but my source was solid.

Frank relished his reputation as a lady killer and his anger about gossip items like this was usually feigned, but on this particular score he clearly wanted to backtrack. I guessed the husband in Morocco had gotten wind of my report and issued some threats of facial rearrangement.

"That broad I walked out with was the hat check girl. I was only help-ing her find a taxi in a dark and dangerous part of town."

"How dark was it?" came a voice I recognized as Sammy Davis Jr.'s Amos 'n' Andy voice. This prompted more background hilarity.

"Henceforth," said Frank, "you will never again mention a broad I happen to go out a door with, especially if said broad has a certifiably violent husband. If you forget that, your prize will be a very unpleasant subdural hematoma."

"And how subdural would that hematoma be?" came a voice. Dean Martin's.

"Asshole," yelled Frank, slamming down the phone.

CHAPTER 2

Luckily I kept the phone pressed to my ear so Sid didn't hear Frank's thundering sign-off or the ensuing dial tone and therefore didn't realize the call was over. Telling Sid that Sinatra had called me an asshole and the entire Rat Pack had just enjoyed a humiliation gangbang with me as its guest of honor did not enhance my professional standing, so I pretended the conversation was still in progress.

"Thanks a million, Frank, I appreciate the kind words and flattery. Now tell me more about that huge deal. Pour on the details."

I grabbed a pad and pencil as if I had to take notes. In fact, I did fake a note, the name LIZ TAYLOR scrawled in large letters, which I made sure Sid could see. Then I made a gesture to Sid, waving him out of my office—the big-time columnist was busy gathering news, gimme a rain check on the chew-out. It worked. The whole thing turned into a plus. It never hurt to snow your boss, banking a few victory points for a rainy day.

With Sid gone, I thanked Dawn, explaining that I figured she'd come up with the Sinatra call to fake out Sid.

"I'm good but not that good," she said.

But she was that good. No, she was great. A street girl from Queens with a ton of sass and vinegar, loyal, fast on the uptake. She would have been a beauty too if not for the large and slightly hawkish Roman schnoz she got from her father, my old Army buddy Leo Linguino, but she made up for it with a neat figure and trim hips that only a twenty-four-year-old could sport. She was not averse to swiveling those hips in the newsroom and when the horny hooting and howling began, she was brazen with the upraised middle finger and the big smile.

"My mom and dad will be so thrilled at this," she said. "Imagine me on the phone with *Sinatra*. I almost told him I was free tonight if he wanted to get together for some pasta fazool and a roll in the Wesson oil."

She winked and did her best swivel back to her desk. Then she returned, curious. "So what did he say? Sinatra."

"Called me an asshole."

"That's what he called you the other time."

"Yeah. He's steadfast in his opinions."

I pretended it didn't bother me. But it did. Who liked it when one of the world's top stars kicked you around like a turd?

Dawn sensed my hurt feelings and bought me a Baby Ruth bar out of the vending machine.

She said, "You realize Sid's in a state of arousal now. He's going into the editorial meeting to crow about the Sinatra/Liz Taylor scoop his best columnist's getting. What are you going to do, given that you have nothing?"

The thing about Dawn: She grasped the concept of cause and effect, the concept of consequences. Most of the people I know wouldn't know a consequence if it bit them in the ass.

I replied with an anecdote. "I was at a banquet a few years back for a prominent journalism honcho, Richard Creighton. He got up to speak, utterly shitfaced, knee-walking drunk. He says, 'There's one secret to success and tonight I'm going to reveal it for the whole world to know.'

"Then he takes another big noisy slurp of his scotch and stretches out the dramatic pause. Then he reveals the big secret: '*Always lie.*'

"This stunned the audience. He then tried to tack on 'Words to live by' but somewhere between 'to' and 'live' he stumbled and fell backward off the dais. Gone. Never to be seen again. To this day I don't know if he got hurt or what. The scene was topnotch slapstick, movie comedy at its finest. I should give it to Billy Wilder."

"You're telling me you'll just feed Sid a straight lie?"

"I'll say it was a heads-up on a movie deal but the deal went south, like most deals do. If it comes north again we get first dibs."

"So you've got no story for tomorrow's paper? Sid'll be beaked at that."

Beaked. Meaning annoyed but to me the mention of beakage called attention to her hooked proboscis. I was thinking I adored this girl and if I ever fell into money, I'd treat her to a nose job. She'd be something else with that one flaw repaired. Sinatra *would* want to slide around in Wesson oil with her.

"You got anything promising for tonight?" she asked.

No. There was zero on the calendar for that night. Zilch. No events, no parties or promotions, no big stars in town. It cut right to the deepest fear in the heart of a columnist: coming up short, not having enough to fill his column.

"Nothing but nada," I said. "I could be in deep do-do. I need B-copy. Plumb the crap pile. Whip the tipsters into action. We'd better get going."

I turned to the phone as Dawn hustled back to her desk where she thumbed through the "crap pile," a stack of press releases plus scraps of papers with scrawled wisecracks submitted by nebbish ghostwriters. Flacks called in these lines hoping I'd attribute them to their clients, many of whom had never said a witty thing in their lives.

My calls achieved nothing except making me sound desperate, which is bad for business. People should think I was rolling in material, that I was a magnet for it. The truth was that I'd had many experiences of hitting two A.M. with nothing to write and my night editor, Brian Mahoffey, clamoring for copy.

So I'd had to sit down and spin something out of nothing. Speculating. Rehashing old stories. Spending a lot of words on descriptions or remembering things that happened on that date five years ago. All of which were excuses for having nothing new. But in the columnist trade, it was what you wrote *when you had nothing to write* that proved your mettle and won the plaudits of your peers.

Dawn came back holding a press release. "This one caught my eye," she said. "It's about a girl singer making her debut at Chez Dee, in the Village."

"Chez Dee? It's not a hotspot, Dawn. It's a sleepy dive with French music and enough customers to fill half a phone booth."

Over the years I'd been to Chez Dee two or three times, at most. The Village had never been my natural habitat. It's too Bohemian for a square like me and I never saw the charm of sulky phonies like Jack Kerouac. I liked Norman Mailer one-on-one but if a crowd gathered around he would start showing off and looking for a fight.

I said, "What is it that catches your eye?"

"The name of the singer."

She circled the name: Elvire Coutansais.

I said, "An ungainly moniker, huh?"

"Who would go on stage with a name like that? I can't even pronounce it."

I called upon the soldier French I'd picked up in the war. "El-veer Coo-ton-say would be my guess. Not too catchy, eh?"

"But what else have you got?" asked Dawn. "What is it that beggars can't be?"

"Hoosiers?"

"*Choosers*."

She stared me down. Finally I shrugged in resigned agreement and picked up the phone, dialing the number on the Chez Dee presrel. The owner came on, Dee Harkovic. She had the kind of husky voice you can't develop without at least a half million cigarettes. Unfiltered. (I once caught Bogart smoking Kools. He said, "I smoke these *between real cigarettes*." Everybody loved that line when I printed it, but it turned out that Bogie had purloined it from someone else.)

Dee Harkovic said, "Believe it or not, I haven't had a nibble on a press release for at least five years."

"It might be another five but I'm scraping the barrel," I said. Dawn shot me a scolding glance for being rough with Harkovic but, like everyone I worked with, I was simply sharing my anxiety with the rest of the world in case they didn't have enough of their own.

"Tell me about the songbird."

"Elvire? She's adorable with a sweet voice. Sings French songs, like most of my singers."

"What kind of songs? Lost love? Yearning? Passion? Blues? Torch? Cabaret?"

"Mainly pastoral."

"*Pastoral?* What's pastoral? As in *pasture*? Because New Yorkers just love songs about pastures. Especially pastures knee-deep in cow shit. I was hoping for a Piaf type. Or a sultry mademoiselle with curves, like Denise Darcel. Is she sexy? How old is she?"

"Twenty-six but not a lot of curves. She doesn't have the Piaf sound but she's got the sparrow body. Five two, ninety-eight pounds. You could fold her up and drop her in your coat pocket."

"How am I going to titillate my audience with this? How does she titillate *your* audience?"

"My customers don't want titillation. They want peace. They come in for a few glasses of wine and some nice music. Come by and hear for yourself."

"I don't think so. But I'll give you a mention in the column tomorrow."

"No kidding? You're an angel, Chick."

I tapped out a couple instantly stale paragraphs and added a little embellishment about the singer's petite size and saucy Gallic charm. The plan was to hold these paragraphs in reserve as a desperation fallback, using them only if I couldn't dredge up anything better. I rolled the page out of my Royal and should have pocketed it but wasn't fast enough because Sid was back, reading over my shoulder.

"Brussels sprouts," he declared, which was his term for a story that was so unappetizing you wanted to toss it to Fido. "Dress it up or deep-six it."

Fortunately Dawn was taking a call from Dali's flack who furiously disputed the part about setting fire to the menu. The doodling and the two-hundred-dollar offer were okay—the flack bumped it up to fifteen-hundred dollars—but not the arson. It wasn't much but I could use it to spark a fight with the competition, chiding them for sensationalizing. Maybe start a feud that would provide spicy warfare and a few column inches over the next few days.

The French chanteuse story was out; the second-day Dali story was in. But I wasn't excited.

Sid gave me a look and said, "I'm going across the street."

Meaning he was going to cross the street on the way to the bar. And I was being summoned to join him. So a few minutes later I followed him across the street.

Sid drank Manhattans—I always thought it was an out-of-character choice for an unfancy guy like Sid—and had one waiting for me. I'd learned to steer clear of booze on working nights, ordering water in a short glass and pretending it was a see-through beverage like gin or vodka (celebrity drinkers get wary if you're not raising a glass to your lips at least as much as they are). My job required hanging out in bars and restaurants from evening till two A.M. and raising too many glasses was a professional hazard: Even gossip writing required a clear head which you don't have when you've been slurping the sauce. But Sid would have spotted the water ruse and under the code of manly drinking it was an insult to abstain from the real stuff. So I had the Manhattan. My advice on Manhattans: Don't let the cherry make you think it's a benign drink. It's a wicked drink, utterly malicious.

* * *

"I was just up in the throne room with the Brothers," Sid told me, gloomily shaking his head as he lit up a foul-smelling Between the Acts little cigar. "They said I was hanging by a thread."

"*You*? But you've been with the paper twenty years."

"And guess what? You're hanging by the same thread," he said, exhaling cigar smoke that nearly caused me to retch on the bar.

"Chick, you get credit for churning out some home runs and a lot of extra-base hits over the years but lately they say you're losing your 'verve and vivacity' as Duffy puts it. Kingsley was less genteel. He said you're smelling up the page."

"Like that cigar is smelling up this bar?"

"I'm serious. You're nearing rock bottom."

"Rock bottom? I thought I was near the top. I haven't heard any complaints."

"Maybe you don't have the ear you used to have."

Floundering slightly I asked, "Where'd Duffy get a phrase like 'verve and vivacity?' That's way above his verbal level."

"It's probably from one of his Yalie friends from the golf club bitching about something you wrote. Or maybe the brothers have a bone for bringing in a columnist with a hotter name, a circulation-booster."

"Oh," I said, cockily. "Like who?"

"Like Herb Caen, out in San Francisco."

"Herb Caen is great. Not for New York but great."

"The Anuses see it different. They think enough greenery will buy him out of Frisco. Which is ridiculous, he's Frisco through and through. Of course a chunk of his paycheck would be the money they'd save by firing you."

It started to hit me. I took a big sip of the Manhattan and felt my eyeballs water so bad I thought they'd fall out on the bar and roll off onto the floor. The Anus Brothers were always making threats and we lived with it but this one hit me in the solar plexus. I knew I'd lost my zest for gossip writing but I didn't think it showed.

Maybe, like a ballplayer, I was just in a slump. I'd had the feeling that *everyone* was in a slump. After the war we thought everything would be rosy, but the rosiness became grayness and the current miserable winter added coldness to the grayness. People were in the dumps, needing a lift, a laugh, something to light up their imaginations, but nothing was happening.

Especially on the celebrity front. The bad weather was keeping even the luminaries tucked in their hotel suites. Instead of cavorting in public they were tube-gazing like everyone else, watching the cowboy shows and cop shows and quiz shows. Last night, for example, there was barely a famous face to be found. Nobody (except possibly Dali) was getting drunk, nobody was flashing cleavage or throwing punches, and nobody whispered anything juicy to Uncle Chick. I'd used up all the lousy ghostwritten wisecracks I had in reserve, done a few plugs, groused about the weather, and taken a few limp shots at the mayor. I got the column finished but, yeah, it lacked verve and vivacity.

I knew I wasn't exactly ebullient about my job but the thought of being fired gave me a shiver of dread. My gossip identity was established and it'd be close to impossible to shift back to regular reporting. So it was gossip or out the door. And that would be a blow because I had a decent paycheck and needed it because I was paying most of the upkeep for a disabled ex-wife who spent her days smoking and knitting. With no salary, how could I keep her in cigarettes and wool?

What would I do? Would I have to go back to peddling wigs, which I did after the war when I was busting my ass working my way through NYU night school (with help from the GI Bill).

"Sid, what are we gonna do?"

"What you mean 'we,' Kimosabe?" he said, stubbing out his cigar. "Look, I'm demotable. They'll give me a job on the copy desk, for a while at least. You, you're a byline with an above-average salary they'd love to take off the books. Plus your girl Dawn Linguini goes too."

"Her name is Linguino," I protested, but of course she was doomed to be called Linguini. The thought of her getting the shaft because I got the boot was a kick in the chops. I tried to argue for her but Sid said, "Hey, why do we call these guys anuses? Part of it's because they don't care how they treat people. Firing people makes them think they're real businessmen."

"What about my readers? I'm part of the reason they buy the paper."

"Even more of them will buy the paper if Caen's writing for it," he snickered. "He's the class of the field. You're the ass of the field."

This was just manly razzing but I'd lost my legendary sense of humor. "What can I do?"

He shrugged. "It might be too late. But try perking things up in the pizzazz department."

"I'm doing the best I can. It's winter. There's no stories."

"Chick," he said, cutting off my whine, "are you going to finish that drink or put it in a savings account? Finish up and we'll do a refill for the road."

I finished as the next round arrived. That wasn't smart but I needed Sid and if he wanted me to have another drink, I'd do just that.

"Readers don't want brussels sprouts, Chick. Give them Baked Alaska, something with flames coming out. Make it *juicy*. People read gossip for juiciness. It's not news, it's an *escape* from news. So either get juicy again or start fixing up Duffy McAdoo with willing blondes every night."

Grimacing, he downed the Manhattan in a single gulp, popped four or five Life Savers, and stood up to go. "Sit here for a minute and think it over. You're on the hot seat, Lamb Chop. Do something."

CHAPTER 3

Do something?

I'd be glad to do something, but what?

People are always giving you advice but it's not helpful unless they tell you exactly *what* to do and *how to start doing it now*. The reason you need advice is because you don't *know* what to do or how to start.

So how was I going to start coming up with Baked Alaska? I worked hard, knocking myself out six nights a week writing my column, pouring every ounce of pizzazz into it, and it wasn't enough. So what could I *do*?

Well, I could drink more. Instead of pushing my Manhattan away like a non-idiot, I sat there and sipped it down. My reasoning was: Two Manhattans might jar me into a new reality, a bolder way of looking at things.

An example of the difference between giving advice and actually helping someone was what I did for Dawn. Five years earlier, she was just out of high school and spinning her wheels. Her father, Leo, called me up and instead of the usual joshing about our army days he sounded tense and anxious as only a father of a floundering teenager could be.

He told me Dawn refused to consider the garbage jobs most girls were getting—hair styling, waitressing, secretary, etc.—but couldn't find anything else. Leo and his wife, Betty, were scared she'd fall in with the local element, by which he meant the sons of the many Mafiosos who infested their Queens neighborhood. These young hoods were louts but they had cash and testosterone and they knew how to have fun. A spirited and good-looking Italian girl like Dawn would not escape their clutches indefinitely.

Leo and Betty were proud people who didn't ask favors, but in their distress they turned to me. This was flattering but I worried that they thought a byline in a newspaper made me a man of wisdom.

I'd known Dawn since she was ten, when Leo and I got back from overseas. I saw a lot of her parents in those days and she grew up before my eyes. She called me Uncle Chick and I loved her like a daughter. Like her salt-of-the-earth parents, she was solid as an oak. She had far too much sense to be tempted by Mafia morons, though I knew concerned parents always fear the worst.

I was the only grown-up Dawn knew who worked in Manhattan and wasn't blue-collar. She'd always been curious about newspapering and always pressed me for inside stories. I wondered if part of my own respect for the values of journalism came from hearing myself explain them to her. The idealism she felt—I'd felt it too in those days—bounced back at me from her eyes. She seemed to have an instinctive appreciation of truth, integrity, accuracy, public responsibility, and so on.

For her fourteenth birthday, I invited her to join me on an actual reporting assignment, which that day happened to be a trial. She took the subway into Manhattan and I met her and took her downtown to the courthouse. During the trial she was attentive and whispered good observations. After the trial, the judge sent a bailiff to invite her up to the bench. The judge told her he'd been watching her; he said he was pleased to have such an alert young lady in his courtroom.

In school she came to life as a student, doing especially well in writing. She was obviously a natural journalist but if you said anything about her working for a paper you got a darkened face, a scowl, a flare-up of temper which I interpreted as anger because she felt that as a female she had little chance of getting a newspaper job. Which of course was true.

I, on the other hand, had passed easily through the gates, a perfect job candidate. I was a vet from the Bronx with a brand-new college degree. I could spell and write a decent sentence and I was willing to live on slavish weekly wages which, to quote a fellow writer, were "in the high two digits." I didn't care about money. I loved being a city reporter and on one of my early stories, a fire at Radio City Music Hall (which turned out to be a false alarm), I was backstage and met some Rockettes including the high-kicking, big-smiling, redheaded Alida Minskoff, who'd escaped from Feasterville, Pennsylvania to come to Manhattan to find fun and excitement. We started dating and the fun and excitement flowed into a storybook NYC romance.

I was riding high. Great job, great girlfriend. Then things got even better. The paper needed a new gossip columnist and people pushed me for the job. I was a comer, fast and hard-driving and I had a knack for the snappy wiseass patter that clicks with gossip. I didn't want to leave real reporting. Like most reporters I looked down my nose at gossip. But a nice combo of praise and a raise changed my mind.

It's not that I wasn't somewhat fascinated by famous people, and I knew exactly when that fascination began. I grew up just a short walk from Yankee Stadium where kids were let in free to watch batting practice before games. The 1920s were glory years for the Yankees and I often went home with balls slugged and signed by immortals like Ruth and Gehrig.

But the player who interested me most was the legendary Ty Cobb of the Detroit Tigers. One day my friends and I were hanging over the field-level rail on the visiting team side watching Cobb warm up before a game. For some reason he stopped and walked over, heading right for me.

"Who you staring at, mutt?" he said.

"Tyrus Raymond Cobb, the Georgia peach," I said, demonstrating for the first time my instinct for sucking up to celebrities.

"Hey, that's pretty good. What's your name?"

"Chick."

"What kind of name is that? Chick like in chicken? You chicken of me, kid? You better be. I'll jump this fence and whup your puny ass and not give two shits for what happens next. What's your last name? Chickenlooper or something like that?"

"Lopritz."

"Sounds like a Jew name."

"My mother's not Jewish so I'm not Jewish," I said.

"You got a quick tongue and that's a Jew trait," he said, but he smiled. He snatched a pen away from another kid, wrote something on a baseball, and tossed it to me. Then he walked off laughing.

I took a glance at that ball and right away jammed it in my pocket and wouldn't show it to anyone, though my friends begged to see it. I took it home and showed it to my parents. The inscription said, "Fuck you, Jewboy, from Ty Cobb." My mother was aghast, my Jewish father was apoplectic. They ordered me to throw the ball in the trash. Instead I hid it and kept it for years until the ink faded.

I wasn't hurt by the Jewish thing. What fascinated me was the lesson I learned: that a famous ballplayer wasn't necessarily the person portrayed in the sports pages. There was actually a real person underneath his fame. In Ty Cobb's case, the real person was a vicious asshole but the point—it sounds stupid but I was eight years old—was that famous people are humans and not gods, that every one of them has a real self, a secret self they hide from the public, and you could get an inside glimpse of that self if you got close to them and got to know them a little.

Since then I'd been intrigued by who celebrities really are. Every time I'd met one I'd tried to dig down and see what they were hiding. That was exciting in my early days dealing with famous people and I shared every detail with Alida who, after a whirlwind courtship, became Mrs. Chick Lopritz. She quit the Rockettes and took a day job selling lipstick and perfume at Bloomingdale's while spending nights as my sidekick on the celebrity circuit.

We were a great couple and my column, titled "Chick's Clicks," took off like a rocket. Ads on the sides of buses showed my picture—with a fedora cocked on my head and a cigarette on my lips (even though I don't smoke). Famous people called to brown-nose for column mentions. I got free tickets to everything and drinks and dinners were "on the arm," meaning nobody handed me a restaurant or bar bill. Inside the newspaper my stature kept rising. They moved me out of the newsroom and gave me an office of my own. It was a shabby little cell but to me it felt like the ballroom of the Waldorf-Astoria.

So then around 1953 comes my sit-down session with Dawn. I took her to lunch at a HoJo's in Queens and she was picking at some fried clams when, without any advance thought, I blurted, "How about a newspaper job?"

"How about no way, no how, no chance, forget about it?"

"I mean it," I said. "You come to work at my paper. As my assistant."

"Don't shit me, Uncle Chick," she said. "I'll give you three reasons why there's no newspaper job ahead for Dawn E. Linguino: I've got no college degree, no experience, and no dick."

"I'm gonna try," I said.

She thought about it for a minute and said, "I love you, Uncle Chick. I think you're full of it but if you pull this off you'll have the greatest assistant in history."

I went to Sid the next day, pleading with him to hire her, and he told me to forget about it. So I did a cagey thing: instead of fighting him I said okay but made him promise to meet her for an interview. Just talk to her, I said. Give her a little advice and send her on her way, no strings attached. He did it and loved her, as I knew he would; she was a New York girl through and through, the best.

But Sid's backing wasn't enough. Some business-side monkey tried to block her hiring so I went up to the Anus Brothers' office and handed my resignation to their secretary. Back in the newsroom ten minutes later

Sid was reaming me out for being crazy when the aforesaid monkey scurried over looking nervous and said he had reconsidered and was processing paperwork to add the Linguini girl to the payroll. A week later she walked in wearing a tight black skirt and black sweater and started as my gal Friday.

It was as good as Christmas for her, and for me too. The best part was that it was payback to Leo, going back to a cold morning in 1945 when we were running across a scraggly field in Germany after snipers opened up on us and I tripped on a root and fell, smashing my kneecap on a rock. The knee went dead. It simply refused to function as a knee. I could not get up. I knew the knee would come back to life in ten seconds or so but by then I wouldn't need a knee or anything else.

The snipers zeroed in and bullets whizzed around my head so close I recall thinking that I could reach out and catch them. I lay flat and pressed my face into the ground as if I were digging a hole with my nose, trying to get lower and stay under the fire. I was not optimistic. I figured that a square foot of frozen dirt outside of Coburg, Germany, was the last I'd see of this earth before everything went dark.

My buddies screamed at me to get up and run but I couldn't. And then Corporal Leo Linguino, to whom I had not been formally introduced, was standing over me hoisting me like a sack of potatoes. He was strong as an ox—and later became even stronger as a baggage handler at LaGuardia Airport where he's now a supervisor. He pulled one of my arms around his massive shoulders and we hobbled forward, me on one leg as bullets sizzled through the air around us.

Our situation was so hopeless we were actually laughing. After a few steps the feeling in my knee started coming back and in a few more steps I could run, and we made it to safety. It was a sorry day for German marksmanship (to our amusement the three teenaged snipers who later came out of the woods to surrender all wore thick spectacles) but it was a lucky day for me because without Leo coming along I would have ended the day as fertilizer on a German field.

That was the beginning of a great run of luck—coming home alive, getting a degree, finding my job and Alida. But now the bitter sting of Sid's warning and two Manhattans seemed to be telling me the party was over. Life was taking back the red carpet. My canoe was racing down Shit Creek and there were nasty rapids ahead.

A small insult seemed to make the trend clear: The bartender asked if I wanted a refill and when I shook my head, he said, "Hey, you're the gossip writer, aren't you? I seen your picture on the side of a bus."

I nodded with fake modesty, enjoying the recognition, and he said, "You write my favorite column, 'It Happened Last Night.'"

"That's not my column," I said. "That's Earl Wilson's column."

"No kidding? So who are you? You're not Wilson. You're definitely not Walter Winchell. You're not Ed Sullivan."

I'd had my hand in my pocket to pull out a generous tip but somehow I couldn't dig up any change for him.

Out on the street I paused for a deep breath of cold fresh air. I stood there hoping I'd be struck by a bolt of divine guidance or maybe a bus. But nothing happened.

It was too early to begin my rounds. The celebs didn't start showing up till eight or nine at the earliest. I decided to do an evening version of my usual before-work routine.

Most days I made two stops on the way to the office. I left my apartment in Hell's Kitchen around one P.M. and walked to Forty-Ninth Street for a brief visit to Saint Malachy's Chapel. I'm not religious but the old line about there being no atheists in foxholes is true and having been in foxholes I was not an atheist. I rarely said prayers or asked favors of the Man Upstairs but I did offer a grateful tip-of-the-cap for bringing me home from Europe in one piece, plus I'd learned that sitting in Saint Malachy's for a few quiet minutes, which I called "a few in the pew," felt like a spiritual rinse-off after a night of slinging the sleaze.

It didn't hurt that Saint Malachy's was "the actors' chapel." Broadway stage actors stopped in for prayers before and after performances and a few screen actors including some stars were known to come in too. I wouldn't be averse to adding a few items about celebs at worship to my column, but so far, I'd achieved no star sightings.

The church was near empty and chilly. I sat there for a while, blank-minded. Then I worked on getting into the right frame of mind for my next stop, a visit to my ex-wife.

* * *

ALIDA LIVED in the apartment we'd shared until the divorce when Alida's widowed older sister, Alberta, moved up from Pennsylvania to take care of her. Alberta moved in and I moved out, renting an el cheapo apartment in Hell's Kitchen.

Because I rarely made evening visits, I used the pay phone on the corner outside Saint Malachy's to let Alberta know I was coming over. It was too late to pick up flowers or chocolates but I searched a few newsstands for a sewing or knitting magazine. I couldn't find one but it didn't matter because Alida didn't read them. Reading put her to sleep.

It never failed to astonish me that only a few years earlier she was my high-energy nightly partner in my club-hopping peregrinations. Bringing her along was a stroke of genius. She had an open, sunny personality and her red hair and dancer's grace made her distinctive, as if she were a celebrity herself. She was great at putting people at ease and she was a pistol with one-liners. Most celebs couldn't sustain a high level (or any level) of repartee so a reporter with a gift for lively chitchat could add considerable perk to an otherwise lackluster evening.

Because of Alida, celebs *wanted* us to sit down with them. She could squeeze into a booth with a star (especially reticent characters like Hank Fonda or Monty Clift) and pretty soon said star would be yakking nonstop and probably spilling some quotable beans. And maybe allowing Alida to grab a snapshot or two with the little Leica she carried in her purse. Alida made me more popular too: I was a guy who loved his wife and hit the clubs with her every night, not just another sad sack lone wolf newshound on the prowl.

Was I a sad sack without her? Was her fade-out the point when my zeal for gossip hunting sprang a leak, when my sense of exciting forward motion hit the wall? I think back to those days and nights and wonder: Where did they go? What happened to the light in her eyes and the brightness of her smile and the explosive laugh, not to mention her gusto under the sheets?

I miss all that but it's gone, and it went fast. One day she was a sparkling forty-year-old; less than a year later she was more like a fogbound eighty-year-old: befuddled, bitchy, given to hysterical rages and inconsolable weeping. The worst part was that we could barely talk anymore. Her comprehension came and went in agitated outbursts, thoughts slipped away, fantasies and oddball reactions were baffling. She was still fairly strong and her hands were steady so she could knit though she could not follow a pattern and the sweaters she made were big enough for dinosaurs.

I took her around to every doctor on Manhattan island including high-priced specialists recommended by top celebrities, but they couldn't help. They said she was depressed (hey, it didn't take Julius and Ethel Rosenberg to ferret out that secret) and gave her pills which didn't help or made her worse. I was not going to subject her to electroshock or a frontal lobotomy and I was not going to commit her to a nuthouse unless it became absolutely necessary, which doctors said it probably would because the alarming pace of her decline indicated that her time was limited. Six months or a year, who knew?

Most of my time with her was a struggle; most of the rest of my time was dotted with sudden pangs of loss and a sense that this couldn't be happening. I had a hole in my heart that couldn't be filled. I found myself mourning someone who wasn't dead, missing someone who was still alive. This torture was undoubtedly doing damage to my sense of reality. I wasn't as sharp as I used to be and it might have showed in my journalism. I also found that for the first time in my life I was moody, surprising myself with mean or erratic behavior.

Divorce was her idea, not mine. I was ready to stick it out with her to the final curtain but she was insistent on it and clammed up when I asked why. I did my best to stall but finally accepted it. I paid the rent for Alida and Alberta; a modest inheritance from their father covered most of their other expenses. It seemed like an okay set-up, given that it was utterly terrible.

As Alberta led me into Alida's bedroom I braced for the familiar tobacco smell and the painful sight of my once-radiant wife. She was in her easy chair, wearing her bathrobe. A long Pall Mall hung from her lips and her hands were busy with those ever-present knitting needles. Her red hair had faded, her eyes were dull, her skin was as white and thin as paper and not tempting to kiss, but I did, giving her a chicken peck on the forehead and saying, "Hello, dear, how's everything?"

I'm not a guy who uses "dear" but somehow I always felt a surge of tender affection as these visits began. (By the time they ended I was eager to escape.) She still recognized me and nodded.

"So what do you girls do at night?" I asked with false cheer.

Alberta said, "It just so happens that it's time for our whiskey sours. Care to join us?"

Given the two Manhattans coursing through my veins and a work night ahead, I didn't want to say yes. But I didn't want to say no. It sounded like the whiskey sours were the high point of their day. Obligatory. Alberta went to the kitchen and mixed them in a noisy blender.

A strong impulse from long ago made me want to tell Alida about the conversation with Sid and my worries about being fired, but of course I had to choke back that topic. She'd either be distraught or baffled. Instead I searched my recent memory for something upbeat.

"I ran into Shirley MacLaine the other night." I said. Alida had liked Shirley, as I did. I'd stopped by Jilly's (a big Sinatra hangout but he wasn't there) and there she was, magnetic and wearing what appeared to be a see-through blouse (close verification seemed inappropriate). She gave me some funny lines and loony chatter which I used in the column the next day.

Alida asked, "Is Shirley still doing it with Jeffery?"

I'd been through this sort of thing before. I could wrack my brain for a week trying to figure out who Jeffery was and then realize there was no Jeffery. There was no Vincenzo from Milano and no Fernando from Rio.

"Jeffery's a fairy anyway," she said. "She should cut off his stones."

I let this pass. I was groping for something to say when Alberta carried in a tray holding three whiskey sours, big ones served in tall glasses with cherries on top.

"What else with Shirley?"

There was nothing else. Except the see-through blouse. It didn't seem right but there was nothing else to say so I mentioned it.

Alida was unfazed. "Did I ever get Shirley's measurements? She's a big girl, isn't she?"

This was a remnant of gossip column professionalism. I'd always been shy about asking actresses for measurements but Alida jumped in and never failed to get them, often after cornering the actress in the ladies' room and teasing out the magic numbers. Measurements of busts and waists and hips had become close to mandatory in the column world. *Buxom* was a highly coveted adjective, along with *bosomy, voluptuous,* and *curvaceous.*

Alida and Alberta were showing no mercy to their whiskey sours, drinking them like lemonade on a hot summer day. I took a good swig of mine. It was powerful.

I asked, "What are you knitting?'

"A sweater for Andy to wear to college."

Andy was our teenage son. Not really. We had no kids. We'd planned on three or four little redheaded monsters but missed the boat.

Moments ticked by as we sat awkwardly. Alberta asked if I'd like another whiskey sour. I declined. Alberta said, "We never have more than one. Ten minutes later we're out like lights."

I bet. In her day Alida had handled more than her share of booze but now the alcohol hit her like a hammer. I wanted to split before she conked out.

Alberta asked to speak with me in the kitchen.

"She's getting worse," said Alberta. "She controls herself when you're here but otherwise she's difficult. Too much for me, Chick. But here's what I want to ask you. I've found a woman who can come in and help out."

She waited. I was supposed to give permission, which I did with a nod.

"She's from Germany. Is that okay?"

"Why wouldn't it be?"

"You fought Germans in the war."

"It's okay. If she can help, it's okay."

"Her name is Frieda Waldschneider."

"Lovely, rolls off the tongue," I said. Alberta was not swift and didn't realize this was a wisecrack, so I added, "I don't care. It's fine."

"She can start tomorrow. I was hoping you could chip in a little extra. This is expensive."

"Of course," I said.

But my thinking was: What happens if I get fired and can no longer chip in?

I said, "Gotta go, Al. Gotta put the nose to the grindstone."

She gave me a hug. I went back to the bedroom and kissed Alida.

"What's your first stop?" she asked. "Toots Shor's?"

"Sure, that's as good as any."

"Give that lovable lug a big kiss for me."

I polished off the last of the drink and hurried out. I was glad to be on the street again.

CHAPTER 4

Hoping Alida's suggestion would bring me luck, I made Shor's my first stop.

As I walked in, I beheld Jackie Gleason in full life-of-the-party mode. He was three sheets to the wind—maybe more than three sheets, maybe six—and waving a glass of booze (with pinky raised) as he circled the round bar in the front room, backslapping and carrying on boisterously, hurling insults and wisecracks to the amusement of the assembled multitude. In contrast, as I took a few steps into the dining room, I saw Joe DiMaggio sitting in dour solitude in Toots's own booth, which is on the left as you enter the room.

This might sound promising: two big names, two targets of opportunity for the Big Game Hunter of gossip. But experience told me there was very little column juice to be squeezed from these two. Yes, I could and would describe Gleason's whirling dervish shtick but it would be unsatisfying because I'd have to do it *without quotes* because not a word he said was printable. And I knew I'd get nothing from Joe D, who made a point of looking away when he saw me. People thought Joe was a classy gentleman because he was handsome in a well-tailored suit (contrasting with the rest of us who looked like shapeless blocks in our off-the-rack outfits) and because of his modest-seeming restraint, but he was anything but modest and his restraint was just about being dull as an eggplant, especially when accosted by reporters. Gleason, on the other hand, was anything but dull but in my humble opinion he was manic-depressive and at this moment he was so manic and so schnockered that I knew I'd never corner him for a quote. And maybe I didn't want to because nobody had faster mood swings or a meaner Irish temper than Jackie Gleason.

I was chatting up the maître d' when Toots himself appeared. Toots and Alida had been the best of pals and he knew all about her hard times. "Tell me all about that redheaded doll of yours," he roared, throwing a heavy arm around me and dragging me to the bar where he signaled the bartender to pour me a big one, which turned out to be bourbon on the rocks. As with Sid, it was a drink I couldn't refuse. I passed on Alida's greeting and he grilled me about her condition, veering off into an intense but hard-to-follow yarn about some other woman with a bad illness.

I appreciated his big heart and concern but it wasn't getting me any column items and he brushed off my prying questions about his celebrity customers. Maybe the reason celebs hung out in his joint was that he talked a lot but knew what *not* to tell.

At last I fought my way out of Toots's grip, claiming I had to visit the john, where someone in one of the stalls was throwing up spectacularly. A guy standing at one of the urinals caught my eye and said, "That's Gleason in there. Har de har-har."

Unusable for me. Vomiting is off-limits as a column topic.

I moved on. Sardi's, Barbetta's, Jilly's, Frankie & Johnnie's, and even a quick peek into the Copa which I can't stand because of the deafening music (Alida loved the music and hit the dance floor with panache). Then I went next door and checked out the Hotel Fourteen bar (a frequent celebrity trysting spot but the trysters must have been canoodling elsewhere). Then I scanned the bar and busy tables of Danny's Hide-A-Way where the boisterous crowd included not a single gossip-worthy face. Where the hell were the celebs? Was it "Hide From Chick" night? I moved downtown to Keen's Chophouse where my usual luck failed me (judges, political bigwigs, and wheeler-dealers always in boozed-up blabbermouth moods, except tonight) and then even more downtown where I looked for colorful and inebriated artists (at the Cedar Tavern) and writers (at the White Horse). There were plenty of both but none with a famous name or a quotable line.

I was wasting time riding around in taxis but coming up with nothing. I called Dawn and asked if the tipsters had phoned in anything and the answer was no. I asked her to keep working the phone and hang around the office (all hands on deck as we faced the emergency of nothingness) till I came in to write.

I glanced at my Bulova and saw midnight coming at me like a bull in a Chinese restaurant. I decided to gamble on something different, moving out of my usual perimeter and heading down to the Village. At first I blanked on the name of the place where the French singer was opening but it came back to me, Chez Dee. My cab driver knew where it was and we got there without much trouble.

Chez Dee was obviously a former cellar, four steps down from sidewalk level. There was no name in lights, just a door with the joint's name painted in the blue, white, and red colors of the French Republic. Soft music floated up as I entered.

Inside, the light was so dim I had to stand there blind as a bat while my eyes fought for vision. A woman took my elbow and I knew it was a woman because she was on the stout side and pressed my arm into her ample breast as she led me deeper into the room.

"I'm Dee," she said.

"Chick Lopritz," I said. It felt strange to say my name. Most show business cognoscenti recognized me and I needed no self-intro.

"Didn't think I'd see you here," she said.

"I didn't either."

Spot lit on a small stage, seated at a piano, was the one and only Elvire Coutansais, singing in a voice that was indeed sweet but very small, as if she were singing to her kitty. The audience was either quietly respectful or maybe there was no audience at all—it was too dark to know. Dee guided me to a table no bigger than a pizza pie and sat down with me. A nearly melted candle flickered on the table. A waiter reached over my shoulder to put down a well-filled glass of red wine. At least it tasted red.

I said, "I guess you're not wasting money on electricity."

"My customers like it dark. Maybe they're here to hide from the world. Myself, I've been hiding here since '46."

My eyes were catching up and I could finally see her face, which was sad but likable. Pushing sixty.

"The item's not running tomorrow. My editor killed it."

"Damn. Why?"

"Boring."

"So why are you here? Slumming?"

"I don't know. Looking for something with pizzazz, because I'm told I'm short on pizzazz."

That last remark was meant to signal cynicism. Dee must have recognized the self-pitying tone after years in dark bars.

"I read your column," she said. "You've got enough pizzazz to go around."

I nodded at the stage. "So this is Elvire?"

"It isn't Richard Nixon."

All I could see was a little face, pale as the moon, with a valentine shape. She was wearing a dark dress so in the spotlight all you saw was her disembodied face. Her voice was so soft it was barely audible. I knew right away she wasn't worth an item in my column. She wasn't a story. She was a dud. And that made me a dud for being there listening to her. And that made my mood even worse.

"She needs some pizzazz, too," I said. "More than I do."

"She's new, give her a chance. She's unpretentious."

"Unpretentious doesn't flip the flapjacks in this town."

I could feel a mix of peevishness and anxiety coming on. I was wasting more time and this would not amount to anything. "Cute girl with tiny voice sings in tomb-silent nightclub" was not knock-'em-dead material.

"Her set's almost finished. I'll send her over."

I thought: why bother? But I sat there, savoring a moment of self-pity. The high from the booze had peaked and was now plunging into woozy dejection. The dismal prospects for that night and every night to follow, whether I had a job or not, pulled me even lower. The image of the ruined Alida was a hook in my heart, ripping and tugging painfully.

Elvire sang two more songs. They were in French and I spoke only soldier French, not pastoral French, so I had no idea what they were about but guessed they were ballads describing farmers tilling the soil or watching hay grow. Then Elvire said, "Merci, messieurs, dames, à bientôt." She got a scattering of applause, the spot blinked out, and when the room lights came up a notch, she was gone.

Thirty seconds later she slid into the chair Dee had vacated, delivering a new glass of wine.

* * *

"Bonsoir," I said. "Je m'appelle Chick Lopritz. Do you parlez anglais??"

"I'm from Ohio."

"I guess the English-speaking part of Ohio."

She ignored my wisecrack, or didn't get it.

"I'm from the town of Worthington, just north of Columbus. I have a good French accent because my parents are French and I took French in school."

"So you're an Ohio girl who took French in high school? Very glamorous. My readers will be thrilled."

"I don't understand," she said.

"So what brings you to NYC, Elvire?"

"Don't lots of young women come to New York? Seeking more fulfilling lives."

Sure they do. Alida was one of them. Looking at this girl, fresh off the boat from the hinterlands, gave me a surge of nostalgia for Alida's joyous early years in New York when the dream actually came true. But the other side of nostalgia was a stab of sorrow about the next part of Alida's story, the cruelty of her brain going on the fritz. The thought of it made my mood even surlier and infected my attitude toward this poor child sitting next to me. I told myself: Do not blame her for being young and hopeful, do not punish her for not being Edith Piaf or being useless as a column item.

Not her fault. Don't be a jerk.

"Yeah, they pour in, don't they?" I said. "Stars in their eyes, like chicks rushing into the wolfhouse. A year later they're brokenhearted and maybe knocked up and riding the choo-choo back to Hicksville. Back to Mom and Dad and the old boyfriend. His name is Wayne or Ralph and he works in the lumberyard and bowls on Saturday night and so much for excitement and fulfillment."

"My goodness," she said, trying to smile.

"It's an old story. Be careful, okay?"

"Okay," she said. Her smile was gone. I'd wounded her.

"There are always exceptions," I said, weakly trying to reverse my negativity. "Let's hope you'll be one of them." I washed this down with a gulp of wine.

"Do you think I can succeed in New York? As a singer?"

I started to say, "Not a chance," but that was too mean even for me and what did I know about cabaret singing? I was a pop music/show tunes guy. The singers I knew were Broadway belters who sang like they feared you were about to go deaf. I'd been at parties talking to singers who would haul off and sing a whole song at full volume six inches from your face and believe me, that's too close.

Elvire was too small. The voice, the body, everything was small and New York doesn't get excited over smallness. On the other hand, I was beginning to realize she was somewhat adorable and had a faint facial resemblance to Audrey Hepburn, though no face could equal Audrey Hepburn's. I'd met Audrey a few times. About three seconds in her presence and you're madly in love. Which reminded me of how much I missed love.

"So, Elvire, you're an imposter here, pretending to be French."

"No. I pretend nothing. I sing the songs my parents taught me. That's all. I don't tell stories or jokes."

I thought: You should try, because your act is pretty close to weightless. But I said, "What did you do in Worthington, Ohio?"

"I drove a taxi."

I laughed. Elvire behind the wheel of a taxi clashed comically with the image of the brash cigar-chomping New York cab driver. It turned out her father owned a fleet of two cabs and she was one of his drivers.

She added, "Sometimes I worked in the nursing home. My mother is a nurse."

I looked at her for a long moment, expecting more but nothing came. This wasn't the usual show biz interview, where the interviewee chatters a mile a minute trying anything to impress you, dropping names or gabbing about upcoming glory or telling some bullshit story from their past. Celebs dread dead air but Elvire was no celeb. She was an authentic person.

"Dee says you write for the newspaper, Mr. Chick. Why are you here tonight? Is there news here?"

"No. That's the problem."

"What kind of stories do you write?"

Her innocence and vulnerability irritated me. And her question embarrassed me. I would have liked to say I wrote about defense policy or art criticism rather than celebrity drivel.

Instead I said, "I talked to Sinatra today."

She looked quizzical.

"Frank Sinatra? You've heard of him in Ohio?"

"Of course," she said. "You personally talked to him?"

"He called me."

"Frank Sinatra *called* you? Why?"

"We had a difference of opinion about a column item."

I meant to leave it there but there was such wonder in her face that I continued. "I wrote that he'd gone home late one night with a well-known married actress, but he claimed he only was helping the hatcheck gal find a taxi."

"Maybe he was being nice."

"No, Elvire, he was lying. If you're a superstar you can have a pajama party with just about any woman in the house and you don't choose the hatcheck girl."

"Frank Sinatra went to a pajama party?" The image amused her.

"No. No. He schtuped the actress."

"I don't understand. He did what?"

"They did the deed," I said. But she still didn't get it. "They had sex. Don't they have sex in Ohio?"

She could not find words. Frank Sinatra having sex with a hatcheck girl at a pajama party?

I went on: "So I'm guessing Frank got a ring-a-ding-ding from the husband who threatened to pulverize his ass so he came up with the phony story about the taxi. And then he blamed *me* for everything and had his butt-boy rat-pack listen in on the call."

I couldn't forgive myself for being so unkind to this little bumpkin, but I wasn't thinking about her. Was my column really smelling up the page, as the Anus Brothers said? Would they actually fire me? They'd never get Herb Caen away from San Francisco but they could always find somebody for my job, even upgrading some clever little Sammy Glick from the newsroom.

She said, "I don't like this story."

"Maybe you should have stayed in Worthington," I said.

"Do you like writing things like this?"

I gave her a world-weary shrug and drained the last of the wine.

She looked at me with something between a stare and a glare.

"There should be love," she said. "You should not do serious things without love. Good night, Mr. Chick."

She stood up and vanished into the darkness. And that happened to be just the moment I realized I didn't want her to go. I wanted to toss a lasso and reel her back in. I even thought of getting up and pursuing her through the shadows and dark tables while calling her name, but that would be pathetic and I was pathetic enough already.

So I just sat there. The alcohol I'd consumed during the evening was catching up with me but not in a happy way. More in a stagnant, anxious way. I wanted to go home and go to bed, but of course that was not an option. I still had a column to write. And I still had nothing to write about.

I got up and navigated unsteadily to the exit. What I was thinking was that, even though Elvire's style was not blunt like Sid's or Sinatra's, I'd just been called an asshole for the third time in one day. Even in my line of work three is too many.

CHAPTER 5

People often asked how I submitted the column. Sometimes I did it by phone, dictating to somebody in the newsroom. Sometimes I scribbled it out by hand back at my apartment or while sitting at a bar and had a copy boy taxi over and pick it up. Sometimes I went back to the office and banged it out on my trusty Royal, which is what I did that night around two thirty A.M.

Something was churning in my mind but it wasn't buttermilk. Whatever it was I couldn't bring it to the surface.

Dawn was waiting for me and we compared our slim pickings. She had a little more on the Dali story. I had the DiMaggio and Gleason sightings and some other small stuff, but otherwise bupkis. I hesitated when I got to Chez Dee because the story was a loser but also because I didn't want to relive my dickhead behavior with Elvire. But Dawn sensed that the Chez Dee experience was under my skin and dug it out of me.

"I don't get it," she said. "Sounds like nothing to me. Was something going on with this Elvira?"

"It's Elvire, not Elvira."

"Have you got a crush on her?"

"Are you kidding? No, she's ten years too young and twenty pounds too small."

Dawn gave me a look, then let it pass. "How many Manhattans with Sid?"

"Deux," I said, holding up two fingers.

"What did he want to talk about?"

"He said my column's leaking pizzazz and the Anuses are bitching about it. I could be in trouble. Sid's in trouble too. And you too."

"These things come and go. You'll figure it out. Why don't you just sit down at the typewriter and have some fun. Relax and enjoy yourself. Aren't you the guy who says, 'Don't be a drip, just let it rip'?"

She was right. When I relaxed and enjoyed myself, the great columns often appeared, as if dictated by celestial messenger. But when I pushed too hard, the fun went away. That could be the cause of the no-pizzazz problem. I needed to recapture the devil-may-care frivolity I had when Alida and I felt like we owned the night.

I sat down and started tapping the keys, writing a few lifeless sentences as I waited for momentum to click in. But it didn't. Everything I wrote was flat, went nowhere, built no energy. I looked out into the newsroom and saw Brian Mahoffey with his feet up on his desk having a smoke, waiting for my copy. I figured I was just having a little spasm of writer's block—every writer gets them—and the sole solution when this happens is to just keep throwing yourself against the block until it gives way and imagination surges back.

The truth was, I felt a little panicky. I was glad Dawn couldn't see it but I was feeling it. And maybe I'd had other recent nights when I'd had the same feeling that I *just didn't have it* and couldn't do it. On those other nights I'd bumbled through and gotten away with it. Maybe tonight was the night I *wouldn't* get away with it.

I asked my Royal for some help. I fed it some new paper and tried again, this time thinking hard about Chez Dee, Elvire's face in the spotlight, the dreariness of the room. My mind came to rest on that scene. Something said: Build on this. Watch quietly.

So I tried that. Eyes closed. Fingers dangling over the keyboard, waiting for instructions from headquarters.

Sid, who's worked with countless writers, told me once that even the best writers have times when they go haywire, briefly intoxicated by a writing direction that turns out to be wildly misguided though it seems at the moment to be excitingly brilliant. Suddenly this was happening to me. Inspiration arrived without knocking. I let the words come, feeling a high-flying sense of mastery and maybe a little bad-boy mischief as I hammered the keys, rushing to keep up with a flow that carried me deeper and deeper into here-be-dragons territory.

FRENCH SONGBIRD IN SMASH DEBUT
ENCHANTS DOWNTOWN CROWD
WITH SEXY SONGS OF LOVE
CHICK'S CLICKS, BY COLUMNIST CHICK LOPRITZ

"There should be love," she said. "You should not do things without love."

These were the words of Joan of Arc (place holder—I'd think up a better name later) last night in a tête-à-tête with Yours Truly after wowing the opening night crowd at cozy Chez Dee in Greenwich Village.

The jaded Village audience melted like a snowflake in Palm Beach as the lithe-and-lissome blonde wandered the vocal highways and byways of a repertory honed in record-breaking runs in Paris and Berlin.

What sincerity—and yet what sex appeal! What an exciting aura of romance about her, and what an enchanting new face arriving just in time to chase away the blahs and blues of February.

By midnight, word of her riveting performance and heart-grabbing chansons d'amour had spread like urban wildfire. The line outside Chez Dee stretched around the block and halfway to Toronto.

The late show was even more blammo than the early version. And pardon me if I sound like a softie snorfling into his Kleenex but I think the Chez Dee crowd would agree: love was in the air, romance was making a long-awaited comeback!

So, mes amis, Yours Truly has the honor of scooping the entertainment pages of Nouvelle Yorque as I extend a Chickian welcome to the new toast of the town, Joan of Arc!

There it was. I needed more to pad out the column so I tacked on quickie updates to the Dali story and a few paragraphs on Gleason cutting up at Shor's (not mentioning his prodigious yorking in the men's room) while DiMaggio brooded in the main room.

I needed a good name for my singer. Somehow an old French lyric popped into my mind: "*Sur le pont, d'Avignon, l'on y danse, l'on y danse.*"

Dancing on the bridge in Avignon. I loved it.

I called Dawn in. "You know any French girls?"

"Sure, I went to Catholic school. Half the girls were French."

"Give me a couple first names of French girls you remember most. Sexy ones."

"Sexy? Anette was sexy. Claire, who got pregnant and had to move to Nyack. She was *too* sexy. A pink-cheeked virginal blonde named Sandrine— all the boys were spazzmodic about her. She wrote poetry and seemed kind of artsy. Otherworldly."

"Bingo," I said, crossing out the Joan of Arc placeholders and writing in the new name.

Sandrine D'Avignon.

What a name! A superlative name.

I proudly showed Dawn the finished column. She sat down and read it, then looked up in dismay.

"What the fuck is this?" she said. "I don't get it."

"What don't you get, Dawn?"

"Is this a joke or something? A fantasy? This isn't real, Chick. You can't put this in the newspaper."

"I turned brussels sprouts into Baked Alaska."

"*Baked Alaska?* This Sandrine character is nothing like your little hayseed Elvira. What's come over you? Are you drunk? Cross this all out. Play it straight. Describe the real Elvira instead. There must be something interesting about her."

I pretended to think. "I'm not coming up with anything," I said.

"What was she wearing?"

"A dark dress buttoned up to the chin."

"That's no help. Does she resemble anybody, any famous person?"

"No. Well, maybe a slight touch of Audrey Hepburn."

"Yes! That's it. *The new Audrey Hepburn opened last night at Chez Dee's.* Everybody loves Audrey Hepburn. My father, my brothers, they'd commit genocide for Audrey Hepburn."

"Audrey's tall. This girl's small."

"So she's the *short* Audrey Hepburn. Who gives a crap? Just tell it. Embellish if you have to. So what if it's a little dull, you won't get fired for it."

"Sez you," I said. "Dull is now a firing offense."

"So is making shit up. And this shit is totally made up, Chick."

I said nothing. I was having a strange swirling light-headed feeling as if my axis had tilted and I was sliding into a new orbit. Very peculiar. I knew I was breaking the rules and I'd never been a rule-breaking guy but this seemed different, an exception everyone would welcome. How could they not love it? I loved it. I was kind of thrilled by it. I'd gone from panic to manic.

Dawn was on her feet, inches away from me as if she meant to physically block me from carrying the pages out to Brian Mahoffey's copy desk.

She looked stricken, shaken, ashen. "Are you hearing me, Chick? You can't do this. Tear it up. *Please.*"

I smiled and took my pages out of her hands but didn't tear them up.

"Chick, the Anuses are already down on you. This will be the last straw. Your career will be FUBARed."

FUBAR—military lingo meaning Fucked Up Beyond All Recognition.

I moved her gently aside, threw my coat over my arm, and walked past her.

"Got a good one tonight, Brian," I said, dropping the pages in front of him as I headed out merrily into the night.

CHAPTER 6

It was a classically boozy thing to do, a goofball impulse turning into a reckless, delighted, profoundly ill-advised moment in which normal restraints stepped out for a cigarette and left me unguarded against a nasty gang of fears and ragged emotions.

My anguish over Alida and my loneliness as she faded away.

My disenchantment with my job and my fear of losing it.

The sour taste caused by my meanness to poor Elvire who, the more I thought about her, the more I liked.

Also, the accusation of pizzazz deficiency. That really burned my bacon. So, with the help and support of two Manhattans, a whiskey sour, a glass of bourbon, and at least two glasses of cheap wine, I'd flipped the bird at everything that oppressed me. I'd slammed down the pizzazz pedal in a headlong, heedless display of "verve and vivacity." I'd created Sandrine D'Avignon out of thin air, journalistic boundaries be damned. I'd brushed off Dawn's urgent warnings. I knew what I was doing was wrong—and I loved it. I went home feeling exuberant.

I went to sleep smiling. But the smile was long gone when I woke up, feeling a sickening wave of reality.

What had I done?

I begged memory to tell me it hadn't happened, it was just a bad dream. When that didn't work I threw on my clothes and headed for the office, hoping I could somehow douse the flames before they got any bigger. I couldn't get a cab, so I took the subway and as the train rocked and roared, I found myself thinking about how Alida invented people, like our non-son, Andy, or Shirley MacLaine's nonexistent boyfriend, Jeffery. I had done the same thing with Sandrine. But Alida had a medical excuse. I had no excuse.

And now I was going to pay for it.

* * *

I SNEAKED into the building with my head down and climbed the back stairs, hurrying to my little office on the far edge of the bedlam of the newsroom.

Dawn pointedly did not look up.

"Sid's looking for you," she said in a flat voice. "Lots of messages on your desk."

She could not look me in the eye. She despised what I'd done. I was a traitor to journalism and I was a fool.

"Mrs. Harkovic's called four times."

"Mrs. Harkovic is who?"

"Dee of Chez Dee. The owner."

Okay. She wouldn't be happy. I took a trip to the john to gather myself. Washed the hell out of my face. On the way back, a copy boy stopped me to ask Sandrine's measurements. He said, "I'm guessing something like 34-23-34. Good but not bimbo, not excessive. Other guys are betting curvier."

I don't get the fascination with measurements. I didn't invent this fascination—a rival columnist did that—but it worked like gangbusters and I had to play Monkey See, Monkey Do. The one measurement I think of fondly was the 37-23-35 attributed to Janet Leigh. On a sunny day last summer, I was walking across Fifty-Second Street and saw her getting out of a taxi outside the 21 Club, wearing a figure-hugging white dress, a broad-brimmed white hat, and white pumps. What a sight she was. Movie-star perfection. My mind snapped a photo that would give my brain cells daily pleasure till the end of my days.

And Janet was nice too. She recognized me and stopped to chat and I was knocked out that she remembered Alida by name and expressed concern about her. Then she told me about her next movie, a Hitchcock picture. "Tony Perkins kills me in a shower," she said with a big smile. "I'm stark naked, of course. You'll love it, Chick." And I did love it, not just as an image for my personal delectation but as a five-star leading item and titillater for the next day's column. Then she gave me a wink and a cheek smooch and left me standing there. I watched the restaurant doors fly open for her; I saw men inside 21 jumping back as if a monarch was making her entrance.

But now I had to put aside luxurious memories of Janet Leigh and face Sid Lepanzer, who was bounding across the newsroom like a Jewish kangaroo. He threw his arm around my shoulder as we entered my office.

"You did just what I told you, Chick: *pizzazz*."

"But maybe a little overboard on the pizzazz, huh?"

"Word-of-mouth has been sensational," he said, grinning. "I heard people talking about it on the subway this morning. I walked through the newsroom and they were all yapping about it. The Anus Brothers called—they loved it. Loved it."

"*Loved?*"

He stared at me. "Hey, it was only a half-dozen paragraphs but this Sandrine, she hit the spot. Struck a chord or something. These things are all about timing. People are just in the mood to read about a beautiful young woman coming out of nowhere and lighting up the town. What the hell's wrong with you? You look like you just puked."

I didn't get it. I smiled. I'm guessing it was a weak smile. I'd expected beheading for falsifying a story but instead I was being congratulated. *No one realized I'd made it up.* How could that be? And it was being talked about—instead of instantly forgotten like most columns.

I had survived. For now. But my next thought was: If this was a hit, it wasn't going to go away. My trouble was just beginning.

I looked around for Dawn. I wanted to give her a "Can you believe this?" shrug which she would answer with a shrug that replied, "Beats the hell out of me." But she wouldn't meet my glance.

"Just one question," Sid said, pulling the door shut behind us. "This songbird sounds a thousand times more interesting than the one you were writing about in that B-copy last night. Plus she seems to have a different name. Explain."

"You told me to dress it up. Baked Alaska, remember?"

His voice dropped to a whisper. "I didn't tell you to win the Nobel Prize in bullshit. Tell me you didn't fake this thing. Please tell me that, Chick."

I thought of Richard Creighton saying, "Always lie." So I tried it: "The other French girl, Elvire, was a fill-in, she's not even French. Sandrine's plane from Paris was late. Elvire just warmed up the crowd till Sandrine arrived."

He exhaled. Ordinarily Sid was hard to fool but this time he was *motivated* to be fooled. He did not want to go to the Anus Brothers and tell them the story they loved was a fake and, worse, that they had a humiliating scandal on their hands.

"Chick, you could be onto a star-is-born scenario—with legs! An exciting newcomer on the scene. She adds warmth to a dull winter. She becomes a star. She's worshipped and adored. A great New York story. This yanks your ass out of the fire just as the flames are licking at your butt. Get down to the Village tonight. Pounce all over this story. Smother it. No, don't wait for tonight, get down there *now*. Find new angles. Wring it like a sponge."

Dawn called, "Mrs. Harkovic's on the line again."

"Gotta take this, Sid." He went off on an eager mission, probably upstairs to build suck-up momentum with the Anuses. I sat down and took a breath.

Dee Harkovic had been around, she wasn't going to be hysterical. But she was pretty goddamn serious, with the theme being, *what have you done to me?*

"My phone's ringing off the hook. People are walking in off the street to make reservations for tonight. They want to see the great Sandrine. Did you mean Elvire? Elvire is a darling but she's nothing like this Sandrine."

So, an immediate obstacle to following Sid's order to follow Sandrine: Sandrine would not be performing at Chez Dee's tonight *on grounds of nonexistence.*

"Chick, I don't get a mention in the paper for years and when my lucky day finally rolls around, you do *this* to me. I'm going to get blamed for no Sandrine. What am I going to do?"

"Close," I said, thinking fast. "Lock the doors and put a sign on the door saying Sandrine had an accident."

"What kind of accident?"

"Well, she's glamorous, she lives fast and free, challenges life, tests the limits. So that means she fell off a motorcycle."

"Sorry to be an idiot but how can a nonexistent person fall off a motorcycle?"

"She was rushed to the hospital."

"What hospital?"

"The one they rushed her to."

"I have to close my club because you went nuts on me?"

"Just for tonight," I said, "while this blows over. Tell your customers the staff's so distraught about Sandrine's accident that you've given them the night off to be at her bedside. And make sure you tell your people not to spill a word of this, tonight or ever."

"My people won't spill. They've been with me for years. Very loyal."

"And what about last night's audience?"

"The place was near empty. You saw it yourself. And they were just the regulars. I'll ask them to stay mum about the great Sandrine. No, I'll tell them Sandrine performed after they'd gone home."

"I'll call later," I said, and hung the hell up.

My heart was pounding. I was starting to realize I'd stepped out of one life and into another.

CHAPTER 7

Dawn came in, still withholding eye contact.

"One of the Anuses wants to see Sandrine's show tonight, although I just heard you telling Dee Harkovic there won't be a show because this nonexistent woman's going to have a motorcycle accident."

"Which Anus? Duffy or Kingsley?"

"Duffy. You're supposed to get him the best table in the house and introduce him to her."

"Duffy's a wolf, right, a real horn-dog. He'll want more than a table."

"Yeah, all the girls steer clear of him."

"Dawn, call Dee Harkovic. Tell her to reserve her best table for Duffy McAdoo and be prepared for a lecherous shithead."

She finally looked at me. "Is this a switcheroo? We're now telling her *not* to close?"

"Right. Forget closing. Doors open wide. Let the crowd in. Give Duffy his table up front."

"Yeah, but how do you provide the French chanteuse? Elvire doesn't sound like a suitable fill-in."

My brain wheels were spinning fast. "Okay, here's what we do. Just before the show we'll have Elvire get up and make the sad announcement about Sandrine's accident. Elvire being very emotional. Have her say that Sandrine's heroically vowed to get out of her hospital bed and come to the club and sing, even if it's just one song."

"Yeah, Sandrine's a real trouper. But what happens when she doesn't show up because she's either near death or nonexistent?"

"You keep harping on nonexistence."

"Don't joke about this, Chick. This is so stupid I can't stand it. You're in deep shit and spiraling downward every minute."

"And have a photographer meet me at the club."

The stress of all this conniving gave me a powerful urge to puff on a cigarette. I hadn't smoked in years but I bummed one in the newsroom and took it up to the roof, hoping I could calm my nerves and think of a way to put an end to the Sandrine lie before it got worse.

Then I saw the obvious way out: *Sandrine could die in surgery.* A dramatic scene in the emergency room, exclusively reported by Yours Truly. Doctors fighting to save her life. Sandrine, barely conscious, singing in a whisper, inspiring everyone with her bravery.

There'd be loose ends all over the place but I could bull my way through with the force of grief, dismissing all unwelcome questions on grounds of bad taste in view of the young artist's tragic demise. Her death would give me a great tearjerker column and a few aftermath columns mourning her loss. Then it would go away. My breach of journalistic ethics would be unnoticed and unremembered.

But some nagging instinct fought back. Sandrine D'Avignon was a rare and special creation, too good to toss away. I'd stumbled onto something with her. I'd made up a harmless little item never expecting readers (and my bosses) to be charmed by it. But they were, and it was a once-in-a-lifetime opportunity that cried out for milking.

Yes, there was deception involved, but there'd be no serious damage if I strung it out just a little longer to see where it would take me. I'd make a splash, maybe a big one. Maybe it would be my springboard to the highest level of gossip or something much better.

Keeping her story going would mean heavy pressure—I thought of Charles Dickens sweating over deadlines as he wrote novels in serial installments for newspapers—and my challenge would be harder because everyone knew Dickens was writing fiction while I had to fool the world into thinking I was writing fact. It would not be sustainable and sooner or later Sandrine would face an abrupt termination. But no one would be hurt. A week later it would be forgotten. It could be my big break.

Of course part of me knew this was ridiculous. But I was revved up and not in a mood for sober judgment. I flicked the cigarette out into the night and felt a lot better. I would take my chances and maybe I'd hit it big. Sandrine got a reprieve.

* * *

DEE GOT nervouser and nervouser, phoning repeatedly throughout the day. She wanted to have an early and a late show but finally realized the motorcycle drama could only be done once. She wanted to add a door charge for a midnight show but came to her senses and dropped the idea, since she'd have to refund the door charge when Sandrine didn't show. She wanted to get advice from her lawyer. I said, God no, don't do that.

Sid told me the protocol on Duffy was for me to hang around outside Chez Dee and greet him, bowing and scraping, as he arrived. I was tempted to defy the regal protocol and let Duffy McAdoo emerge from his limo without my fawning assistance, but I didn't need to add insubordination to my list of firing offenses. So I stood there watching customers push through the door. There was a genuine air of excitement. It did not take a sophisticated eye to ID the crowd as Village hipsters rushing to get a look at the hot new face before the uptown squares came running.

McAdoo's limo pulled up, discharging two couples plus himself. I'd reserved a table for him and me; now there would be six of us, if I was included.

"You're Lopritz, yes?" he said to me, showing off to his dipshit friends. I'd met him dozens of times, each time feeling his contempt as he stared down at me because he is about six foot six, a skinny drink of water, notably chinless and sporting a very prominent Adam's apple. How he could be a successful womanizer with that face and neck amazed me—I suppose it was testimony to the value of wealth, position, and horniness. The two other couples were standard issue rich young adults—the men were Ivy League twits; the blondes were Bronxville blue bloods. That's all the description you need. I barely glanced at them the whole night.

The lights were half-up inside so the crowd could find its way around. There wasn't much to see; small wooden tables and chairs, bare walls, a foot-high riser large enough for a singer and piano. Elvire, wearing an unseasonable and very Ohio-ish polka dot dress, sat at the piano, playing something the conversation drowned out.

Dee's waiters pulled over the one table big enough for six of us. I had the photog grab some flashes of us. McAdoo ordered champagne and scanned the room snootily.

Midnight came and went. The crowd was fidgety. Elvire's piano music came to a halt, which seemed to signal a transition to showtime. Elvire got up and left the room.

An uncomfortable few minutes went by. Then from somewhere I couldn't see there was a commotion including raised voices and a current of tension. Elvire reappeared and picked up the mike.

"Ladies and gentlemen, I have the most horrible news," she said in her tiny voice, as the crowd quieted down to hear her.

"The wonderful Sandrine D'Avignon has been in a very bad accident. On her motorcycle. Just a little while ago, as she was coming here to perform for you. She has been taken to the hospital. They say it is quite bad but we are hopeful."

With that she broke into tears. Convincingly genuine tears. She stood sobbing, sniffing, dabbing her eyes with the sleeves of her dress. Her performance was so good I almost forgot she was faking it, unless she wasn't—perhaps the thought of another person's accident so wounded her innocent heart that she was authentically moved by it even though she knew it was false.

I scanned the room and spotted Dee Harkovic, standing near the entrance. Our eyes met. She gave me an eyebrow gesture that said things were going well so far.

Elvire regained her composure and continued. "Sandrine has begged doctors to let her to come here tonight, in a wheelchair, so she can sing just one song to thank you for coming, but the doctors say absolutely not. I think she is very brave. Our proprietor, Dee Harkovic, would like to say something."

Just in time because the shock was wearing thin. A pissed-off rumble was percolating around the room. People were feeling disappointed, perhaps cheated. Dee stepped up on the riser and gave a philosophical smile.

"French music is appropriate to the sadness we feel now. But I must beg your indulgence; there will be no entertainment tonight. The restaurant staff has asked me to shut down immediately so we can be with Sandrine at the hospital. I am so sorry to send you away like this. Please leave your names and phone numbers at the door and you will be invited as priority guests when Sandrine is well enough to return."

The photog flashed shots of Elvire and Dee and then hurried to the door to shoot people heading for the exit.

Duffy McAdoo stood up, radiating pique. "Well, ain't this the shits," he said loudly. "Shall we go to Harlem? Small's Paradise?"

They swept out. The photog jumped in front of them for an exiting shot.

Duffy didn't waste a nod or a word on me. It was an opportunity to display his journalism leadership but he didn't see it or didn't bother. He could have instructed me to call the cops to get the story on the accident, to rush to the hospital to get the surgery and bedside angles, to find out the extent of Sandrine's injuries and gather reaction to the shocking news, perhaps even to call Paris and Berlin where she'd recently performed (to internationalize the story), and to have the photog snap a posed photo of Duffy consoling Dee.

But Chick Lopritz did not need to be told what to do.

SHOW BUSINESS HEARTBREAK!
TRAGEDY SNATCHES GLORY
FROM FRENCH SONGBIRD
CHICK'S CLICKS, BY COLUMNIST CHICK LOPRITZ

Yours Truly was there. I saw the beginning. Last night I may have seen the tragic end.

I was there Wednesday night when the meteor of Sandrine D'Avignon flamed across the night sky. And I was there last night, a witness to wrenching despair as the shocking news exploded in the faces of a hip downtown audience: the brilliant chanteuse Sandrine D'Avignon was fighting for her life after a nightmarish motorcycle accident.

Witnesses said D'Avignon skidded out of control while attempting to steer clear of an elderly pedestrian who'd fainted and lay helpless as traffic roared toward him. D'Avignon waved an arm to alert motorists behind her but the motion unbalanced her. She lost control and hit a curb, flying over her handlebars on a flight path that ended in a bone-crunching collision with merciless asphalt.

She lay there, crumpled and unconscious.

Ahead was a night of surgery rather than a scintillating onstage performance at Chez Dee in Greenwich Village where a capacity crowd awaited her, eager to hear the voice that recently thrilled Paris and Berlin.

The audience—and Yours Truly was part of it, seated upfront with publishing mega-honcho Duffy McAdoo—was stunned by the announcement of the accident. We filed out in a solemn grieving procession after proprietor Dee Harkovic said club doors would be shuttered so adoring staff could rush to the singer's bedside.

"There are no words to express my shock," said McAdoo. "This beautiful and talented young woman is the toast of Europe. We were so eager to welcome her to our shores in her first visit to America. And of course all of our prayers are with her."

At press time, the hospital refused comment but an inside source tracked down by Yours Truly said there was reason to hope: "Her condition is grave but she's showing extraordinary courage. She will not succumb to adversity."

Meet me in this space tomorrow for an exclusive update on Sandrine's condition.

CHAPTER 8

The bosses gave the story thermonuclear play, splashing my column on the front page with photos and more photos inside. Our rival papers had paid no attention and they were aced out, caught with nothing. There would be furious fuck-yelling in their city rooms but the Anuses were in heaven.

To me the motorcycle crash was just a simple lie to avoid producing a physical Sandrine. Knowing the story was false, I had no emotional reaction to it, but the public went for it hook, line, and sinker. The image of the beautiful young woman flying over her handlebars and then being at death's door produced a shocked and heartfelt response. The drama of Sandrine becoming a star was good; her tragic accident doubled or tripled the story's impact.

An hour after my column hit the streets a crowd started gathering outside Lenox Hill Hospital in response to a rumor of Sandrine's presence there. People pushed into the lobby carrying flowers they hoped to present at her bedside. Others stood on the street in a vigil, waving handmade Get Well posters they hoped Sandrine would see from her window. A hospital spokesman using a bullhorn tried to convince them that Sandrine wasn't there; they channeled their Sandrine emotion into hooting him down, calling him a liar.

Thus from the lunatic fringe of fandom came the first sign of what was to come, a preposterous but passionate citywide relationship with a woman who didn't exist. I didn't need a crystal ball to know this thing was not going to blow over. The demand for more about Sandrine was clamorous and palpable. The newspaper would milk it shamelessly. The Anuses would lash Sid into a frenzy and Sid would lash me like a dog team yipping across the Yukon in a race toward a new vein of gold.

My conscience—what was left of it—was in turmoil. I enjoyed being the creator of a hot story, but I wrestled with guilt and fretted about repercussions. I knew my guilt would get worse as I perpetrated an ongoing daily scam, telling lies in every sentence, enlarging the Sandrine story and dicking around unforgivably with the trust and emotions of my readers.

I foresaw other things too. Increasingly elaborate lying would create weak spots, factual discrepancies, and checkable details that would jump out to anyone looking into the story's veracity. Probes by reporters were sure to come. Fending them off would be increasingly exhausting. And given that I lacked a criminal mentality, living with the lie would create personal tension that might drive me into rash and regrettable behavior.

Part of me even hoped for a fast disgrace, a downfall that would expose the lie and free me from it. But in those first few days there were no signs of truth rising up to smite falsehood. The public's appetite for more and more had the momentum of a tank battalion, crushing doubt and skepticism beneath its clattering treads. The story's incredible credibility went unchallenged.

In the newsroom, the nonstop ringing of phones was deafening. Colleagues I barely knew loitered around my office holding cups of coffee, dangling lines like, "Hey, that column on the French singer was a dilly." Then they stood there hoping the compliment would tempt me to reward them with a nugget or two of insider dope on the plight of Sandrine.

Sid was gleeful, as if he'd gone to Lourdes and been cured of his bowel obstruction. When I saw Sid happy, I knew it was because the Anus Brothers had smiled upon him. His first words were about Duffy McAdoo's joy at seeing himself linked to Sandrine and how much he loved his photo on the front page (the headline was STAR SINGER FIGHTS FOR LIFE/ PUBLISHER CALLS FOR PRAYERS) along with the quotes I'd put in his mouth. Sid confided, "It didn't hurt that his sibling rival Kingsley is envious as hell."

Only Dawn held back. She was the only person in the building, besides me, who knew the whole story. The difference between us was that she still had integrity.

Sid led me into my office and closed the door.

"So Chick, did you start this rumor about Lenox Hill? Because the hospital is having a shitfit. Their bigwigs yelling at our bigwigs."

"It wasn't my rumor. Rumors like that just start on their own."

"So where is she? What hospital?"

I shook my head. I had no answer. If I was going to tell lies I would have to learn to think fast and be prepared for moments like this.

"Don't play dumb, you quoted a hospital source so you know what hospital."

"Of course I know the hospital." I considered the mountain of lies that loomed ahead of me and was tempted to stop right there and throw my cards on the table.

Nah, the ship had sailed.

"Sid, if I tell you the hospital, you won't be able to keep it secret. Duffy will squeeze it out of you. Or someone else will. Then we'll lose control of the story. It won't be exclusive anymore. Everybody will jump in to get a piece of it. So to keep ownership of this story for you and me and the paper, I have to keep it secret from everybody."

"Okay, I can probably sell that upstairs," he said. "But hit this story hard. We'll kick the bejesus out of the competition. They'll be all over the place just looking for her while you'll be getting her innermost thoughts."

Then he hesitated. "Chick, just tell me everything's on the level."

"Yeah. Everything's fine. We're covered. Watch me rock, Daddio."

He gave me a dubious look, then turned away.

I looked out at the newsroom. It was one of those exciting days when the newsroom comes to life, when things are humming, pulses are pounding, everyone is hammering typewriters or shouting into phones or taking rushed, alligator bites out of sandwiches while dripping mustard on their ties. I was miserable. And then I knew what I wanted.

I wanted to get laid. Not just laid but everything. Enveloping. Total escape from reality. Curl up with some warm luscious body and blot out the insane situation I'd created.

But there was no luscious lady I could turn to. This area of life had been defunct since Alida's troubles began. My despondency obliterated my sex drive. You'd think that hanging out every night in clubs packed with some of the most stunning women in the world would have got the blood moving south again, but not really. In fact I'd had dinner with none other than Sophia Loren (and eight other people) just the week before and she actually teased me about having no girlfriend. It became the talk of the table and Sophia's husband, Carlo Ponti, broke in with a gesture signifying frantic masturbation and that brought a round of uproarious laughs. It was funny but a little rough on my dignity. Sophia Loren was at the top of the list of women I didn't want thinking of me as a whack-off artist. (The next day Ponti sent a great bottle of wine and a note saying, "Just in fun." Nice gesture but I guarantee Sophia made him do it.)

Duty called, so I put my sexual longing on hold. Maybe I was emerging from the grief phase of my life but that would have to come later. I had to churn out a column; I couldn't be sniffing around like a teenager with a boner. You know the old lesson about amour: the more desperate you are for it, the more you're not going to find it.

* * *

ONE PLACE I knew there was no chance of heated amour was Alida's apartment. I had plenty of time for a visit because there'd be no barhopping or gossip hunting that night. I didn't have to go out looking for stories because the content of the column had been decreed: Sandrine and nothing but Sandrine. I knew I'd be coming at it from a hospital angle but that was the limit of my inspiration so far.

Alberta opened the door with an uncharacteristically sly look on her face. She closed the door behind her and stepped into the hallway.

"*Achtung!*" She gave me the Hitler salute. Then she stepped back and let me into the apartment. I realized the Nazi joke was about the new nurse. I'd forgotten about her.

Alida's bedroom was an immediate surprise. Its gloomy disheveled quality was a thing of the past. The overflowing ashtray was gone. Alida looked fresh and well-scrubbed in a pressed white blouse and black skirt. She was wearing lipstick, something I hadn't seen in a long time. And there was no knitting in her lap.

"Are you humping the French singer?" she asked.

"Alida, this is an improper way to address your former husband," came a new, firm voice, that of the nurse, Frieda Waldschneider. She stood a few feet away, keeping a servant's distance, though her bearing was more master than servant. She was close to six feet tall with posture so straight it seemed military. She wore black-rimmed glasses, a loose dark sweater, black pants, and snow boots. Her blonde hair was tucked up in an old-fashioned shop girl cap. She was in her middle thirties, I guessed, with strikingly chiseled features and creamy skin that radiated health and vigor. I thought: She is a poster girl for the Aryan race. Hitler would be thrilled to see her.

"I have made improvements which I hope meet with your approval," she said. "A disorderly room and sloppy clothing is bad for Alida's mental condition. And today we have made a brisk walk for exercise."

Alberta clicked her heels like a German officer. Frieda clearly caught the mockery but ignored it.

I asked Alberta, "Are we having whiskey sours tonight?" but Frieda cut off Alberta's reply, saying, "Alcohol is forbidden for Alida, in her condition."

Alberta said, "I could make you one, Chick," and I accepted the offer. This German babe was giving me the jitters. Searching for something to say I complimented her nearly accent-free English.

"I've been here since after the war so I have many years to perfect my English. But the way New Yorkers speak is more difficult."

"More difficult than what?"

"The English that is spoken in Nevada. Where I was. I am new here, looking to get my start. New York is the place to build a life. New York is what counts in America. Everything else is second."

"New Yorkers love to hear that tune," I said. "They eat it up."

After a little awkward dead air I said to Alida, "I don't see your knitting, dear. Did you knit today?"

Frieda jumped in. "She is making a sweater for your son."

Alberta returned with the whiskey sour. "Sorry, no Schnapps tonight," she said.

"The French girl," said Alida. "Is her face wrecked?"

"Oh, no," I said. "Bruised, but she'll be fine."

"Tell her to not land on her face next time she falls off a motorcycle."

There were a few more uncomfortable sentences before I was seized by the urge to make a getaway. Frieda offered a handshake. Her fingers were long and cool, her grip was confident.

Alberta followed me into the hallway.

"How do you like the new warden?" she asked.

"Well, she's a frosty one."

"Soon she'll be getting command of her own regiment."

Alberta was enjoying the Nazi joke and doing pretty well with it.

"How's Alida taking it?"

"She likes the action and attention. This woman has drive and energy. I don't have either, Chick."

"I'll send a check tomorrow."

As I walked down the hall Alberta shouted, "*Jawohl, mein Kommandant!*"

I looked back and we smiled at each other.

* * *

GOOD REPORTERS—and I used to be one—know you have to see things with your own eyes, so I made a swing by Lenox Hill Hospital.

A cold night had thinned the crowd and there were only a dozen die-hard Sandrine lovers left, holding their Sandrine posters. When I revealed that I was Sandrine's chronicler, they clustered around to bombard me with questions, assuming that my presence confirmed the rumor that she was hidden somewhere inside the hospital. I hadn't started the Lenox Hill rumor but I made a mental note to spread rumors that she was in other big hospitals so her fans would rush around from one hospital to another and the mystery of Sandrine's whereabouts would become an enticing sidebar to the story instead of a hole in it.

I pulled out my notebook and started asking questions, trying to put my finger on the emotion that drew people to Sandrine. I lived in the world of celebrities every night so I knew a little something about the magnetic pull of fame and fantasy, and this seemed to be a classic fairy tale: a beautiful young princess in a tragic collision with fate.

I noticed right away that they wanted storybook stuff and dismissed everything else. I was ad libbing biography about her childhood in France or brothers who'd died in the war—they didn't care. I mentioned her literary aspirations and a woman said, "No, Sandrine would never bury her nose in books, she would go out and seize life." I was going to quibble—hey, lady, Sandrine is *my* invention, not yours—but stopped myself. Let everyone have the pleasure of designing his or her own Sandrine.

It seemed to be taken for granted that Sandrine would survive her injuries. Their script for her required a heroic recovery and a weepy happy ending. But for now they wanted to know if injuries had marred her beauty, whether her singing voice was intact and even whether her injuries would make her unable to have babies. A man asked me about her figure; the next question would have been about her measurements but I turned away. We do not discuss the measurements of a princess.

Then I took a light punch in the shoulder and turned to look into the grinning face of Carmen Basilio.

In my view, Carmen Basilio was one of the great welterweight boxers of all time and a warm and likable human being unless you were in the ring with him getting your ass kicked. I'd met him a few times after his big wins, when he hit the nightclubs and the celebs fought to touch him.

Basilio had a rough voice, a pug's flattened nose, and his face was a mask of scar tissue but he had a surprisingly nice smile. We shook hands and here's my advice: Shaking hands with Carmen Basilio is to be avoided if you don't want your hand broken. He could bend steel with those hands.

"Whacha up to, Chickie? I seen your column on the mademoiselle. What a knockout, eh? Hey, maybe you can give me her number?"

He chuckled to show he was joking and I, of course, chuckled back. He asked how my wife and kids were doing—a standard nice-guy question, he had no idea if I had a wife and kids and I then asked about his wife and kids not knowing if he had any.

I asked what he was doing coming out of a hospital.

"Hey, always looking for a scoop, eh?" he said, with another shoulder punch. He told me he'd come to Lenox Hill to get his eyes checked.

"Tell your readers the peepers are hunky dory," he said. "Sugar Ray throws any trick punches, I'll see them coming a mile from Tuesday. Good line, eh? A mile from Tuesday. Maybe you'll put it in your column?"

"Sure I will, champ."

Then he insisted on driving me downtown in his champagne-colored Caddy. The ride included a monologue about his epic slugfests with Johnny Saxton who, Carmine insisted, had Mob ties. That was an old story.

I got out at Fourteenth Street and hoofed it down to the Village. I was on a hunt for inspiration and wanted to see what was cooking at Chez Dee.

CHAPTER 9

The sign on Chez Dee's door said "Closed" but when I gave the door a nudge it swung open so I strolled in. Chairs were upside down on the tables and the place felt empty until I heard music and realized it was Elvire alone at the piano, playing and singing almost inaudibly.

She didn't see me coming and I startled her.

"Mr. Chick," she said, smiling. "Looking for Sandrine?"

"She's hard to find," I said.

"Oh, I bet she is." Maybe Elvire had a sense of humor after all.

She said, "I read that a reporter had called every hospital in New York, New Jersey, and Connecticut without finding her."

"Yes. But no one says she's unfindable because she doesn't exist. Instead they say her location is a big secret, a big mystery. It makes the story better."

With a little smile she kept playing her piano.

"By the way," I said, "your performance making the announcement was fantastic. Those tears were ultra convincing."

"They were real. I know there is no Sandrine but she exists in my imagination. You know about imagination, Mr. Chick. You invented her. I think it was wonderfully creative. Dee is here. I'll get her."

"Elvire, I want to apologize for being a jerk."

She was already moving behind me and I couldn't see her face but she put her hand on my shoulder and rested it there for a moment.

I sat down on the piano bench and tickled the eighty-eight, playing "Three Blind Mice," until Dee's voice came out of the darkness, "I didn't expect to see you back here." She approached carrying two small glasses. Cognac.

"Returning to the scene of the crime," I said. "No hard feelings, I hope?"

"Of course not. We all have to do our jobs. Of course the way you do yours is beyond my comprehension."

We took first sips of the cognac, which was old and deep and flavorful.

"What am I going to do tomorrow night?" she asked.

"Put up a sign: Sandrine promises to return when she is well. Otherwise business as usual."

"What made you do it, Chick?"

"You mean creating Sandrine? It's hard to say. Lots of things. Elvire and I had a conversation about Sinatra and I was being an ass but she said something very sincere and simple about love. And that stuck in my mind and maybe it had something to do with Sandrine coming to life. And maybe"—I looked around to make sure Elvire was out of earshot—"maybe Elvire is where the Sandrine idea began."

Dee widened her eyes. "Now there's a surprise. Elvire's a lovely girl but I don't see much resemblance to what I take Sandrine to be."

"Which is what? Tell me."

"Physically, I see Sandrine as beautiful and sexy but in a very pure way," Dee said, smiling as she sipped her cognac. "Emotionally, a European-style modern woman, smart and hip. But she has secrets. She's driven by art and demons. Her needs are deep. She lives the fast life, so the motorcycle was a perfect fit."

"Wow," I said. "This is Class A material, better than anything I'd thought of."

Dee laughed as I whipped out my notebook, scribbled notes on what she'd just said, and asked the simple question that all reporters know often produces the best answers: "What else?"

"What else?" She thought for a moment. "She is unattainable. Unattainability is a large part of her appeal."

"Excellent."

"Unpossessable. Unforgettable. Unappeasable."

"What do you mean by unappeasable?"

"I don't know. A challenge. Can't put out her fire. Can't fill her up. Can't fuck her enough. She needs more than you can give. She is on a different level from you."

"Keep going."

"She's someone you search a lifetime for and then you see her and say, 'There she is at last.' Or maybe you never find her."

Then she stopped.

"Dee, this is so romantic."

"Do you think I listen to French music every night without becoming romantic?"

"No, it's more than that."

"I was young once," she said. "Maybe I had a little Sandrine in me, or wish I did. Maybe all women do. Look, you're onto something with this. You'll have to figure out what it is. I doubt if you can pull it off, but I hope you do."

"Pull what off?"

"A joke or a hoax or a nice little fantasy, whatever you're doing. Or a work of art. That's what Elvire thinks. She thinks you're an artist."

Nobody ever called Chick Lopritz an artist. This was amazing. The people who thought Sandrine was real were entranced by her but two people who knew Sandrine wasn't real were *also* entranced by her. I realized how little I understood about this character I'd created.

Dee stood up and headed into the darkness.

"Can I sit here awhile?" I asked.

"I'll send out another glass," she said.

* * *

**SANDRINE FIGHTS BACK
SAW ACCIDENT COMING
"A MILE FROM TUESDAY"**
CHICK'S CLICKS, BY COLUMNIST CHICK LOPRITZ

Yours Truly pens this column by candlelight from Chez Dee in the Village.

The joint is empty, dark as Tut's tomb and twice as lonely. It was here that Sandrine D'Avignon made her American debut the night before her motorcycle accident, a tragedy that touched countless hearts and created a New York legend.

"Unattainable. Unpossessable. Unappeasable." That's how Chez Dee proprietor Dee Harkovic describes Sandrine. "She is the kind of romantic character you search a lifetime for and then you see her and say, 'There she is at last.' Or maybe you never find her."

And finding her is a challenge. Her location is the biggest secret in town. Crowds in the grip of "Sandrine fever" followed a false rumor and swarmed Lenox Hill Hospital, creating chaos. Predictably they'll follow similar rumors tomorrow.

Reporters are mystified but Yours Truly has picked up a few tricks of the newshound trade and the reward was a few minutes at her bedside last night at a medical location whose name will remain hush-hush for fear of attracting rampaging herds of fans.

They were a few minutes I'll always cherish.

She was beautiful and still, lying beneath a sheet pulled up to her chin. Her face is bruised, but not badly. Her voice is whispery and hoarse. She is weak but smiles sweetly. Her eyes are clear.

There was no damage to her soul or spirit. As for the rest of her, the docs are concerned but optimistic.

"All I remember," she said, "is the old man crossing in front of me when he tripped and fell and lay motionless. He looked like a kindly gentleman, like my papa.

"His life was in great danger. I knew I would crash as I swerved to avoid him. I saw the crash coming a mile from Tuesday, as we say in France. Then everything went black. Perhaps I will write a song about it."

I mentioned a rumor that she had been signed to make her return singing from the stage at Carnegie Hall.

"No, no. My loyalty is to Chez Dee. I so regret that this accident ruined my performance there and my first visit to New York, where I have always wished to visit and perhaps to live. To me, New York is what counts in America. Everything else is second."

Her eyes welled up. "I had planned to include my favorite New York song. Singing that song to a New York audience will be my dream as I fight my way back."

But which song? What song did you want to sing to your New York audience?

She smiled and said, "A very slowed-down, poignant version of an old classic."

A nurse entered the room and whispered that my time was running out. But lying there looking up at me, Sandrine put all of her courage into a heart-wrenching sample of a song she clearly loved.

Somehow I knew it would be "The Lullaby of Broadway."

Readers, do me a favor: close your eyes and imagine this beautiful young woman in a hospital bed, clinging to life but struggling to sing this high-spirited song we all know and love.

Her voice is thin and fading. Her eyes fall shut. Her lips mouth a few last lines and then she is still.

The nurse tugged gently on my elbow.

"Sleep well, Sandrine," I said, pausing to touch her hand.

Signing off in Sandrine's words: "There should be love."

CHAPTER 10

The "Lullaby of Broadway" scene was a show-stopper. Everyone wanted more Sandrine. They *cared*.

For example: while I could have gone to the office and reveled in success I preferred to savor it quietly so I did a few in the pews at St. Malachy's and then stopped for a cheeseburger at a luncheonette where the waitress wrote "TSBL—Margaret" on my bill.

I called her over to ask about the TSBL.

"It stands for 'There should be love,'" said Margaret.

It was Sandrine's line. Actually Elvire's line. The line I used as the closer for the Lullaby column. It sounded highly cornball to me but maybe I was missing something about the state of human sentiment. Were people feeling unloved in a loveless world (or was it just *my* world that was loveless)?

I called Dee. "Dee, do you know what TSBL means?"

"I heard it this morning. My older granddaughter's using it. Her friends too, when they say goodbye to each other, as in, 'See ya later, Chrissy, TSBL.'"

"It's from my column. I got it from Elvire. I'm calling to thank her for it."

"Really? I'll tell her when she comes in. By the way, she's got a boyfriend now. And hey, thanks for the column mention. We're reopening tonight."

Somehow it bothered me that Elvire had a boyfriend but I didn't give it much thought. Dee and I ended our call TSBL-ing each other.

I realized I didn't need to go to the office, ever. I now had only one task per day, the Sandrine column. I didn't have to prowl for gossip. I didn't need to work the phones or scrounge for news or feel desperate when I couldn't find any. If Marlon Brando slugged a paparazzo or Tennessee Williams got busted at a sex joint downtown, I couldn't care less because Sandrine was the only thing that mattered.

What was new about this was that it was all taking place in my mind. I wasn't reporting facts, I was creating fiction. Fiction gave me the liberty to create Sandrine *as I wanted her.*

But how did I want her? My first thought was that I could create a replacement for Alida. But some cautious instinct warned me away from this; I'm no psychologist but it seemed like something that could backfire in a bad way. I dropped it. And besides, Sandrine wasn't for me, she was for readers.

So who was ideal for readers? A wholesome type, like Dinah Shore or Doris Day? No, Dinah and Doris were beloved but too safe. They were not fascinating. They stirred no promise of an exciting ride to a place you'd never been. They were careful to *not* be sexy. You could not imagine torrid coupling on a beach with Dinah Shore or sweaty car sex with Doris Day.

Sandrine would be different. She had to be likable and certainly not slutty but her appeal had to go beyond a great smile and nice voice and blonde hair. Dee had been right on the money: Sandrine had to be mysterious, passionate, and elusive. Dee also mentioned purity, not in the sense of chastity but more about her unsullied pursuit of higher things, art and meaning and love and whatever.

Creating a woman like this was a tall order, probably beyond my talent. Sandrine deserved a better author than me. But I would give it the old college try. I went back to my apartment, put on a pot of coffee, and let her rip:

"SILVER DAWN OF AVIGNON"
SANDRINE WAS A NIGHT RIDER
ON THE BACKROADS OF FRANCE
CHICK'S CLICKS, BY COLUMNIST CHICK LOPRITZ

I am at her bedside. Her life-loving spirit is winning but only by a nose against the pain of her accident and surgery—and there might be more surgery this week.

Is it life-threatening? No answer to that one.

"Risk rides with you on the motorcycle," Sandrine told me in a whisper. "Risk carries you to the border of life and death. You sense death waiting for you. But you must put aside the fear because fear makes you blind to discovery."

Working Ma Bell's transatlantic circuits I learned that Sandrine D'Avignon wins high respect in European racing circles. The racing fraternity excludes distaff cyclists but Sandrine is welcome on practice runs, where her riding skills earn praise.

English racing champion Rory Delafine said her daring technique showed character as well as skill. "She has a champion's embrace of speed and the willingness to let speed take her to otherwise inaccessible places in her soul."

Delafine, formerly a Royal Air Force fighter pilot, is rumored to be an ex-lover of D'Avignon's, but his British discretion forces a gallant "No comment" to every journalistic probe of his love life.

"But I'll say this, actually," said Delafine. "I have never met a woman more absolutely hypnotic and utterly wonderful as Sandrine. Any man would do or give anything for her. Yet there is a sense that a man would only weigh her down. For now, speed is her only lover."

When I passed on these comments from Rory Delafine, Sandrine's eyes teared up. She would not address intimate matters but said Delafine had taught her "not just how to ride but the why of it too."

She described nights in the South of France, taking long rides on country roads, roaring through the dark at reckless speed, laughing and singing, "approaching catastrophe a thousand times but always relying on my instincts."

In the aftermath of breathtaking rides, she told me, she would sit up for hours, tingling with adrenaline, with music in her ears and songs in her heart.

Many of the songs featured in her performances were penned on such nights. Among them is her signature hit, "Silver Dawn of Avignon," which includes her most famous lyric, "There should be love."

TSBL!

Meet me here tomorrow as the Sandrine Watch continues.

✳ ✳ ✳

It's NOT easy to write this stuff. My normal column-writing voice was Broadway smart-ass, not soggy romantic. And somehow I felt that the Sandrine I was getting to know in my own mind would be embarrassed by the artsy-fartsy stuff about her, but it seemed to be what readers wanted.

It was also a strain to figure out what came next in her story. I created the option of another surgery as a way of putting the story on ice for a few days to give myself a time-out. My next column described her being wheeled into the operating room for perilous surgery. I urged prayers and crossed fingers for luck.

So here was another chance to kill her off. But readers wouldn't stand for it and I realized I didn't *want* her to be dead. Several times I'd caught myself worrying about her, as if she were real. The one mistake you cannot make, I warned myself, is to be self-duped. A liar cannot fall for his own lie, though I could see it was possible if you wanted to believe it. In fact Elvire, who knew the truth, telephoned and asked for the music and lyrics to "Silver Dawn of Avignon" so she could add the song to her act as a tribute to Sandrine.

"But you know the song doesn't exist," I told her. "I made all of this up, Elvire. And TSBL comes from *you*. You know that."

There was a long pause, which I took to be disappointment, and then she said, "Of course, Mr. Chick. But I thought there might have been a real song."

She wasn't the only one. For the hell of it, I went by Colony Records to see what would happen if I tried to buy a record of Sandrine's famous song. Inside the store I was asked to put my name on a long list of people who would be notified by phone when "Silver Dawn of Avignon" records became available.

Sandrine thoughts swirled through my mind but pointed me nowhere. I needed someone to talk to and it had to be someone who knew what I was going through. I phoned Dawn and asked her to meet me for a drink at Smith's Bar.

We needed to talk. She had been icy since the Sandrine thing began, as if I'd betrayed her.

"I'm on the way," she said. "It'll be good to get out of here. Everyone is pestering me about Sandrine. The phone never stops."

* * *

I WAS at the bar waiting for her when the waiter tapped my shoulder and told me I had a phone call. Who would call me at Smith's Bar?

I walked to the end of the bar where there was an old pay phone hanging on the wall between the men's and women's rooms. It was not an especially fragrant place to stand.

The phone was hanging by its cord. I picked it up and said a tentative hello.

"Sergeant Lopritz? This is Corporal Linguino."

"Leo?"

"Yeah. Betty's on the extension."

Betty and I exchanged hellos.

"Dawn said this would be a good time to catch you while you're not busy with a million things."

"Yeah, she's on her way up here right now."

"I know, but she wants us to talk to you before she gets there."

That worried me.

"Dawn told us all about the French girl, how you made her up and so on. I know it's a big secret but it's safe with us, you know that."

"Sure, Leo. I trust you two and Dawn more than anybody."

"Dawn's upset, Chick. To her it's like you've sinned against the church. She looked up to you like a paragon of I don't know what."

"Journalistic values," said Betty.

"Right," said Leo. "But now you're making stuff up and that's wrong. You know that, don't you, Chick?"

"Sure I do, yes."

"Good. At least you know it. So tell me why the hell you did it?"

"I'm a little fuzzy on that, Leo. I don't really know for sure. Haven't you ever just done something unexplainable, without any thought or a good reason?"

"Yeah. I picked you up on a battlefield. There was no good reason for that."

We all laughed. It was a good laugh, a tension breaker.

"Look, Leo, I wish I hadn't done it but I did. And now I'm kind of stuck with it. I've thought about just admitting it but the paper wouldn't let me do that in print and if I did admit it to my bosses, they'd just fire me and have someone else take over the column and the Sandrine saga. And I'd be singing 'Buddy, can you spare a dime.'"

"Nah, you'd do okay, you'd do fine," Leo said.

"What's the right thing to do? Is there something you or Dawn wants me to do? Say it and I'll do it."

"No, we're not that smart. You're the smart one."

"Not lately."

"So look, let me tell you what I said to Dawn," Leo said, and I heard a quaver in his voice. "I said, hey baby, this is Chick. *Chick.* He's in a spot. It don't matter what it is. He's our best friend, we're his best friends. He did a great thing for you and he loves you. So forget what he did with the fake singer thing. You be loyal. Be on his side."

"And what did she say to that?"

"She cried a little."

"Cried?"

"Maybe the first time since kindergarten."

Dawn is no softie. If more women were like her, Kleenex would be out of business. Crying was unbelievable. I was moved by it and almost shed a tear myself. But suddenly I was being crowded by a tough-looking Irish guy who looked like a thug in the Westies who wanted to use the phone and was giving me hurry-up looks. So getting weepy was not a choice for me.

Betty said, "She cried because Papa made her understand what's right. She's going to be loyal. She'll stand by you all the way. No more giving you the shame-on-you guilty sign, you know, the thing with the forefingers."

Leo said, "It's all straight now. I gotta get off the phone."

"I don't know how to thank you, Leo," I said.

"Fix me up with Anita Ekberg," he said.

The Westie heard Anita Ekberg's name coming out of the phone and made big-tit gestures.

Now it was just Betty and me on the line. She said, "What's the scoop on Alida?"

"Not good, Betty. She's having a hard time."

"And it's a hard time for *you*," she said. "You're all alone, you work too hard, you're living in a shitbox apartment, you're probably drinking, and you spend all your time with these celebrities who don't care about you. Get yourself together. You could get another job. Leo could get you a job."

"Unloading baggage?"

"No, Leo could get you some kind of white collar job at LaGuardia. It's not writing a fancy column but it wouldn't be so bad. What you really need is a good woman, Chick. Follow your own advice with this TCBO thing."

"I think you mean TSBL."

"Yeah. Anyway, when this is over, you'll get on the train and come out for an osso bucco that'll knock your brains out. We'll eat and laugh like old times. Okay?"

"Thanks, Betty. And thank Leo. And Dawn."

The Westie was doing mocking thank-you gestures.

"She'll walk into that bar two minutes from now. No more trouble between the two of you, okay? And Chick, you need anything, you call."

I was hanging up the phone when the Westie yanked it out of my hand. I grabbed it back and clubbed him senseless with it.

Not really.

CHAPTER 11

I'd barely dented my Schlitz when she walked in, cute as a button. Guys who'd been hanging glumly over their beers perked up like spring had come. They studied her every move as she climbed the barstool next to mine.

"Had any good phone calls lately?" she asked, smiling.

"Yeah, just got one from a nice couple in Queens."

The bartender came over and she ordered a Seven and Seven, a vomitous drink (Seagram's Seven Crown mixed with 7 Up) but I withheld comment. She opened a manila envelope and emptied out a pile of message slips.

"Anything interesting in there?"

"The interesting thing is that everybody's buying in. Mayor Wagner wants to give Sandrine a citizen's medal for saving the old guy. A Supreme Court justice is in town and wants to introduce her to his grandchildren. Justice Frankfurter. That's a judge's name, *Frankfurter*? He should get a job at Nathan's."

She gave me a straight look in the eyes. "You're fooling everybody, Chick. This is like the greatest con of all time."

"I didn't mean to fool people."

"Yeah but you're doing it. But no more about that. It's above my pay grade."

I gestured at the message slips. "What do they want, these people?"

"All kinds of things but what gets me is that they seem to think they know her. In fact, there've been two calls from people who claim they *do* know her. One of them told me he's her surgeon and wants to check her stitches. Are you kidding me? The other was a woman who said they shared a hospital room and stayed up all night talking and discussed things too personal to reveal, though she wants to reveal them to you so you can put them in your column and slip her a hundred bucks."

"Have we heard anything from the competition?"

"No, but they're coming. They'll find a way in. They're hungry bastards. TV is calling too. The *Today Show* wants her to come on when she's up to it."

"That's network television. Interest has gone national?"

"Oh, yeah. Did you forget you're syndicated? I got calls from Chicago, Baltimore, Louisville, Charleston, Saint Lou. New papers are picking you up. You're syndicated to a lot more than you used to be."

"How many?"

"One fifty-six and rising."

"Wow. Is circulation up?"

"Sure. I don't know numbers but it's way up."

"Sid's enjoying this? I bet the Anuses are happy as pigs in shit."

"Sid's on Cloud Nine. Maybe Cloud Ten. How about you, Chick, are you enjoying this? You're the talk of the town but I can't see you pulling this off much longer. Enjoy it while you can."

"Are you okay with it, Dawn?"

She didn't answer. I could see she wasn't listening to me. I'd lost her attention just as I wanted to ask her an important question, which I did anyway. "Dawn, do you like Sandrine?"

"*Like* her? Whaddaya mean?"

She was staring intently into the mirror behind the bar.

"Do you have any emotion about her? I mean, if you met her, would you like her?"

"What are you talking about? She's not real." These words were said absently, unlike her next words: "Do you see the big guy at the table behind us?"

I followed her gaze to the mirror and saw the guy she was talking about. He sat alone at a small table, a barely touched glass of beer in front of him. He was about forty with broad shoulders and a wide face and blond hair peeking out from under a smart-looking fedora. His expensive overcoat hung open to reveal a pinstriped suit that looked European. This is not the normal ensemble at Smith's Bar in the Hell's Kitchen neighborhood of Manhattan.

He looked back at me with a flat gaze when I looked in the mirror.

"He's watching us," Dawn said.

"Maybe he's just admiring the merchandise," I said, glancing at her rear end curving over the barstool. She shook her head. "If he was putting the eye on me, I'd know it. He's watching *you*. He probably followed you in here."

"Maybe we're imagining things?"

Now she was locked on, staring right at him, making bold eye contact. Then she spun around, jumped off the barstool, took a few aggressive steps toward his table.

"Okay, so who the fuck are you?"

Dawn is a spunky gal.

"I beg your pardon?" he said.

"Why are you sitting here?"

"Why? To drink. After work I enjoy a beer, though American beer disappoints."

"You don't like American beer? Are you a Red."

"A Red? You mean a Communist?" He laughed. "Not at all. A Communist would not know good beer from bad beer. In fact he'd prefer bad beer."

"Where'd you get that accent?"

"I'm Dutch, from Amsterdam. I learned English while attending Harvard University before the war. I am now an international trader in silver."

"That thrills me to the depths of my soul."

He smiled. "I would like to buy you and the gentleman a drink. There's a question I need an answer to and I'm certain the gentleman could provide it."

Dawn glanced at me for guidance and my guidance was that I preferred evading questions to answering them, so Dawn turned back to him and said, "If you want answers, buy a newspaper."

He shrugged. "I feared you'd be uncooperative. This is an important matter and I hoped it could be done amicably."

"Amicably? If you want amicability I could introduce you to my friend Rocco Arace. His brothers Tony, Joe, Vincent, and Tino are amicable too. All told, that's over a thousand pounds of amicability. And I've got other friends."

"I have friends too," he said, frowning.

Dawn was getting started on an invitation for his friends to meet her friends when I saw trouble coming and interrupted. "Dawn, enough. *Basta*."

She heard me and broke it off, giving him a final glare before wheeling around and returning to her barstool.

"Let's have another belt and see what he does," she whispered.

So I ordered another round. I tried to avoid looking at the guy but Dawn kept a steady eye on him until he got up, walked toward us, and said, "Another time, another place."

Then he walked out, without a backward glance. He was a bozo. Six three at least and built like Bronko Nagurski. I'd interviewed Bronko a few times when he came through New York as a pro wrestler long after his football career.

Dawn said, "I think he's a private eye hired to track you and show the way to Sandrine. Maybe he didn't want to talk to you with me sitting here."

"He's too well-dressed to be a private eye," I said, but the suggestion threw a scare into me. Not just because the guy was imposing but because the reality level had been raised. This wasn't a fantasy exercise going on in my head. This guy was real and if he worried street-smart Dawn Linguino, maybe I should be worried too.

She said, "Who would hire him? The other papers? To crack into the Sandrine story?"

"No. Private dicks cost money. Newspapers are too chintzy for that."

"Maybe this is just something that comes with your new territory. You're a man of mystery and that attracts nutjobs. What about calling the cops?"

"It's a thought. I don't know what the cops could do but it would make a good angle for the column. But it might also put the idea into other nut-jobs' heads and I'd have a bunch of them coming at me."

She said, "Okay, but if you see this guy again, give me the high sign. My friends from Howard Beach would love to reason with him."

* * *

THAT NIGHT I lay in bed feeling awfully alone. Dawn had urged me to enjoy the Sandrine experience "while you can" but I wasn't really enjoying it and I knew that "while you can" would be brief.

I knew I'd be caught.

I was amazed I hadn't been caught already. But few news stories were really checked out. Huge factual discrepancies could last a long time before anybody corrected them or connected the dots. Often the dots were *never* connected because as every reporter knew, connecting dots wasn't easy: Old records were a mess, phone numbers were lost, key people had died or moved on, people were lazy or too busy to help or too suspicious to help or just too stupid to help. And proving a negative—that something *didn't* happen—was usually impossible. A better way to check out false stories may come along someday but at this point in the history of journalism real digging just wasn't going to happen unless an especially persevering reporter got a scent of a story and had the time, skill, and budget to stick his nose into it.

Smelling a rat was one thing, catching the rat was something else.

On the other hand, the Sandrine story was meteoric and meteors demand attention. Scrutiny would come and when it arrived, would reality destroy Sandrine? And me? Would I lose her? Were she and I linked in a doomed flight from reality?

Betty was right: I needed a woman. And she had to be a special woman. The Sandrine I had in my head was special. Crazy as it sounded, I'd developed a feeling for her.

Lying in bed that night, gazing up at my ceiling, I had a strong sense of her presence in the room, hovering above me. I murmured something to her, she seemed to whisper something back.

I was shocked. I knew she wasn't there but I waited, silent and holding my breath, hoping to hear her voice. Nothing happened. I sensed her slipping under the covers beside me, reaching a silky arm across my chest. I listened to her soft breathing. I heard the sound of my thumping heart.

CHAPTER 12

March 3–8, 1958

When morning came I sneaked a hopeful peek to my left to see if she was in bed with me. No such luck. Had I been dreaming? It didn't feel that way. She'd been a real-seeming presence but I'm not a guy who buys in to fantasy relationships.

The experience left a romantic glow that lifted my spirits, a nice change from the heaviness I'd felt since the Sandrine episode began. I wanted to put this energy to work, to make the most of the story I was building about Sandrine instead of being reluctant about it. I would start by hurling her into the grand swirl of life.

NO MORE HOSPITAL BLUES!
SANDRINE TOURS CITY WITH YOURS TRULY
CHICK'S CLICKS, BY COLUMNIST CHICK LOPRITZ

"Miraculous"—that's how the docs described it.

"Magical"—that's what she called it.

"Risen from the bed!"—that's how I put it.

Call it the Resurrection of Sandrine D'Avignon, who not only survived life-saving surgery but climbed out of bed to manage a few halting steps on her own.

In glowing spirits she pleaded for permission to take a brief excursion outside.

All she needed was a friend to push her wheelchair. She turned to the person who's been at her side nearly nonstop since her medical ordeal began.

Yours Truly.

The docs set a two-hour limit for Sandrine's afternoon parole. We bundled her up and hit the streets.

Where to start?

"Rockefeller Center," she said. "I have always dreamed of watching the ice skaters."

So we did, with Sandrine gripping my hand excitedly as the skaters whirled by.

"I was a reckless skater as a girl," she told me. "I loved it but I was no—what's her name—Tenley Albright."

(See this column two years ago for my interview with figure-skating immortal Tenley Albright after she grabbed the gold medal at the 1956 Olympics.)

She loved it. She clapped and cheered, she clasped her hands over her heart. Some of the skaters felt her magnetism and responded with waves as they flashed their showiest moves on ice.

Sandrine said, "Think of all the young lovers who've stood here watching the skaters and holding each other tight. And think of the millions who've wished to be here and the millions who will come here."

It was an only-in-New-York scene.

"Where next? The Empire State Building? Central Park?"

"No," she said. "Something with meaning for you."

So I wheeled her across Forty-Ninth Street to one of my favorite Manhattan venues: the Actor's Chapel at Saint Malachy's Church.

"I should come here before my performances," she said, sharing my pleasure in the church's modest and peaceful interior.

As we sat in the quiet church I told her the story of TSBL.

"Ah yes, I always say that to my audiences. I'm sure I said it at Chez Dee. And now New Yorkers are saying TSBL to each other? That is so charming."

She beamed with pleasure. "I am falling in love with New Yorkers. Can I give you a kiss which you will pass on to every-one in the city?"

Could I say No?

It was a lovely kiss.

Which every New Yorker should savor.

TSBL. See you tomorrow as the Sandrine Saga rolls on.

This column gave me an idea for a good continuing theme: a mov-ie-montage romance between Sandrine and New York.

In my next few columns we did the town. The wheelchair vanished, limping gave way to striding, frailty became vigor. There was pink in her cheeks and wind in her hair as we did the Circle Line, the Staten Island ferry, the Statue of Liberty. We saw her splashing through midtown's snowy slush, chatting in cozy, sexy restaurants, and waving happily from a hansom cab clippety-clopping through Central Park. Of course when I say "we saw" her, that means only in word pictures painted by Yours Truly. No one actually *saw* her, though many just missed her. Some people claimed to have seen her and that was good for me, adding veracity.

I started doling out Sandrine coverage on a not-every-day basis, to keep readers hungry for more. On other days I returned to my normal gossip routine. One night stopping in at Louis & Armand's restaurant on Fifty-Third, I encountered the ABC anchorman John Charles Daly. Daly jumped up at the sight of me, throwing an arm around my shoulder and leading me toward a quiet corner where he improvised a pitch to share the Sandrine story: It would always be my story in print, of course, but he would own it on TV. The network exposure he'd provide would get me nationwide fame and maybe a book deal leading to a movie deal.

Daly was tall and debonair, forceful, somewhat inebriated, and he had that fabulous radio voice—the very same voice that was the first to announce the news of Pearl Harbor and the first to relay the report of FDR's death. It was hard to say no to him but of course I had no choice: There was no Sandrine for ABC's cameras to shoot.

Daly kept pressing and I kept evading and finally he gave up in frustration, peevishly swerving onto the Journalistic High Road and lambasting me for not getting "deeper" into the Sandrine story. He said my columns had a superficial hack-writing sound and read like The Little Golden Book of Sandrine. Why had I not captured more of her real character? And why the hell had I failed to produce a single photo of her, since readers were eager to know what she looked like. My excuse was that her face was still bruised from the accident.

"You're botching this, Lopritz. You are revealing a colossal lack of imagination. You've got a great story but you just don't get it, do you?"

But *he* was the one who didn't get it.

It never occurred to him that the story was utter bullshit. Not bad reporting but bullshit.

My appearances in the office became infrequent. I was treated like a star but my colleagues were, of course, professional question askers and sooner or later their questions would trap me into bad answers. Indeed the press was starting to come at me. Dawn took their messages which I ignored but I dreaded the day when I could no longer outrun the jabbering jackals of journalism (forgetting that I was a card-carrying jackal myself).

Dawn kept asking if I'd spotted the Dutchman she'd confronted at Smith's Bar. When I said no, she told me I lacked street instincts and wouldn't notice him until he was knifing me, or whatever.

I MENTIONED earlier that Janet Leigh, decked out in white from head to foot as she entered the 21 Club, was the most spectacular woman I'd ever seen.

Move over Janet. You are now in second place in the all-white outfit/ stunning woman category.

And who was the new winner? The astonishing answer was Frieda Waldschneider.

Alberta, leading me into Alida's room, whispered, "You're gonna have a cardiac when you see this," and she was nearly right. There stood Frieda, except she was not the same dowdy Frieda. She was transformed into something resembling a stage satire of a sexy nurse. Her black-framed glasses and dull baggy clothes were gone, replaced by a gleaming white nurse's get-up, but no real nurse looked like this. Her skirt was tight and short, her legs were astounding with lean muscles stretched taut by high heels (don't all nurses wear high heels?), her buttons seemed about to burst under the bulging pressure of her breasts, and she wore a tiny nurse's cap atop a mane of golden hair.

I gaped at her until Alida barked, "Hey, I'm here too, you know."

Of course Alida felt diminished by Frieda's impact. So did Alberta. So did I. Regular mortals seldom gazed upon such fabulous specimens.

"Alida is doing so good," Frieda said, flashing a cover girl smile. "It is heartwarming to see her great progress." She illustrated the heartwarming concept by clasping her hands over her Himalayas.

Alida said, "I thought she was Kim Novak walking in. She won't tell me her measurements. But I'll get them."

The rest of us laughed awkwardly.

Frieda put an arm around Alida's shoulders and said to me, "Alberta tells me Alida was known for her wit when she accompanied you to meet the movie stars, yes?"

By this time I'd added up two and two. Frieda had found out I was the chronicler of Sandrine, the hottest story in New York. This made me a man with a place in the world which in turn made me a potential stepping-stone to opportunity, and opportunity was what her heart desired. So she had launched a charm and beauty offensive with me as its target.

She sat down on the edge of Alida's easy chair, a motion which included a breathtaking crossing of the legs.

Alberta dragged in a kitchen chair for me and I sat, face to face with Frieda.

"Move closer so we can talk," she urged, so I inched the chair forward. "Tell us all about Sandrine, tell us everything."

Alberta dragged in a second chair for herself and I faced the three women in what seemed like a rehearsal for a press conference about Sandrine. I felt the trepidation I'd feel if such a conference ever took place.

"She's—" I went blank. I had created Sandrine in words but now words failed me. Dee's melodramatic adjectives were obviously inappropriate—unattainable, unappeasable, etc.

Frieda said, "Describe her beauty."

"Yeah, she's really beautiful. And she has other nice qualities too. She's nice. Intelligent. Writes songs."

"She has blonde hair? How does she wear it?

I'd never thought of this. I said, "In between."

"Does she have a boyfriend?"

"Not that I know of."

"Does she smoke?" asked Alida.

"I don't think so."

The three women stared at me, waiting for more about Sandrine. All four of us were thinking hard but hiding our thoughts. I had a strange feeling that the three women all grasped something about my relationship with Sandrine, something I was too dumb to figure out.

CHAPTER 13

Dee Harkovic was on the phone, sounding rattled.

"This guy came in with a lot of questions about Sandrine. You ought to hear this."

I jumped in a cab and raced downtown.

"At first I thought he was a cop—and he made no attempt to show he wasn't," she told me. "That's unethical, isn't it?"

"Did he show a badge?"

"No, but he had a cop style. Speaks in a growl. Came on like I was guilty unless I could prove otherwise and it's unlikely that I could prove otherwise."

Could it be the Dutchman from Smith's Bar? I asked if he was a big well-dressed blond guy with a slight accent. She shook her head. I asked if Elvire was in the bar when he came in.

"No, she's having dinner with her boyfriend. And probably some horizontal enrichment. She'll be back soon."

"Okay, continue."

"The guy's first question was, 'Do you know Sandrine D'Avignon?' and I said, 'Of course I know her.' And that surprised him. Chick, you've mentioned me in your columns about Sandrine. How could I say I don't know her?"

"Why was he surprised?"

"He said, 'You're the first person I've talked to who's actually met her.' Then he asked me to describe her. I said, 'Hey, you want descriptions, ask Chick.' And he said, don't worry, he would."

"Then what?"

"He asked what hospital Sandrine was taken to and where the accident took place."

"Both of which you don't know."

"That's what I said. And he said you visited her at her bedside so how the hell can you not know what hospital it was?"

She smiled and paused for effect. "So I said, 'Do you know Maurice Chevalier's middle name?' And he said, 'What the hell does that have to do with the price of oysters?' And I said, 'I got into a cab with a bunch of very upset people. Somebody said the hospital's name and we went there. I forget which one. Where did the accident happen? I never asked. So I don't know. Sometimes you don't know. I ask you for Maurice Chevalier's middle name and you don't know. It's Auguste, by the way."

"Good answer," I said. "Totally useless to him."

"My husband, rest in peace, was a lawyer. Represented all kinds of bums in the Village. He used to say, when your client is guilty—as his always were—change the subject, challenge the accuser's motives, do a lot of sneering and snorting. Confuse the questioner. Baffle the jury."

"So was this guy confused?"

"Yes. He said every fact in your columns failed to pan out. There was no Rory Delafine, the English racer. He said no one in the French music world had ever heard of Sandrine D'Avignon. Nobody in Berlin either. I asked how he found that out. Did he telephone every nightclub in Paris and Berlin? Does he speak French or German?

"He said, 'I didn't say *I* made the calls. My paper's cheap about paying for long distance.' And I said, 'Somebody *else* made the calls? I think you're full of crap.' And he said, 'No, this is solid. It's been professionally investigated."

"By who? Did he name the source?"

She shook her head. "No, but this is where I started thinking something fishy was going on. Do cops come in and say *somebody else* has already investigated this and I'm just following up? So I said what I should have said earlier: 'Who the hell are you?' "

Elvire walked in with her boyfriend. I would have expected an artsy type but he was a clean-cut graduate student at Columbia studying European language and culture. Wore a sports jacket and tie. Introduced himself as Martin, I didn't catch the last name. He left but said he'd be back to watch Elvire's show.

Dee filled Elvire in on the story of the guy with the questions. Elvire listened in alarm, a hand over her mouth in what reminded me of a silent movie gesture, a heroine seeing a stagecoach going off a cliff.

"So, Dee," I said. "Did the guy identify himself?"

"He said, 'I'm a newspaper reporter. You've seen my byline on the front page many times. Alvin Percy.' He seemed to think I would faint at how exciting his byline is. Do you know this guy?"

"Al Percy—sure I know him," I said. "Our papers are constantly at war. He's a bully. And a bulldog. Heavyset. Kind of a muddy-looking guy."

"That's him. Muddy's the right word for him."

So, finally, a sign of trouble, the first significant challenge to Sandrine's credibility. I would have preferred that it came from someone other than Percy. He was a schmuck but not an incompetent schmuck. He'd done big stories. He was aggressive and willing to play dirty.

Dee said, "I sent him on his way, though he'd said he'd be back to interview Elvire. I said Elvire would say just what I'd said."

Elvire nodded vigorously. It occurred to me that she and Dee were forming a mother-daughter relationship. Good. I liked them both.

Before leaving Dee's I used the phone to call Dawn and asked if I'd had any calls from Al Percy.

"In the last two hours, only a dozen," she said. "He wants to meet you at ten tonight at P.J. Clarke's. He said if you're a no-show you'll regret it."

"I'll regret it either way," I said. Then I had a good idea. "Dawn, why don't you join us?"

I figured her presence would disrupt the mix when I sat down with Percy, maybe throwing him off his game. And she might pick up on something I missed. Dawn had the instincts of either a good journalist or a mid-level Mafia boss, meaning among other things that she had a nose for bullshit and spotted trickery or bad motives faster than most people.

* * *

WE STROLLED into Clarke's fashionably late, about ten forty-five. The place was jammed and noisy. I glanced at Table 20, Sinatra's table, and was glad he wasn't there. Then I ran into a bouncer I knew and he told me Percy was waiting in a back booth.

Percy was surly, scowling at Dawn.

"Who's she?"

"My grandmother."

Dawn kept a straight face. Percy was momentarily speechless so I jumped in first.

"Al, I hear you've had someone investigating the Sandrine story. I remember when you could do an investigation on your own. Who's feeding you?"

"Someone who knows what he's doing. But I'm asking the questions tonight, Chick. And here's the first one. What are you up to with this thing?"

"You mean Sandrine? I'm telling the story of a wonderful young woman who came here from France, encountered tragedy, and is now transcending it. Don't tell me you're not moved by it."

"I might be if I didn't smell a rat the size of Montana. Why is it that Dee Harkovic and her little singer and you are the only people in the world who can confirm even laying eyes on her? And why do none of the very few facts you give check out? I think you're working a scam and I want to know how and why."

"Did you talk to Rory Delafine?"

"No such person. Doesn't exist."

"I don't quote people who don't exist," I said, hearing a muffled snort from Dawn. "And who's the genius who says Rory doesn't exist?"

"My source."

"Who you won't name. Al, when I needed quotes from a top English cyclist I found Rory Delafine and got the quotes and I did it in a matter of minutes. But you still can't find him. Here's a hint: *The World Motorcycle Racing Almanac.*"

Dawn burst out laughing at this invention. That was a slip but she saved it by saying, "Pathetic" in a jab at Percy's investigative skills.

"You say she had a motorcycle accident but there's no police report. No hospital record. I checked 'em all. You say she was all over Manhattan and took a hansom ride and so forth but nobody credible ever saw her."

"Nobody recognizes her because they don't know what she looks like. And they won't find out till her facial injuries heal. But the real thing, Al, is I've got one of the greatest stories of all time and I own it. You think I'm gonna give you a map to the stream where I panned this gold? You just want a piece of it."

"*I want to see her,*" he said, pounding the table. "In the flesh. I want to ask her questions. I want to find out what you're up to. The way I see it is it's about dough. It's always sex or money but I think this one's money. You're just trying to keep your rag of a newspaper from going down the toilet. And that's exactly how I'm going to put it when I phone Duffy and Kingsley McAdoo tomorrow. Or when I write this up for tomorrow's paper. Whichever comes first."

"Al, you're right. The story *is* selling newspapers. Lots of them. Guess what: Newspapers like good stories because they sell newspapers. You think the McAdoos will deny that they like revenue?"

"You've got no story, Mr. Percy," Dawn said. "Nothing. Just a list of facts you can't confirm. If I said Abe Lincoln walked into P.J. Clarke's and danced a naked cha-cha on the bar last night but you can't find anyone who saw it, does that mean it didn't happen? Or does it mean you did a crap job searching for witnesses?"

"She's right, Al," I said. "You got nothing. You're the hero of zero."

With that I did a theatrical double knuckle rap on the table and stood up. "Thanks for the drink, Al." I realized we'd never even ordered a drink.

"Have you ever heard what they call me?" he asked. "They call me Al 'No Mercy' Percy. And no mercy is exactly what I'm going to shove up your butt. Get out of here and take your grandmother with you."

Dawn gave him the finger. We turned and stalked out.

A chill wind was blowing down Third Avenue.

"How'd we do?" asked Dawn.

"We spun him around. Ticked him off. Gave him a headache. So far he hasn't gotten beyond focusing on a bunch of shaky facts. He hasn't realized that the facts are shaky because the entire story is bogus. John Daly's a better newsman but he didn't see that either. Percy's got nothing concrete but he'll write a story tomorrow and it'll hurt us no matter how weak it is. It'll plant doubt. We'll be on the defensive."

"We've had calls almost since the beginning questioning things you've said in the Sandrine columns but you're right about nobody catching on to the underlying bullshit. By the way, I loved the way you came up with *The World Motorcycle Racing Almanac*. I'll be referring callers to it. Maybe also *The French Cabaret Gazette*."

"Dawn, why do you think people believe the Sandrine story?"

"I don't know. People love stories and this is a nice one and it keeps getting more interesting. Or maybe they just believe it because it's in the paper. People say they don't believe what they read in the papers but they do."

"Maybe because they *want* to believe in Sandrine. Maybe they *like* believing in implausible things." I was thinking about how much I'd liked believing Sandrine was in bed with me. And I'd liked the emotion it left with me.

"I don't know, Chick, but here's what I want to know: Who's doing Al Percy's legwork? Who's this source of his?"

"I have no idea. But it worries me that somebody sharper than Percy is in on this. Somebody who wants more than a headline."

* * *

KINGSLEY MCADOO took the call from Al Percy.

Kingsley regarded reporters as slime and undoubtedly handled the call with the two qualities he was famous for: disdain and denseness. A transcript of the conversation would have made hilarious reading: on one side, a slob journalist bellowing about flaws in a story (a story that from Kingsley's viewpoint was spurring sales at a time when his paper needed all the spurring it could get); on the other side, an obtuse but alarmed aristocrat responding with thickness and arrogance that must have driven Al ten yards beyond apeshit. It is inconceivable that Al came away with a single coherent quote or anything usable from Kingsley McAdoo.

That was the good part. The bad part was that Kingsley then called Duffy who called Sid who called me. I was summoned to an early meeting, forcing me to skip the church and the visit to Alida's apartment where I'd looked forward to another tantalizing glimpse of Frieda Waldschneider.

"What in the world was that *cretin* fulminating about?" Kingsley asked (meaning Percy) as we took seats in the ninth-floor conference room, which offered a great view of the Hudson River and a nearly life-sized oil portrait of Chester McAdoo. Chester, hors de combat in a home for geriatric zillionaires on the Hudson's upper shore, had been the paper's chief executive for decades, screwing up only by fathering the two snobby sons now entrusted with the paper's stewardship: Duffy, whose primary goal was intercourse with every woman in the world, and Kingsley, who had no known goal but walked around in a cloud. Duffy was an odd-looking stringbean; Kingsley looked and seemed closer to normal until he got to the second or third sentence of any thought. Both were way over their heads and irascible when forced to run their business. The company lawyer, MacAndrew Warren Tisdale, who looked to me like a former Anus Brothers prep school buddy, sat at the far end of the table thumbing through a stack of papers.

My thought was: Nothing good for Sandrine could come out of a meeting like this. Those people did not understand her, they did not care about her, they were not her author or protector. They were meddlers with wrong motives. They would become increasingly involved in her future and no decision they made would be right.

Kingsley said, "Can't we just tell him to fuck off and leave us alone?"

"That would be inadvisable," said Sid. "He calls himself No Mercy Percy and it sounds like he's determined to attack the Sandrine story. And he has outside investigative assistance of some kind."

"This is of dire concern," said Kingsley. "The man is inimical to our interests. He makes me wish murder was still legal. Can we get some kind of injunction or sue him, MacAndrew?"

MacAndrew shook his head gravely and dismissively.

Kingsley couldn't find a light for his cigarette and it seemed to be making him agitated. He turned to Sid and said, "Match me, Sidney," and Sid fumbled around for a match, his annoyance obvious to me but not Kingsley.

"It sounds like sour grapes on the part of this Percy guy," said Duffy. "Cliff got all the facts about Sandrine and Percy got nothing, so he's pissed."

"It's *Chick*, Mr. McAdoo," I said. "Not Cliff."

"Either way," Duffy said.

Kingsley said, "Let's not overlook the financial ramifications. Circulation has jumped up. It could jump back down if this rodent has his way. A serious down-jump and we're sodomized and once that happens we're totally fucked. That's what we're looking at, gentlemen. It's Biblical."

Sid said, "I think we all agree that Chick's done a great job and the story still has a lot more mileage. What we have to do—"

"When do we get to *see* this broad?" demanded Duffy. "I went down to that joint in the Village and saw nothing but some sniveling French peasant girl. Now I want to see Sandrine. Sorry but reading Cliff's word-pictures is not enough. When the hell is she going to *appear*?"

"It's like she doesn't *exist*," cried Kingsley.

Well. Stop the presses. Let the record show that of all the people who'd been fascinated by the Sandrine story, the first person to stumble onto the bare fact of her nonexistence was a gibbering idiot, Kingsley McAdoo. Fortunately he was so stupid that *he didn't know he'd figured it out* and because he was so stupid *the others paid him no attention*. His insight was left behind as the discussion rolled forward.

Sid jumped in, reaching hard for a solution, probably intuiting that something was deeply wrong. "I think we gotta build credibility step by step with concrete verifiable facts that silence the Al Percys of the world. If there is any reason to go hazy on particular details, so be it, but—"

Kingsley interrupted. "If we don't, every hack in the city will smell blood and be on us like one of those saber-toothed walruses. We'll be ripped to shreds. Duff, can we go see Pop? He'll know what to do."

"No, King," said Duffy. "Pop is senile."

Then he turned to me. "You've got to *produce* her, Chuck. Show King and me she's everything you say she is. Then we'll back you 159 percent."

"Here's an idea," said Sid, making a noble effort to turn the tide. "We just ignore Al Percy's story. It's a one-day story anyway, a potshot by an envious competitor. The public wants the Sandrine story to keep going the way it is. So let's not throw bumps in the road because we're momentarily disrupted by Al Percy."

"No, my way is better," said Duffy. "We screw Percy by bringing Sandrine out in public where she'll confirm every fact we've reported and make him look like a ten-gallon bag of horse turds. Then she'll go on with her life, with Chip covering it in his columns and our press runs getting bigger every day. We'll sell more ads and papers than we even sold in Pop's day. How's that sound to you, MacAndrew?"

MacAndrew nodded sagely and approvingly.

"So that's it," said Duffy. "Chip, work out the plan for introducing Sandrine to the world. Meeting adjourned."

* * *

SID AND I rode down in the elevator.

I said, "He calls me Cliff, he calls me Chip, he calls me Chuck. Does he even know who I am?"

"In his country club world there are lots of people named Chip and a few people named Cliff or Chuck but no one named Chick. The name doesn't exist for him."

We continued riding in silence, looking at our shoes.

"You've got to produce this woman," he said.

Sure. Of course.

But she was not produceable. My enthusiasm for the Sandrine story, which had been rising, was now falling again. I wanted to confess to Sid. I wanted to get everything off my chest, admit my guilt for making up a phony story, and blurt out answers all to the questions I knew Sid had.

The doors opened.

Sid, glaring straight ahead, said, "Find a way, goddamn it, and no dilly-dallying."

CHAPTER 14

I called Dawn into my office and told her what had happened. I hoped I didn't look as worried as she did.

"What are you going to do?"

I shook my head.

"Can you get someone to pretend to be Sandrine? An actress?"

"That's an obvious solution but think about it. It's got to be someone who's totally unknown because you don't want her recognized. You don't want old boyfriends or neighbors coming forward and exposing her. She has to be able to speak French and sing and drive a motorcycle like a pro. She's got to look and sound and act like the Sandrine I've described. And she has to be willing to work for almost nothing because I've got no money to pay her and when this whole episode is over she has to be willing to vanish forever and not pop up to discredit the whole thing. Where do I find someone like that?"

"I see what you mean," Dawn said, shaking her head in agreement.

She'd carried in several cartons of mail addressed to Sandrine c/o me. Fan mail. I'd never really seen fan mail. Most of it was from teenage girls, often scribbling on pink stationery with hearts and TSBLs drawn in everywhere, but adult men and women wrote too. There were romantic propositions (from both genders) and a few detailed sexual propositions but most of the letters were childlike in their wholesomeness. I was touched by their readiness to offer love and trust to a person they'd never seen or met, a person who was barely plausible, a superficial creation in a newspaper column.

Then a second thought kicked me in the head: If these people were pathetically needy and vulnerable to fantasy, *so was I*. In fact *I* was even more pathetic because (as I was starting to realize) I fell for her too and I *knew* she was a fantasy. What a vein of loneliness and need I had tapped into, theirs and mine.

I was guilty of everything people would say when they found out the truth but I had to keep going. I had to write a column. I saw right away that I could make SANDRINE ANSWERS YOUR QUESTIONS a recurring column idea. A good (and easy) idea was highly welcome; I was running out of them as I exhausted the Sandrine-falls-in-love-with-New-York scenario, writing seven full-length columns about her so far plus several partial columns.

Dawn and I read letters for almost two hours. We underlined every possible reader question in red and I composed answers for the ones we liked. I also tossed in a few questions of my own, including one in which Sandrine announced that she was considering a public appearance. I figured this would signal Duffy McAdoo that I was moving in the direction he'd ordered.

SANDRINE ANSWERS YOUR QUESTIONS
CHICK'S CLICKS, BY COLUMNIST CHICK LOPRITZ

Sandrine feels a tremendous obligation to her fans.

"They write the most wonderful letters and every one is unique," she said, pleading with me to turn over the Chick's Clicks column to her for a day so she could answer some of the questions that come at her in bushels.

Q. Sandrine, what are your measurements?

A. I know the answer in centimeters but not inches. So sorry!

Q. We're dying to see what you look like. When are you going to show us?

A. Soon. My bruises are almost healed. But I must be convinced that people really want to see me. Please tell me so by writing a letter c/o Duffy & Kingsley McAdoo at this newspaper.

Q. How is your singing voice?

A. Fine for speaking but not yet for singing. There was some vocal cord damage and my voice is weak. But I have wonderful doctors.

Q. Do you miss performing?

A. Oh yes, *certainement*. There is something so warm and exciting about bonding with the audience. TSBL, of course. It is almost like sex—am I allowed to say that?

Q. Will you ride your motorcycle again or do you fear another accident?

A. I am already riding. That was me roaring through the city late last night—I hope I didn't wake you! My dream is to ride a motorcycle at top speed through the California desert, sleeping at small seedy motels by day and riding from dusk to dawn.

Q. Did the accident affect your ability to have babies?

A. There's no damage to that part of my anatomy. All I need is the Right Man, and perhaps he has already arrived.

Q. What? Are you saying there's a man in your life now?

A. Maybe. He's someone I've met here in New York and he is very special. But it would be bad luck to speak about him before anything develops.

Q. Are you interested in marrying or just sowing wild oats?

A. I love wild oats but not sewing.

Q. Who is your idea of a really attractive man?

A. My former boyfriend Rory Delafine, for one. James Dean, who was very much like Rory, must be on the list. Robert Mitchum. Senator Kennedy. Albert Camus. Being French I am attracted to writers and intellectuals, especially existentialists. And I love Charles DeGaulle, who is so grave but has such a cute and tremendous nose.

Q. Do the French really eat snails? Do you?

A. Visit me in France and I'll show you.

Q. Are you a bohemian?

A. I don't know. I've never been there.

Q. Who is your favorite singer?

A. Billie Holliday. And I love the songs of the Belgian musician Jacques Brel. And the Everly Brothers.

Q. What was your experience during World War II?

A. It was a very hard time. I was with my family in the south of France. I was only a teenager but for a year I was a courier in the Resistance, which is when I fell in love with riding motorcycles at night. But the war is something I don't like to discuss.

Q. Do you wear exciting lingerie?

A. I'll say this: For a thousand years French women have passed on to their daughters the arts of femininity. This is why French woman are so attractive at all ages, and if a French woman is poor and has just one outfit, that outfit is perfectly chosen to highlight her beauty and sex appeal. And that goes for her lingerie as well. And I am a French woman so what do you think?

"It's a good mix," said Dawn, reading my draft. "What's this about the man in her life?"

"An idea I'm planting for future columns."

"It's you, right? Are you working yourself into the male lead in the Sandrine fantasy?"

I didn't answer, I didn't know.

I said, "My favorite answer is the one about sending a letter to the Anus Brothers. I'm betting on an avalanche of mail. It's great hype plus it'll give me a few days to come up with a plan."

"You're sounding like the Old Chick again," she said.

Yeah, but I'd had enough for the day. The session with the Anus Brothers and reading all those fan letters had sapped my spirits. I hung around for a while, schmoozing with other reporters and wasting time. Then I called Alberta and said I'd come by for a visit, stopping off on the way for a restorative few in the pew.

It was early evening, heavy with winter darkness.

* * *

It was drizzling when I started walking but in the space of minutes the drizzle exploded into an end-of-the-world deluge. The downpour emptied the streets and made taxis disappear. A whipping wind turned my flimsy umbrella inside out. I gave it the heave-ho and plowed on, defenseless against the elements.

I was hustling across Forty-Ninth Street, hunched over with my hat pulled down to my nose and chilling rain sneaking down the back of my neck, when suddenly I was lifted off my feet. For a moment I thought I'd been swept up by a gust of hurricane-force wind but in fact it was two big bruisers on either side of me, each with iron grips on my elbows. I was carried forward a few steps, spun around, and slammed hard against a brick wall.

One of them, a hat pulled down over his forehead and a face almost invisible through a sheet of rain, got nose to nose with me and growled, "Where is she?"

"She? Who?"

"You know who."

He gave me another slam against the wall, knocking half the breath out of me.

Shock was leaving as fear and pain rushed in, but I could think well enough to know he had to mean Sandrine. But how did those thugs fit into my sweet little princess story?

"*Where?*"

Where?

The answer was *in my brain*, but I didn't want to invite any sidewalk brain surgery to find her.

My reward for not answering was an uppercut to the belly. It felt like a kick from Seabiscuit or Man o' War. I collapsed and they let me sag to my knees onto the rain-soaked sidewalk.

"Stand him up," one guy said to the other.

They hoisted me back to my feet. I was gasping for air and dreading another punch.

"Mr. Drusen wants to see her."

"Mr. Drusen?"

"Hendrik Drusen. You know the name?"

"No."

"You will."

"Give him a big hug from me." It was the best I could muster in terms of spit-in-your-eye Jimmy Cagney defiance.

"When you're ready to tell us where you've stashed her, call your buddy Al Percy and ask him to connect you to Mr. Drusen. And Mr. Drusen is impatient so make it soon or you'll see us again but it'll be much worse the next time. Get it?"

"But who's Henry Drusen?"

"Hendrik."

"Herman? Howard?"

It felt good to sass them but it earned me another huge shot to the guts, followed by a roundhouse punch crunching into my cheek as I sank to the pavement. I wished my buddy Carmine Basilio was here to take these guys on.

Dazed and barely conscious, I sat upright for only a moment before slumping over onto my side, struggling for breath while lying stretched out in a frigid puddle.

When I looked up, the thugs were gone but the rain was still attacking. Water invaded my shoes, which became icy claws gripping my feet. I was deflated; I could not muster the strength or spirit to stand up. It was like being a boxer knocked to the canvas by brutal punches, too senseless to move while the referee counts him out. I flashed back to my facedown experience on that battlefield in Germany when I waited for a bullet to split my skull. I prayed for Leo Linguino to appear and carry me to safety once again but there was no Leo. The street was deserted.

Here it is, I thought: *my punishment for creating Sandrine.* Instead of sitting in a swinging nightclub swapping chatter with movie stars, I was alone, drenched, beaten up, and left on a dark sidewalk with my ribs bashed in and cheekbone throbbing and no help in sight.

Then I heard a screaming engine. A motorcycle. It came toward me, bumping up onto the sidewalk, splashing rainwater on me as it skidded to a halt. Its helmeted rider dismounted and crouched next to me. I did not hear a voice but I felt a warming, encouraging energy. Not just energy but a fortifying wave of love and support. Miserable as I was, I was gladdened by this strange experience. I tried to rally. I rolled onto my knees, got my legs under me, and with a mighty effort pushed myself to my feet expecting to come face-to-face with this blessed Samaritan.

But the rider had withdrawn, remounting the motorcycle, gunning the engine, shooting forward.

Then she was gone.

* * *

I LEANED against the wall catching my breath.

There was a pay phone on the corner and I staggered toward it, feeling like I was going in three directions at once. My teeth were chattering, my fingers were so stiff from cold that I spilled a handful of coins on the sidewalk. On hands and knees I felt around in the freezing puddle until I found a dime to call Dawn.

Dawn flew into an immediate rage and was ready to dispatch a team of Queens maulers to wreak vengeance on the apes who'd attacked me. I didn't think said apes would be back for a while but I asked her to see what she could find on Hendrik Drusen.

"My money says he's the Dutch guy from Smith's Bar," she said. "The two who worked you over are his muscle. They've been tailing you, hoping you'll lead them to Sandrine."

"Why? Dawn, try to figure out why."

* * *

I DRAGGED myself to Saint Malachy's. It was almost empty, just a few solitary worshippers scattered here and there. The chapel was damp and dim but there was something comforting about the smell of burning candles.

Leaning on the pews to brace myself, I walked haltingly to the farthest, darkest corner, just past the confessional booths. I sat down, peeled off my soaking hat and coat, found a handkerchief in my suit pocket, and tried to dry my face.

After a few minutes my teeth stopped chattering. The pain subsided. I was mortified at being beaten up. I did not know what the beating was about or how I'd gotten into the whole Sandrine idiocy or how to get myself out of it. I wanted to shed the lie and tell the truth. The sight of the confessional booths reminded me of my urge to confess to Sid.

The thought of confession got me on my feet again. I slow-walked to the booths. As a non-Catholic I had no idea how confessing worked. Did you sign up for a certain time or come at a certain hour or call the priest for an appointment? What would I say to the priest? "I have sinned. I broke the foremost rule of my profession, I abused my trust, I made up a character who people fell in love with and when they find out it's a hoax they'll be hurt and furious, and now I have to make the lie even worse but don't even know how."

Would I have to say a billion Hail Marys? How do you say a Hail Mary?

I jiggled the door handles. They were locked. So much for confessing. I went back to the place I'd been sitting.

How long did I sit there? Ten minutes? More? I told myself to be still, to wait for my strength to come back, to gather the courage to go back out on the street where those apes might be waiting to begin Round Two. I thought about the motorcyclist. Was she real or just a dream of a man who needed rescuing?

And that's when, to my annoyance, someone sat down next to me. A man, and he sat down close, thigh to thigh. In a church full of empty pews, why did he have to squeeze in next to me?

Without looking at him directly I could tell he was stocky, wearing a heavy coat with the rain sliding off it and a black fedora blocking the top of his face. And maybe there was someone else with him and he was in the middle of a threesome of me, him, and the other person.

Could he be Hendrik Drusen? No, I felt no menace. But he seemed to be waiting for me to say something or at least turn to him. I stubbornly refused to do either.

Finally he said, "Never thought I'd see a gossip columnist in a church."

Familiar voice. I turned to him and saw part of a craggy face which I couldn't make out in the low light. But he knew who I was. Therefore he might be a representative of the species I write about: celebrities.

Yeah. He was a celebrity all right. He took off his hat to give me a good look at his face.

Spencer Tracy.

I'd met him once on a visit to a film set in the California desert when he was starring in *Bad Day At Black Rock* (for which he notched a Best Actor nomination) and another time at a Hollywood party where we had a short but enjoyable conversation about baseball.

"Come here often?" I asked, and he laughed.

"It's my fate," he said. "There was a time in my youth when I intended to become a priest. Instead I played one in movies."

"Okay, you're a Catholic in a Catholic church, an actor in the Actor's Chapel. Its all making sense."

"That's better," he said. "How are you, Chick?"

He offered his hand and we shook. Then he gave me a pat on the back. "You look bedraggled, kiddo. Things not going well?"

"I just had a couple guys kick my ass, just down the block from here."

"Muggers? Muggers usually don't come out in this kind of weather."

"They weren't muggers. They were representing a Mr. Drusen. Whoever the fuck he is."

"You might tone down your vocabulary, given the surroundings."

"Sorry."

"You've sure made a splash with those columns about the French singer. Maybe this Drusen character has something against French music. Maybe he's a talent agent trying to muscle in. They can be rough."

There was a female laugh from the other person.

Tracy said, "Have you met Kate?"

Kate. Katharine Hepburn.

She took the cue, leaning forward and removing the scarf that hid her face. I'd never met her.

"Enchanted," she said with a smile, reaching over Spencer's lap to shake my hand. "I've always wondered where the name Chick comes from."

"Just a nickname. For Charles."

"You should have stuck with Charles," she said. "Half the men in my family are Charleses."

I laughed at this. Tracy was so Tracy, Hepburn was so Hepburn. I said, "You two remind me of the stars of a movie I just saw in December. *Desk Set*."

"Glad you liked it," he said. "I've got two more coming out in October, *The Last Hurrah* and *The Old Man and the Sea* in which I co-star with a fourteen-foot marlin."

"Did Hemingway get in the way?"

"He was kind of a jackass but enough said about that. Anyway, I had some free time so I came to NY to see Kate. Tonight we're going to *Sunrise at Campobello*."

"Ralph Bellamy as FDR," she said, in that Hepburn voice of hers. "We love Ralph. We're meeting him for drinks after the show."

Tracy was giving me a good, all-seeing look—and nobody did that look better than he did. "You're in a jam, aren't you, Chick? Tell me about it."

For a moment I forgot it was Spencer Tracy the great actor sitting next to me; I saw him as Father Flanagan, wearing a priest's habit and a kindly but concerned look on his face.

It was my opportunity to confess and I grabbed it. I poured out the whole Sandrine story with Spencer Tracy and Katharine Hepburn as my rapt audience. Of course it's usually the other way around: you're *their* audience.

"So it's all a lark?" Hepburn asked with amazement. "You just created her on the spur of the moment? Isn't that *fascinating?*"

Tracy wasn't quite so fascinated. "Doesn't it sound like a kid who makes up an imaginary friend? Like Billy the Beaver."

She said, "Don't be a chowderhead, Spence. Chick, we are avid readers of the Sandrine columns. *Avid*. You've pulled it off marvelously. Why did you do it?"

"Because he needed to," said Tracy.

That was a surprisingly perceptive idea and it gave me a moment's pause but I was intent on finishing my story. When I got to the part about the McAdoos—I didn't call them the Anuses—ordering me to produce a physical Sandrine, Tracy seemed to light up.

"Frank Capra did a movie just before the war called *Meet John Doe*," he said. "Barbara Stanwyck played a columnist who writes a column inventing this guy John Doe. She needs someone to play the role of John Doe in public so she holds a casting and Gary Cooper gets the job and goes on to be the typical Capra working class hero. And of course Barbara falls in love with him. That's what happens when you make up fantasy characters, right? You need them and you fall in love with them. So find an actress to be your John Doe, your Sandrine. What the hell else can you do?"

"What fun, let's play casting director," said Hepburn. "She's got to be young, which lets me out. She's got to be sexy, kind of tragic and mysterious and French. How about Jean Seberg?"

"Great, but Jean's from Iowa," said Tracy.

"Yes, but she played a young French girl, Joan of Arc. Or how about Audrey? Her French is perfect."

"I'm thinking Betty Bacall," said Tracy. "She does sultry and mysterious better than anybody. How old is Betty now? Thirty-five? Is that too old?"

"Grace Kelly?"

"Too upper crust. I can't see her as a French cabaret singer. How about Leslie Caron? Is she sexy enough? I hear she plays a Parisian schoolgirl in a Lerner and Loewe thing coming out soon."

"I know where you're going with the French stuff, Spence," Hepburn said, laughing. "*Bardot.*"

"Brigitte Bardot? Why not?" he said with a big smile. "She's French and definitely sexy. She's not the world's most accomplished thespian but maybe she could swing it. What do you think, Chick?"

Brigitte Bardot as Sandrine? Was he kidding or was he crazy? Could I walk a world-famous sexpot like Brigitte Bardot into Duffy McAdoo's office and say, "Let me introduce you to Sandrine D'Avignon"? Actually Duffy might love it.

Then I thought: Tracy and Hepburn seemed to have forgotten that we weren't casting a *movie*—we were looking for an absolute unknown who could play a part in real life. I explained that and they both chuckled, coming back to reality.

"But there must be a hundred young actresses in New York who could do it," said Hepburn.

"I don't know young actresses," I said. "I know stars but not unknowns. And I can't hold a casting. Word would leak out and ruin everything. And I'd have to put the girl on a lifetime retainer because if she suddenly showed up on a Broadway stage or soap commercial later on people would say, 'Hey, isn't that Sandrine?' Plus I couldn't find the *right* actress. Sandrine is one of a kind, like you, Kate. Only Sandrine could be Sandrine."

"He's soft on her," said Tracy. "Too bad she's not real."

Hepburn snapped back, "You and I play characters who aren't *real* but people still care for them. Authors fall in love with fictional characters. We're about to see Ralph Bellamy play Franklin Roosevelt and we're going to *believe* he's Franklin Roosevelt and we're going to *care* for him."

Tracy nodded, conceding the point. The Bellamy mention reminded him that curtain time was approaching. He slapped my knee and said, "Chick, we've got to run. You're in a pickle but you'll think of something."

I thanked them profusely.

"We won't breathe a word of this, and that's a promise," said Hepburn. "Go home and put on some dry clothes. You smell like a wet cocker spaniel."

CHAPTER 15

I didn't care about my wetness or dog odor. I knew what I wanted to do and it wasn't visiting Alida. I phoned Alberta, telling her I had to work late. She let me off the hook. Alida had gone to bed after a difficult day with lots of crying. Frieda had taken her for two long walks in Central Park which calmed her down but exhausted Frieda, who'd gone home (removing an incentive for a visit). I promised to come by in the morning.

Then I hopped a cab to Chez Dee.

Outside Dee's I lingered on the sidewalk. The street was nearly deserted and it would have been easy to spot someone tailing me. But I'd either given the apes the slip or they'd had enough punching bag fun for one night.

Inside Dee's, Elvire was singing to a larger than usual crowd. Dee welcomed me and led me to a primo table. Elvire spotted me and interrupted a song to introduce me to the audience. "Ladies and gentlemen, joining us tonight is Chick Lopritz, the columnist who writes about the great Sandrine."

Heads turned. People clapped. A customer across the room shouted, "Why didn't you bring her with you?" and that drew laughter and more applause.

Everyone wanted to lay eyes on Sandrine.

Dee sat down with me. She told me business was booming thanks to the publicity from my columns. "It's been great. Please keep this going."

I enjoyed the attention and gratitude but mainly I just wanted to drink some wine and listen to French cow music. But Elvire had moved beyond the peasant songs I'd made fun of. She'd become more sophisticated without losing any of her gamine charm. She'd also developed stage presence. Her voice seemed less timid. She was no longer a frightened amateur.

"She's blossoming in front of my eyes," said Dee. "She'll never be a Piaf or a Judy Garland or even a Connie Francis, but she's getting confidence now. She's happy. Martin the boyfriend maybe gets some credit. Maybe the Sandrine story helped too. That was a real forget-Ohio welcome-to-New-York event for her."

I watched her sing and it confirmed my earlier thought: Elvire is where Sandrine began. I'd made the Sandrine character larger than life and glamorous for public consumption, but it all started with Elvire's gentle purity and yearning for love. TSBL. That part of Sandrine was what people responded to. The rest—the European dimension, the motorcycles and hospital drama and love affair with Manhattan—was only frosting.

For a moment, but only a moment, it seemed like a brilliant idea to turn Elvire into the physical Sandrine everyone demanded. But it wouldn't work. Elvire inspired Sandrine but she could not *play* Sandrine. She had quality but not *star* quality. She had presence but not magnitude. Duffy McAdoo had called her a little French peasant girl. She would not sell newspapers and she would never be the glitzy package desired by the McAdoos and expected by most of the public. Even Tracy and Hepburn pictured the real Sandrine as a full-fledged screen star.

Elvire came over and sat with me after her set. The tension of our first conversation was long gone. It was hard to believe we'd had such a strained first meeting because we were now relaxed and she was delightful. We discussed Sandrine only briefly, and that was a relief. The conversation flowed freely. I started to realize what I liked about her, and it required inventing a whole new attribute: She was *good to sit with*. I liked being with her and having her next to me. In a quiet way I felt like we were a couple.

When the time came she got up and sang another set and I enjoyed it immensely. I can't remember a better night. At closing time I walked out with her and Dee. Elvire was living at Dee's house in New Jersey and Dee was driving her to and from the club. Martin the boyfriend hadn't shown up, busy with his studies. The night ended with the three of us standing on a street corner in a light snowfall exchanging good-night cheek kisses.

It was about two A.M. and I went home happy. I was glad I didn't have to hit a bunch of nightclubs to squeeze gossip out of half-drunk celebrities.

* * *

SINCE MY divorce I'd lived in an old brick building in a third-floor walk-up apartment looking down at Tenth Avenue. It was an unsavory neighborhood, noisy and a little scary and it had a certain garbage can aroma to it, but I liked the unsavoriness, which offset the overdose of ritziness that came my way on the celebrity circuit. It reminded me that I was not just a tabloid reporter but a tabloid person. Working class background, war vet, a divorced and solitary guy hustling for a paycheck. This was my identity and I went wrong whenever I ventured out of it for more than a few hours of pretending to belong to celebrity world.

My apartment was spare and basic: tiny living room, kitchenette, small bedroom. Its only good feature was a large window that allowed me to observe the street theater on Tenth Avenue. I'd never had a guest, female or otherwise, but people assume a man in my position would inhabit either a Hugh Hefner-style seduction pad or the opposite, a slovenly bachelor pigsty. It was neither, just a nondescript place where I slept and ate breakfast.

My clothes were still damp from lying in the puddle on Forty-Ninth Street. I peeled them off and lifted the window wide open, letting in a gust of cold air that felt good hitting my flesh. I popped a can of beer and returned to the window, elbows on the sill, watching the sparse traffic below. A few street people straggled along. It was a good late-night scene and I was at peace. The storm was gone, the night sky was clear, and I saw Orion up there in the stars, looking proud and strong.

I closed the window and was about to hit the sack when I sensed a tingle in the air, a sensation like an elusive fragrance. I knew it was Sandrine. She was there, in the room, somewhere behind me.

But I was learning the rules of fantasy: If I turned and looked for proof of her presence, she wouldn't be there. I couldn't resist sneaking what I thought was a clever way to cheat the rules: I looked for her reflection in the window. Nothing. All I saw was a naked guy drinking a beer alone in the middle of the night.

"Don't worry, Sandrine. I know you're not real. I won't try to make you real."

But I waited for a reply, hoping the conversation would become real.

"I won't hire an actress," I assured her. "Hiring an actress to play you and writing scripts for her and parading her around deceiving people—I won't do it. Putting some actress into your role would make her you. And *you* would disappear as the new Sandrine filled your shoes."

No response, but I felt I was finally seeing what to do.

"So screw the McAdoos," I said. "Screw Al Percy and everyone else who's yelling for a physical Sandrine. You'll exist in my columns alone, not in some actress's flesh. Elvire called you a work of art and a work of art has its own reality. As for Hendrik Drusen, I don't give a damn what he wants and this is the way to make sure he never gets to you. *If there is no physical you, he can't get you.*"

Then she was gone and I went to bed proud of my defiance and clarity. I suppose I hoped Sandrine would reappear and join me for a beautiful night's sleep, but I wasn't surprised when there was nothing in the room except stillness.

I was halfway to sleep when, with a jolt, I remembered that my Sandrine Q-and-A column coming out in a matter of hours would quote her offering to appear in public if fans wrote letters urging her to do so, which they would surely do.

But I'd just promised there would never be a physical Sandrine. Could I claim Sandrine had changed her mind about appearing in public? Could I declare that nobody wrote letters and nobody wanted to see what she looked like? Could I make up a story about her rejecting fame by running off to a monastery in Spain or eloping to Pakistan with Rory Delafine?

No, I couldn't get away with any of those things or anything else. Had I made it impossible to carry out the vow I'd just made? Of all the forces pressuring me to produce a public Sandrine, I was my own worst enemy.

* * *

In the morning I was getting dressed to go to Alida's when Dawn called.

"Have you seen *TIME* magazine?"

"It's not on my reading list."

"Wanna know the cover story of the new issue?

"I'm guessing I probably don't."

"THE PHANTOM SONGBIRD OF NEW YORK. The cover is all black with a line drawing in white of Sandrine singing in a club like Chez Dee. You can't see her face."

"Read it to me."

The article said New Yorkers were in the grip of a mass fixation on a woman almost no one had ever seen. The fixation was expanding, an unprecedented phenomenon with only a single information source: meaning me, Chick Lopritz. The article called me a member of a "garrulous gaggle of gossipmongers" but gave me a backhanded compliment, saying I was "considered journalistically reliable, by gossip column standards."

"I can't believe they'd write this without calling for my side of the story."

"They did call, many times," said Dawn. "You ignored their messages, along with all the other messages you've ignored. Should I keep reading?"

The article ticked off all the unverified facts Al Percy had threatened me with and went him better with reports from overseas correspondents confirming that Sandrine was unknown in French music circles, had no French passport, no birth certificate, no family in or near Avignon, had not graduated from any French school, or lived anywhere in France. Nor had she sung in Berlin and there was no record of a British aviator and motorcyclist named Rory Delafine.

"The one good thing," I said, "is that *TIME* beat Percy to the story and did it better, so he's left with nothing. But here's my question: Was *TIME's* original source the same source that fed Percy?"

Dawn read on. The article hacked away at every fact I'd invented about Sandrine, discrediting everything. I sensed that I was only a sentence or two away from the guillotine of total exposure, the inescapable conclusion that Sandrine was a hoax.

But the blade did not fall. *TIME* chickened out. I bet I knew why, having taken part in many writers-versus-editors clashes like the one I now imagined, with *TIME* writers insisting on declaring Sandrine a hoax while cautious editors resisted: "What happens if she *does* exist and we've devoted a cover story to saying she *doesn't*? What happens if Ed Murrow's interviewing her on *Person to Person* next Friday and viewers are saying, 'Hey, isn't this the girl that *TIME* magazine says doesn't exist?' How fucking stupid would we look if that happened? How fucking furious would Henry Luce and his henchmen be? How fucking fired would we all be?"

But that didn't mean dropping the story. No, Sandrine was a hot topic and lots of reporting effort had been invested. So my guess was that *TIME* simply played a little dodge ball, altering its course, falling back on its well-known propensity for Big Picture sociological bullshit. If Sandrine could be perceived as *a symptom of a trend* which the magazine could lead the way in reporting, *that* might be something for *TIME's* editors and essayists to plunge into.

And that's what they did, saying that "while the story has more holes than Swiss cheese, it reveals a moment of emotional melancholy in the American psyche, with Sandrine D'Avignon arriving at precisely the moment when Americans are yearning for an antidote to the blues.

"The worst recession since World War II is upon us and worsening. More than five million Americans are jobless. Our father figure, Eisenhower, is aging before our eyes. The Cold War grinds on and the Soviets embarrassed us in the race to space, orbiting two Sputniks months before we launched Explorer I.

"So in a dreary and depressing season, what could be more inviting than a sudden fine romance, a daily serial following the tragedy, tribulations, and triumphs of a beautiful Cinderella who—though unknown, unseen, and undocumented—seems to have captured lonely hearts and provided a splash of color to brighten the grueling gray winter of 1958."

It went on but I'd heard enough and was quite amazed. Sandrine had not only escaped exposure but was given credit for brightening the American mood.

Dawn said the Anuses loved the article and so did everyone else at the paper.

"You're fucked, Chick."

I had no words.

"You're in too deep to get out."

Probably. I was in way over my head.

Dawn again, "Oh, I've got some stuff on Hendrik Drusen. Wanna hear it?"

I was still reeling but tried to listen.

"He's a wealthy Dutch businessman, a trader in precious metals. His family is well-established and has offices in Amsterdam, Sydney, and New York. The New York office is at Sixty-Third and Madison."

"What else?"

"Thirty-eight years old. Former officer in the Dutch army in the war and Olympic athlete. Aside from that, I haven't found much, except for a few old photos that resemble the Dutchman from Smith's Bar. I'm pretty sure it's him."

"Any clue why he's so interested in a fictional cabaret singer?"

"No. No clues," she said.

* * *

ALBERTA LET me in. Frieda had taken Alida on a walk to Central Park. Alberta handed me a sheet of paper. I recognized Alida's deteriorating handwriting.

> Dear Sandrine,
> Yes I want to get a look at you. Please do something in front of the cameras. I watch the

Huntley and Brinkley news every night and will be waiting to see you. I used to be married to chick. My health is total down the hill.
Sincerely,
Alida Lopritz

"She figured you could hand deliver it," said Alberta.

"Okay, I will."

This is what I was up against. Every letter would be an emotional plea to get a look at Sandrine. My plan to deny that plea would break a lot of hearts.

Alberta told me where they'd be in the park, somewhere around Columbus Circle, so I set out to find them and it was easy. Alida could walk but preferred to be pushed in a wheelchair. Frieda, even in a drab and bulky coat, was easy to spot. Both looked unhappy. Alida had clearly been crying and Frieda, who was obviously not cut out for nursing, was exasperated and bored.

Alida recognized me, which was good. Someday she wouldn't recognize me and that would be bad.

"Alberta gave me your letter, dear. I'll make sure Sandrine gets it personally."

"Sandrine is beautiful, isn't she? Young and beautiful and probably with a wowser of a silhouette, like this one pushing me." She tossed a glance at Frieda. "Have you noticed the curves on this babe, Chick?" Frieda was expressionless. "What a pair of bazooms, eh?" said Alida. But she smiled at this. If discussing Frieda's bazooms made her happy, I guess I could put up with the embarrassment.

"What's happening in the park today?" I asked, trying to change the subject.

"Just the usual crap," said Alida.

I could see this was hard on Frieda. I suggested I could take over pushing Alida and Frieda could go have a cup of coffee in peace and wait for us back at Alberta's. This suggestion was greeted with pleasure by both women.

I pushed Alida around for a while, not saying much, but she complained about the cold so I turned her around and we headed home. Pushing a wheelchair is tiring and boring and I was paying no attention to anything when two big men in overcoats and hats approached us.

"Having a nice stroll, Chick?" said one. I knew the voice. One of the apes.

"Mr. Drusen wants to know if you're ready to cough up that location."

Alida spoke up, "Who are these stooges, Chick?"

It took a second or two for the anger to rise in me. No one likes intimidation, especially when walking a helpless woman in a wheelchair. I hadn't been in a fight since the army but I gave the guy a shove and he upped the ante with a shove back. And the second guy stepped in and pushed me from the other side. There was no way to escape and I didn't want to escape, I wanted to fight both of them and didn't care what happened.

My blood pressure was about two million over eighty. But I was cocking my fist and about to throw a punch when one of the thugs shrieked in pain. I looked down to see Alida's knitting needle piercing his inner thigh.

"The next one's going for the family jewels," she cried and tried to stab him again with her other needle when the man screamed "Motherfucker!" and gave her a hard backhand slap which sent her and her wheelchair toppling to the ground.

The other man was watching this in shock and it seemed like a fine time to belt him in the face, so I did. It wasn't a knockout punch but he stumbled backward, rubbing his jaw. I felt good about hitting him and was about to do it again when I heard shouting; the sight of Alida knocked to the ground brought people running from every direction.

The two thugs disappeared. Alida lay on the ground, laughing. People tried to comfort her and help her up but she pushed them away, insisting she was fine, though her cheek was flushed where she'd taken the blow.

"We kicked ass, Chick!" she howled.

We did. And we laughed about it all the way home, the most fun we'd had together in a few years.

* * *

ALIDA REGALED Alberta and Frieda with a surprisingly coherent account of the fight.

"Who were these two?" asked Alberta.

"I don't know. Just looking for handouts, I guess."

"Horsefeathers," said Alida. "They knew your name. Called you Chick. And guess who has a cavity? Yes, it's Alberta!"

Alberta had a dental appointment. She was already dressed in her going-out clothes. Frieda was in her skintight sex-bomb nurse outfit. Her hair was pinned up but a few open buttons revealed a dark and dangerous valley of cleavage.

Frieda said to Alida, "Do you need to take your nap now, darling?

The very suggestion of a nap caused Alida's eyes to droop. Frieda and I got her into bed. She was out cold. I was alone with Frieda.

CHAPTER 16

We moved into the living room where a small tattered couch was the only place to sit.

"She's only got bourbon," said Frieda, pouring us each a hearty slug, neat.

"So, now you will please tell me about these two hoodlums," she said. "What did they want?"

"Sandrine's whereabouts."

"Why?"

"I don't know. They work for a Dutch businessman named Drusen. Why he wants Sandrine's location is a mystery to me."

"He had some connection with her?"

"No, none." I could be certain about this: Sandrine had no past and no connection with anyone. I made her up two weeks ago.

"What emotion do you have about her?"

"Emotion? Well, she's a great talent and a fine person. It's been a privilege to get to know her."

"You sound like a politician," she said. "Why are you evading? Have you slept with her? Do you love her? I think you do."

A cat got my tongue, and it was a tough cat. I'd thought about this, true, but I'd pushed it away because I simply couldn't see myself as someone who falls in love with an imaginary woman. However, since the night she'd seemed to be hovering over my bed and since she may have been there for me when I lay beaten on a wet street and since she'd seemed to visit my apartment, I'd felt some sort of fulfilling radiance that reminded me of love.

Meanwhile the exhilarating moments fighting the thugs with Alida reminded me how great it was to be *with* somebody, to have a partner in the major showdowns of life. It reminded me of how much I needed someone to fill the void as Alida slipped away. A chemistry of need and fantasy had ignited somewhere inside me and preposterousness wasn't enough to blot it out.

"Perhaps it is wrong for me to ask," said Frieda. "I am sometimes blunt."

"No, it's okay."

"You're uncomfortable talking about her?"

I took a slurp of the bourbon.

"You don't fool me," she said, smiling. "I can read men. My existence is entirely about men. Look at me."

She unpinned her hair and let it cascade around her shoulders. She sat up straight and thrust out her chest. A few buttons had become unbuttoned.

"All men want me. I am not bragging. It's the simple truth and always has been. Everything I do is affected by it. If I buy vegetables in the market, the grocery man drops the change on the floor because he's so nervous looking at me up and down. You can call it a cliché but I am a prisoner of this cliché. I am not complaining, this is my gift."

"So what are you reading with me?"

"I think you care about Sandrine one way and care about me in another way."

"No offense but I didn't know I cared about you at all."

"Okay, then I'll button up my shirt to the neck. You'll have to find somewhere else to stare."

We laughed at that, sipped bourbon, laughed again, then went quiet. Then a change of topic.

"Chick, I am sorry, but I cannot continue being caretaker for Alida much longer. I hope she gets better and so forth but deep down I'm not interested. I'm interested in me. See, I'm direct. I have ambition for myself. I want a good life, with money and security and love. And there is no time to waste because I am almost thirty-five and my looks will go. But today I am a sex bombshell. I am intelligent. I have education. My father was a doctor in Germany. I was sent to good schools."

I said, "I know a lot of beautiful women, actresses, some of the most beautiful in the world. Most of them are intelligent. Not always book smart, but intelligent."

"But they're famous and not. I'm nobody. Why? Why do they get fame and fortune while I am taking care of a dying lady whose mind is halfway out the door? I'm sorry to say that." She touched my arm.

"Maybe their talent is more marketable than yours." I guess I was lashing back at her for what she said about Alida.

"I have marketable talent. Not singing, like Sandrine. But I have skills."

"Like what?"

"Well, I know one you would like," she said with a smile. "I can walk around naked wearing a heavy headdress made of bananas and cherries and apples and lemons."

"Sounds like a chorus girl?"

"Yes, I was a showgirl. In Paris, at the Lido. Also in many stage shows in Las Vegas. I have glowing skin and a magnificent figure and this blonde hair and great teeth. See?" She smiled widely, displaying her teeth, a veritable Ipana ad. "And all is natural. Well, not the teeth but everything else. I am what they want for the big revues: a long-stemmed lovely. The Lido loves tall blonde German girls. I am five feet, ten inches. French girls have short legs. Here, watch."

She jumped up and circled the room in what I supposed was the showgirl walk, all straight-backed square-shouldered posture, walking in long deliberate strides while balancing an imaginary elaborate headdress of feathers and fruits and smiling down seductively at the men in the audience.

It was quite a display and I admit my pulse quickened. She reminded me of Monique van Vooren, a Europe-born super blonde actress and gossip column regular I encountered often on my nightly rounds. Towering, perfect-looking, and smart, too, but not what you'd call different from a thousand other statuesque hopefuls.

"You think it's easy to do this? It's not," she said. "Come, stand up and try it."

Before I knew it she'd pulled me to my feet and shown me my place a yard behind her. We walked in a slow circle around the room as she glanced over her shoulder to appraise my progress as a showgirl.

"Never hurry. Stand tall. Make every step a thing of beauty and control. Keep your balance. Never let that headdress wobble or fall. Relax the arms. Expand the chest."

I followed, trying to be a good sport, feebly trying to imitate her. I could barely believe I was doing it. It was funny and we both giggled but she was right, it wasn't easy.

"Feel the audience's eyes all over your skin. Think of yourself not as a naked body but a moving statue by Michelangelo, a work of art. Are you a work of art now, Chick?"

"I sure am," I said.

"Of course you are. Breathe calmly. Keep your balance. Let's do a big turn now. Keep your distance. Don't bump into the next girl. Look at the back of my neck, not my ass. You're looking at my ass."

"How can you tell?"

"I have a rearview mirror."

"Rear view is a good thing to have."

"Flirt with the audience. Sexy smile but don't hold eye contact or you'll lose focus. Hold your tummy in. Be proud of your breasts."

She glanced around to see if I was being proud of my breasts.

I asked, "How does it feel to be naked with a roomful of people leering at you?"

"You enjoy the power. You own their eyes. You're doing well now, Chick. Uh oh, steady, steady. You almost lost the headdress. You might be fired for that. But you're doing well. Want to go around again?"

Sure. We went around again. This time she never looked back, demonstrating the full pro walk. I had to admire her mastery of the form.

When we got back to the couch she said, "Okay, we stop."

We sat. I exhaled and reached for the bourbon. She crossed her legs and removed her heels.

"You enjoyed?" she said. "I hope I have not embarrassed you."

"It was memorable. It gave me new respect for show girls."

"More bourbon?" she asked, refilling my glass.

"You can see I belong in the spotlight," she said. "So I'm asking, why does Sandrine seem to resist the spotlight until today's column when she says she will appear if people write letters? Is this just teasing? She knows everyone wants to see her."

"It's what the public wants but I'm not sure it's what she wants. First of all, there are the bruises on her face—"

"No, be serious. Makeup hides the bruises. Is she shy? She's a performer so I don't think she's shy. She rides a motorcycle so I think she's not timid. Are you keeping her locked up in a room somewhere? Is she your love slave?"

She smiled to show this was a joke but she was clearly interested in Sandrine's whereabouts. Like everyone else.

"Does she need a friend? I mean, a woman friend, someone to talk to. A confidant. I could help her. Will you introduce me?"

"Everyone wants to meet her. But certain things are happening, including second thoughts about showing herself."

"Why would she have such thoughts?"

"People go crazy, you know? Media frenzy. Fans going insane, like with Elvis. Sandrine is not built for that. She is sensitive and dignified. Thoughtful. She finds beauty in solitude and quiet."

"Such foolishness. She'll have enough solitude and quiet when she's old or in her coffin. It is wonderful to be a success with people all over you. So what if they get pushy? So what if fame is not as good as it's supposed to be. You have to push for what you want."

"This isn't the first time someone has asked me to help them get a break," I said. "And I hope you get a break, Frieda, but I don't see any connection between you and Sandrine. Frankly I don't think you have anything in common."

"We are both women," she said, and for a second a dark cloud seemed to come over her, her perfect composure wavering. I had pegged her as thick skinned, but she seemed hurt.

"We need help," she said. "Sandrine says everyone needs love, but everyone needs help, too, man or woman. You help Sandrine. Why do you not help me too?"

"Help you? I'm your employer. I'm paying you to take care of Alida."

She thought for a moment. "I must check on her."

She hurried into the next room. As her absence stretched out, I tried to think. The conversation with Frieda had gone from awkward to giddy to slightly seductive and then to something that warned of sensitive business. The woman was more than I expected. Part of me wanted to make a run from a complicated situation, part of me couldn't resist staying to see how the script played out.

"Alida is fine," she declared, returning. Her arms were folded over her chest and there was a troubled look on her face as she sat down.

"You know, I am jealous of Sandrine. Because she has you. You help her and love her. I have no one like that."

"Don't tell me you can't get a man."

"I can get a man in five seconds but that's not the man I want. I had a man for years. We were together in Paris. You must understand I had bad experiences in the war. My mother died, my father was taken into the army and sent to Russia and never came back. When I got out of Germany my sister was afraid to follow me. I can't find her. I think she's dead. I finally got to Paris when the war was over but along the way I did things that I cannot talk about. And then I met this American, Danny Chone, and he got me out of France. We went to Los Angeles and then Las Vegas. This was 1948, 1949. Vegas was just getting started and we had dreams of being part of it from the ground up. But Danny always fucks himself. He's an angles player—you know the type—always thinking big, always big schemes that go wrong. And he associates with gonifs and no-goodniks. I worked, he did his schemes, and it never added up. Finally I said so long, Danny, and so long, Vegas, I am New York-bound."

"Lots of people come to New York to start new lives."

Suddenly she brightened. "I have a wonderful idea. Of how I can help you."

She jumped up and then sat down close to me. There was highly noticeable jiggle in the balcony and I realized her Maidenform bra had disappeared during the long trip to Alida's room. Panties too, I bet. And she'd added lipstick. Her dark cloud was gone, replaced by blue sky and a new tactic. She put a hand on my knee and smiled.

"Sandrine doesn't want to show herself. I don't know why and you won't tell me. But here's my idea: She doesn't have to show herself. This is exciting."

With that, in a move as fluid as water and as smooth as glass, Frieda hiked up her skirt, threw a leg over my lap and straddled me, arms around my neck pulling me closer for a kiss which, to be honest, startled me and caused a fumbling response. Then she pulled back, rested our foreheads together, and finished her thought.

"Instead you show *me*. I will be the Sandrine who appears in public. I am tall and blonde like her. What do they call actors who perform when the star is sick? Stand-in? Double? Understudy?"

These sentences were uttered breathlessly as she maneuvered to zip down my fly and extract the Leaning Tower of Pisa, upon which she quickly impaled herself. Her move was pure ballet, a marvel of athletic and digital dexterity. It was also a marvel of mental dexterity since she did it while pitching me on a concept which, I had to note, was not only identical to what Spencer Tracy and Katharine Hepburn had come up with but went the next step, providing a specific woman to play Sandrine: Frieda would be the physical Sandrine.

"Sandrine doesn't like to be seen. I do. She wants to be hidden. I don't."

She was pistoning up and down, up and down, as I remained a passive partner pinned between her and the couch.

"She'll never have to face a frenzied crowd. And don't worry about reporters. You will tell me what to say and I'll say it. You will train me. I will be your obedient student. I can do this. I am a veteran performer."

Somehow I managed a counterargument. "You've performed before thousands of men. Someone will recognize you and everyone will find out you're not Sandrine."

"No. Believe me, they weren't looking at my face," she cried. "They were looking at *these*." The last buttons were undone, the white nurse shirt was pulled open and there were the most perfect breasts in the world, soon to enfold my face in their soft and tingling splendor.

Her selling effort lapsed as we went into the clubhouse turn bucking hard for the finish line. I was merely along for the ride but it occurred to me that I was the one supposedly being seduced—instead she was thrilling herself with her big idea. She wanted to be Sandrine. The very idea was orgasmic to her.

"Say yes," she cried. "Let me be Sandrine!"

I said nothing but her momentum was unstoppable. The next few strokes were overwhelming, but she beat me to the finish line and celebrated with uninhibited fireworks like I'd never imagined.

Was she faking it? Not a chance. That was unfakable, unhinged, quivering and trembling. The sound effects as she went over the top were fuller, louder, and perhaps more alarming than anything I'd heard since the artillery barrages of World War II.

Then she deflated, sagging against me, gasping for breath.

Then we heard Alida's voice from the next room: "What the fuck's going on out there?"

Frieda executed an emergency dismount, yanking her skirt into place and frantically rebuttoning as she dashed toward Alida's room.

I tucked myself in and did what men tend to do: I ran for it. Scrammed. And didn't look back till I was a block away.

A Saint Malachy's drop-in seemed inappropriate.

CHAPTER 17

March 13, 1958

For years Ed Sullivan hosted the most popular variety show in the history of television, called *The Toast of the Town* and later *The Ed Sullivan Show*. During all those years Ed never stopped writing his gossip column in the *Daily News*. This made us rivals. We crossed paths often and had a lot in common as veteran newshounds on the celebrity beat.

Ed and I got along decently, which is not to say we trusted each other. Neither of us got along with Walter Winchell, a notorious horse's ass who worked the gossip beat for the *Daily Mirror*. Winchell also did TV and had an audience of twenty million for his Sunday night radio show. I never did TV like Ed or radio like Winchell, which answers the musical question of why I was not in the Top Two among Most Powerful Gossip Columnists.

I'd known all along that the other papers envied my huge score with Sandrine and would try to grab a piece of it, so no surprise when Ed's assistant called Dawn and proposed that Ed and I huddle over lunch at El Morocco. Dawn booked it for one P.M.

But let's move the clock back a half hour, to when I arrived at the newspaper building and saw a crowd gathered to watch a spectacular PR stunt. A platform had been erected just outside the building's entrance. A workman in a third-floor window was repeatedly lowering a basket containing slips of paper to a workman on the platform, whose task was to update a running tally on a big tote board titled LETTERS TO SANDRINE ARE POURING IN. Local television crews were filming the scene. Even before I realized what was happening, the TV guys whirled around and turned their cameras on me.

The number of letters Sandrine had received so far was 4,708. In the two minutes I stood outside the building giving self-serving non-answers to the TV guys, it went up to 4,985.

Upstairs I asked Dawn if the letters were for real. She said, "The count's just a guess but it's true that we're swamped with letters. The mail room's in a tizzy."

"They all want to see Sandrine?"

"You bet. They're *crazed* to see her."

I'd had it in mind to take Dawn aside for a conversation that might help me get a clearer view of the situation. But before I said a word, Dawn pushed me out the door for the Sullivan lunch. As my cab moved away from the building the tote board total was up to 5,299.

El Morocco was hopping. The lunch hour was in full swing, waiters were weaving between tables with trays of martinis, Ethel Merman was braying at a noisy table across the room, and Ed was sitting solo at his personal table. His table had a telephone and he was listening to someone but said "Gotta go" and hung up as I approached. He rose to his feet and did what seemed to be an imitation of himself as TV host, crouching into his reely-big-shew posture and announcing, "Ladies and gentlemen, please welcome on our stage, Charles 'Chick' Lopritz. Give him a big round of applause."

I got into the showmanship with a gracious sweeping arm gesture modestly accepting imaginary applause. We shook and sat and settled down.

He asked about Alida. I asked about Sylvia.

Two flutes of champagne arrived and were left untouched.

"Chick, for openers, cards on the table, let me tip my hat to you for hitting the story of the decade with this French songbird. What's her name?"

"Ed, you know her name and I'm guessing you also know the latest count."

"Yeah, Sandrine's the name and the count's heading for six thousand. And figure that for every person who actually writes a letter, you have a thousand who *intended* to write but didn't get around to it or don't know how to lick a stamp. That would mean a very big number of people want to get a look at her. May I ask who came up with the gimmick of sending in letters? It certainly wasn't your dim-witted publishers—what do you call them, The Two Assholes?"

"The Anus Brothers."

"That's it, yes, and very appropriate. But I'm guessing that asking for the show of support via letters was your idea. Somehow I think you're putting words into the mouth of this young lady, and let's hope that's the only thing you're putting in her mouth."

"Ed, you shock me. I'll have to talk to your priest."

He smiled, and smiling didn't come naturally to Ed's face.

"I'm impressed with your work on this. It brings honor to our much-maligned fraternity. Including the you-know-what at Table 50."

Table 50 was Winchell's HQ in the Cub Room at the Stork Club, which was on Fifty-Third Street, only a short stroll from El Morocco on Fifty-Fourth. I'd never had a restaurant table I could call home. I'd considered Gino's on Lex and Sixtieth but it lacked swank even though Tony Bennett was a regular.

"And if publicizing the letter count was clever," said Ed, "keeping her under wraps all this time was genius. Einstein himself, rest in peace, couldn't have dreamed that up. Create suspense. Build appetite to a fever pitch and then pay it off with the perfect topper when she takes the stage and the crowd goes delirious. That *TIME* cover story pumped the balloon even more for you. So tell me, on the QT if need be, when are you going to pull back the drapes and reveal this wonderful young woman to the world?"

So a powerful man—America's most popular TV host—was joining the army chanting Sandrine's name, urging her to come forth and show herself. I was the solitary soldier standing against that army. Having been in a real army, in real combat, I had a realistic view of how it would end. In two seconds I would be a corpse by the side of the road as the world moved on without me, my millisecond of resolute bravery utterly forgotten.

So rather than putting up a hopeless battle to save Sandrine from celebrity and reality, I made an instant decision to flip the flop, to throw honor and resolve to the winds and surrender. I would play the game the world wanted me to play, because a one-man-stand on a principle I couldn't even articulate would mean losing everything, getting me nothing but a ticket on the midnight train to Shit City, whispering sweet nothings to an imaginary girlfriend.

As I arrived at this big decision, Ed's attention had wandered and he was looking over my shoulder, waving and smiling as he lowered his voice to a confidential whisper. "Take a quick peek over your left shoulder, about six tables along the wall."

I took the peek. All the tables were full, waiters scurrying around. I recognized no one.

"The one with the hair, do you see her? Jacqueline Bouvier Kennedy. Now that is a handsome woman. She's probably talking with a decorator about fixing up the White House when Jack gets in."

I didn't want to be a dumb rube twisting around for a gawk at Jackie Kennedy. I would sneak a glance on the way out.

"So where were we?"

"Sandrine, Ed. Her first appearance before the public."

"Right," he said. "Let me tell you when it's gonna happen. Sunday night. On my show. With Americans from coast to coast tuned in."

The closest thing I'd had to a thought about Sandrine's emergence from nonexistence was a vague image of a cozy event at Chez Dee's. But the Sandrine story had outgrown Dee's. Sandrine's first appearance had to be jumbo, which meant television, and Ed's show was as jumbo as it gets.

"She can't sing yet, Ed. You know that. Damaged vocal cords."

"Forget singing. I don't care about her talent. I just want her to take a bow from the audience."

"Just a bow?"

"Stand up, wave, sit down. That's it. In five seconds she'll be seen by eleven million viewers, minimum. Maybe twelve or fourteen. Look at it this way: People just want to *see* her. If she sings, it could be disappointing. Not everybody likes her kind of music, whatever it is. So just one great blast of TV exposure, imprinting itself on the collective retina of America. It'll be perfect."

"What's in it for you, Ed?"

"For me? Plenty. I get five seconds of the woman everyone from Maine to California wants a glimpse of. We'll plug it and promo the hell out of it. All dials will be turned to CBS. I'll get an off-the-charts ratings number. My sponsors will love it. It'll be a fantastic exclusive, especially after that contretemps with Buddy Holly a couple weeks ago."

(Ed gave Buddy Holly some shit backstage. Buddy Holly gave Ed some shit back. Then Ed introduced Buddy but somehow mispronounced his name. Then the line feed for Buddy's guitar went dead and Ed was accused of sabotaging it. It hadn't looked good, a black eye for Ed's show.)

"Nothing else?"

"Nope. You've got my word. But there's one thing you can do, Chick. Plug her appearance on my show in your column. I hear you're syndicated in over two hundred papers these days."

"Last I heard it was one hundred fifty-six."

"Nah, you're over two hundred. And rising."

Nobody told me. Ed was ahead of me on everything.

"Of course Winchell's got two *thousand* worldwide. So if you want to play in this league, you have to make ballsy moves. So what's it gonna be? Take it or leave it? You're gonna take it, right?"

I tried to commune with Sandrine. I wanted her to be sitting there exuding serenity against the famous zebra upholstery, nodding forgiveness for the decision I had to make. But of course she did not appear. I'd stretched the fantasy to the limit, maybe even falling in love with it, but fantasy had to submit to reality.

Ed said, "Are you going to answer or have you fallen into a coma?"

I whispered my last words to her, "I'm sorry." Then to my surprise I felt her cool hand stroking my neck in a gesture of trust and assent.

Actually it was Ethel Merman's hand stroking my neck.

"I caught the gossip boys gossiping!" she bellowed, for all to hear. "Both at the same table. A single grenade would take them both out and make the world a better place."

We rose and did cheek-kissing. Ethel skipped all foreplay and, with two columnists in her grasp, launched a spiel about a musical she was going to be in, based on the life of the great stripper Gypsy Rose Lee.

"Ethel, aren't you a little long in the tooth to be peeling in public?" joshed Ed.

"I'll never be too old to wow an audience, Ed," she roared. "But I'm not Gypsy. I'm Rose, Gypsy's mama. It's gonna be a smash!"

There was some more suck-up chatter and Ethel went on her way, waving to everyone. I saw her reach across a table for a we're-both-famous handshake with Jackie Kennedy.

"Quite a dame, eh?" said Ed.

"Not a shrinking violet."

"When you say 'violet' all I can think of are Liz Taylor's eyes. I've interviewed her countless times. I don't recall you interviewing her, Chick. But look, back to Sandrine. Ix-nay on the alling-stay. Say yes. We'll shake on it and I'll intro you to Jackie on the way out."

We shook on it.

"You're doing the right thing, boyo. It'll be the perfect launch for you and whatever you plan to do with her."

Plan? Ed planned. I didn't plan. That's why he couldn't be denied.

Jackie was charming. Asked about Sandrine. Said she and Jack were insanely curious to see what she looked like.

* * *

I was at home trying to write a column I didn't want to write when Alberta called.

"What happened with Frieda? She's sore at you. She's going to quit. I don't know what to do."

"I'll call her later. She won't be sore."

Frieda was going to get what she wanted.

* * *

THEY PUT my next column on the front page. Next to it was a big photo of three smiling workmen next to tall stacks of letters. Behind them was a hand-scrawled tally board titled "SANDRINE LETTERS" showing a total of 10,338.

SANDRINE TO APPEAR ON TV!
ED SULLIVAN: "GET SET FOR A REELY BIG SHEW"
CHICK'S CLICKS, BY COLUMNIST CHICK LOPRITZ

"It's more than I ever dreamed of," Sandrine said. "An appearance on *The Ed Sullivan Show*."

The beautiful French singer glowed with anticipation. She was sipping tea (for her voice) in a downtown coffee shop, wearing her incognito outfit: hat, scarf, and no-prescription glasses.

Bowing to the wishes of more than 10,000 letter-writers, Sandrine will finally step before the cameras—and you won't be disappointed!

Expect the Sandrine appearance to come late in the show, a tactic by Ed to build and hold a record-breaking audience.

Be ready—Sandrine's bow from the audience won't last more than a few seconds so have your popcorn popped, put the little ones to beddie-weddie, and lock that barking dog in the cellar.

Sandrine herself requested the ultra short appearance. Millions of viewers will find it all too brief but Sandrine feels that until she can sing again, appearances cheat her fans.

"What do they see except the face of a French girl who is falling in love with America?"

That kind of humility is rare on the celebrity circuit, but it's a circuit Sandrine has no wish to join.

"You sell your soul to be adored by people who don't even know you," she says. "It turns you into someone else and pulls you away from the people you love. I am an artist, not a celebrity."

Don't miss Sullivan Sunday as the Sandrine saga speeds forward. TSBL!

* * *

W<small>HEN</small> I finished writing the column, I had a copy boy pick it up but I kept a dupe and clipped it to a collection of the earlier Sandrine columns. The Complete Works, the entire lifetime of Sandrine D'Avignon in a batch of papers so thin I could stuff it into a manila envelope. Which I did.

I called Frieda, who was as icy as midnight in Murmansk. I guess I thought that having lived through the post-war life in Paris and Vegas, she'd be worldlier about less than debonair sex manners, such as my not staying around to add the proper finish to an intimate encounter. But even showgirls had feelings. I'd done the wrong thing.

I asked her to meet me at Chez Dee because I didn't want to tell her by phone that she was going to become the physical incarnation of Sandrine.

I also wanted to begin immersing her in the role. Meeting Dee and Elvire would instruct her in Sandrine's world and it would be good for Frieda to breathe in the difference between Chez Dee and the brassy stages of Las Vegas.

Frieda gave me a chilly silence and I could hear a big Fuck You coming down the tracks. So I quickly added, "You won't regret it."

She said, "I'll trust you. *Once.*"

As I jumped on the A train downtown I was thinking: There was a new Sandrine in town. Things were going to be different.

CHAPTER 18

The New York subway costs only a dime and the trains are fast but not fast enough. Subway riders are in a hurry to get to their stops before something ugly happens.

The most common dread is contact with a bottom-dwelling, dregs-of-the-earth crazyman. When it happens, the textbook response is dead-eyed urban indifference: ignoring and *never* looking at the crazyman because that look could start the clock on an encounter that would haunt your dreams.

But it wasn't a standard subway psycho who sat down next to me. Unless subway psychos wear expensive cologne. The scent was so head-turning that I turned my head, breaking the no-look rule to sneak a quick size-up peek.

Which revealed that I was sitting next to Hendrik Drusen.

Drusen: the Dutchman from Smith's Bar, the boss of the two gorillas who knocked me down in the rain, threatened Alida and me in Central Park, and now closed in to block me from making a dash for safety. The two thugs had mayhem in their eyes, eager to avenge Alida's needle and my punch.

Drusen wore a natty camel's hair coat with a matching camel-colored fedora and he seemed to be about the size of a camel. His big round face was turned to me directly and he was smiling.

"You may call me Rick."

"I'm not calling you anything," I said, playing the Bogart-like tough guy.

"You have knowledge that is important to me," he said. "I'm hoping we can negotiate a transaction."

I looked at him squarely. He radiated thickness: shoulders, face, nose, and lips. He had blue eyes and wheat-colored hair.

"Your Neanderthals attacked me when I was with a woman in a wheelchair. Do you call that negotiation?"

"It is sometimes necessary to put fear into someone you are dealing with, to show that you will stop at nothing. And don't think you can get away again. If you run we'll catch you. We are former athletes, younger, quicker, and stronger than you. I personally competed for the Netherlands in the 1948 London Olympics."

"Yeah, all these years I've wanted to congratulate you on that, Rick. What event?"

"The hammer throw."

"Ball peen or the kind with the claw."

"Ah, the wordsmith is quick with a wisecrack, but I've heard it many times before. The Olympic hammer is a sixteen-pound metal ball at the end of a metal wire."

"Where can I get one of those?" I asked. "I could use it to kill mosquitoes. So you threw this metal ball and won the Olympics?"

"I didn't win. It was a time of great austerity in my country. There were no funds for sport training. I trained in a park and had very little coaching. It was unfair."

"So how'd you do? Third, fourth?"

"Thirteenth, if you must know."

"Uh oh, out of the money. No medal, eh? Do they give you a tie clasp or something for that?"

The train stopped. Bolting for the door was a thought but I had no chance of squeezing between the two linebackers who blocked my way. The doors closed and the train continued.

"At which stop do you intend to disembark?" he asked.

"I intend to disembark at Spring Street, Ricky. That will conclude our relationship, and it's been swell."

"Our relationship will continue until I learn what I must learn. If I don't, there'll be trouble in River City."

The train stopped again. We were at Thirty-Fourth Street, meaning four more stops to Spring.

I thought for a minute and said, "Rick, do you understand that the cops are going to come between us? I am a prominent newspaperman in this town. I have pull with the boys in blue. I print nothing but suck-up items about Steve Kennedy. *Police Commissioner* Kennedy."

At this point good old Ricky dropped the nice-guy routine and seized my wrist, yanking it behind me and up my back. He was very strong. Another inch and I'd hear the crack of a very painful broken shoulder.

"Where is she?"

"I have some news on that front, but you'll have to let go of me."

The train stopped again while he thought that over and then released my wrist.

I opened my manila envelope and showed him the carbon of my column describing Sandrine's upcoming Sullivan appearance. He read it with intensity and looked up. "She'll be on television? My God."

"Sunday at eight on CBS. Set your dial to Channel Two."

"What does she do on the program? Does she sing?"

"Nope. Just waves to the audience."

"I can see her?"

"You and millions of others."

He seemed stunned.

We pulled in and out of West Fourth Street. Spring was next.

"Tell me this, Rick. You seem to be bright and rich. If you're so hot for Sandrine how come you haven't found her on your own, without resorting to strong-arm stuff?"

"You think I haven't tried? I've paid a fortune to private investigators."

"Investigators?" A light bulb popped on in my mind. "Did your investigators dig up a lot of info which you fed to Al Percy? And when that didn't get you anywhere to *TIME* magazine? I'm right, aren't I? And the idea was to beat the bushes and create pressure for Sandrine to come out in public. Right?"

"Obviously. It was a good tactic. But now I'm changing to a new tactic: Surround the one person who seems to know where she is and force him to lead us to her. And I mean *force* him."

"It's just not possible, Rick," I said. "Go ahead and kill me."

"It would not disturb me to do that," he said. "I killed people in the war. I fought in Indonesia."

"I fought in France and Germany," I said. I didn't know if I'd killed anybody. Fired lots of bullets but never saw an enemy fall.

I didn't like having my life threatened but my next bit of defiant tough-guy dialogue was ill-advised. "Ricky, I bet you were one of those Dutch traitors who fought alongside the Nazis."

His eyes flashed but before he could do anything one of the apes stepped forward and give me a slap in the face so hard it almost knocked me cross-eyed. It was also so shockingly loud that it sent a ripple of panic throughout the subway car, with the other passengers jumping to their feet and clearly intending to get out of harm's way as the train pulled into the Spring Street station.

I stood up unsteadily and joining the exiting throng with a thug to my left, another behind me, and Drusen gripping my right elbow.

"Lead us to her," he commanded. "It's your choice: cooperation or hospitalization."

* * *

I was still reeling from the slap as we got to the street. I grasped at ideas for a clever move but cleverness failed me. I didn't want to lead him to Dee's but nothing else came to me.

Dee looked quizzically at my three large friends as we entered but said nothing, leading us to the same ringside table where I'd sat with Duffy McAdoo and his twit friends the night of Sandrine's bogus accident. I was surprised that Drusen didn't dispatch his thugs to a far corner. I had the sense he wasn't thinking well. Neither was I, of course.

"A lady will be joining us shortly," I said to Dee. "A tall woman, possibly wearing a nurse's outfit."

Drusen said, "Who's this woman joining us?"

"My ex-wife's nurse."

"You go to a nightclub with your ex-wife's nurse?"

"Wait till you see her."

Dee said, "Elvire will be on in a minute."

Drusen ordered a glass of gin, neat. He ordered nothing for me or the thugs. Dee went off into the darkness.

"I haven't been to a hole like this in years," Drusen said, looking around. "Brings back memories."

Elvire appeared, stepped onto the stage, nodded to me, and started to sing. She wore a skirt and sweater and looked womanly and French rather than girlish and Ohioan.

How would Frieda react to this scene? I suspected she hadn't been to a low-key neighborhood dive any more recently than Drusen. If she'd read my columns closely she might recognize the club's name as well as Dee's and Elvire's, but maybe not. She expected me to be alone, offering a make-up gift to atone for my bad manners. Instead she'd find me sharing a table with two beefy hoodlums and a strapping, rich-looking gentleman with a European suit and haircut.

At that point Frieda made her entrance. It was memorable.

* * *

She handed her coat to somebody and posed for a moment. She wore a low-cut black dress, pearls, earrings, her blonde hair was down and she was towering in heels. This look was designed just for me (the message was "here's what you're not getting") but its sexual shock wave swept over everyone in the club and especially to the men at my table. The impact was heightened by her elegant showgirl walk to our table and her facial expression: bristling, haughty, intimidating.

"This is the nurse?" asked Drusen, laughing. He rose to his feet, bowed gallantly, and offered her his hand, which she disdainfully ignored.

I grabbed a chair from another table, squeezing it in between Drusen and me. Frieda sat and crossed her legs as Drusen shamelessly looked her up and down. Elvire kept singing even though Frieda had stolen the attention of everyone in the room.

"Let me introduce Frieda Waldschneider," I said. "Frieda, this is Hendrik Drusen and his friends, Mutt and Jeff."

"I've seen many like them," Frieda sneered. "Palookas."

Dee arrived and asked for Frieda's order.

"Stinger," said Frieda.

"A stinger? Now there's a no-nonsense drink," said Drusen, admiringly. "You seem to be European."

"From Munich but I have lived in America since the war."

"I am from Amsterdam but come here often on business."

I said, "I'm from the Bronx but practice my craft in Manhattan."

Frieda paused, turned to me, and said, "I thought this would be just us."

Drusen whistled, which I took to mean, "This broad doesn't horse around."

I said, "Frieda, you asked to see my column for tomorrow."

She hadn't asked but I handed her the carbons, which she read by the light of the table's dinky candle. The candle lit her face, which showed a glimmer of something—surprise or excitement.

Frieda said, "She's going to be on *Ed Sullivan*? And you have summoned me in relation to this?"

Drusen was listening closely.

I said, "We can only discuss it in private."

"Then let's move to another table."

"*No. You stay*," said Drusen. It was a command, barked with Gestapo forcefulness, which of course added a vibration of menace to the strained mood at the table.

"Who are you?" Frieda asked Drusen. "Why are you here?"

He made a steeple with his fingers and smiled.

"That's a long story," he said. "Would you like to hear it?"

"No," said Frieda. "I don't give a shit about your story."

The thug I called Jeff, the one who'd slapped me on the subway, raised a hand to slap Frieda but Drusen stopped him with a sharp glance.

"I'm going to tell my story," Drusen said. "I think you'll like it."

We all waited. I could tell that Drusen was pleased to have the stage. He said, "I am here to find the love of my life."

CHAPTER 19

"Let us go back to August 14, 1946. I am a major in the Dutch army. I have been sent to Paris for a few days to attend meetings of the Paris Peace Conference. They put me on a committee. Its work was tedious and insignificant and I remember nothing about it. All I could think about—all anyone could think about—was that the war was over. I slept through the meetings but at night I joined other officers seeking entertainment.

"I had been to Paris before the war but of course it was a different city now. Exhausted, shabby, hungry. Everyone rode bikes because there was so little petrol. Even the better restaurants served poor food, though good wines were available. But Paris always has women. Even in threadbare clothing they looked exciting to us. I was twenty-six and like any young man I had a fantasy of Parisian romance."

He paused as a waiter arrived with Drusen's gin and Frieda's stinger. I sensed I would need something strong to get through Drusen's story. I asked for a martini.

"We went up to Montmartre. It was filthy and you had to be careful because street criminals were as thick as rats and people were grabbing your sleeve and wanting something. But August 14 was a beautiful summer night and everywhere you looked something *Parisian* was happening. I remember looking up at a window where a prostitute was standing, pretty and young, wearing a blue-and-white striped jersey which she pulled up to show me her breasts.

"There were dozens of small clubs. We were in our officers' uniforms so obviously we had money to spend and were looking for music and women, so barkers ran out of these clubs and implored us to come in. Which we did. A drink here, a drink there. Lots of music. The women wanted us to buy them champagne. We watched some striptease but it was not very good.

The women were not really strippers, just women struggling to earn a few francs.

"I recall a bit of melancholy sinking in. Some of the others in my group departed before midnight. Two friends and I continued, going from club to club. A few women had joined us, like camp followers. They led us around.

"There were mentions during the evening of a certain club called *La Vierge Antilope*. The women said it was exciting but dangerous. They did not want to go with us. But of course we were brave and adventurous young men. We were soldiers. We could not resist it."

The last thing I expected from Hendrik Drusen was an engrossing tale of old Paris but we listened intently. Frieda was riveted. I noticed that Elvire had pulled up a chair and Dee was standing behind her, listening in, and a few random customers had drifted over, forming a loose circle around the table. Drusen seemed to thrive on having an audience.

"We found a local fellow and tipped him to lead us there. It was a bit of a walk, with lots of confusing turns from one small street to another. I tried to pay attention but I was drunk and all landmarks, like Sacré-Coeur, were out of sight. And then we arrived.

"It was three or four in the morning but the room was crowded and pulsating. It was a place unlike anything I had ever seen or imagined, a fantasy of Parisian nightlife. The music alone was different from ordinary French music. It was played by a live band, very loud.

"It was dark and the smoke was so heavy you could hardly see or breathe. We ended up at a small table and a waiter slammed down three smudged water glasses and then a full bottle with a cork in it but no label. Absinthe. Did we prefer something weaker, he asked, sneering. No, absinthe was fine. I had tasted it a few times before and disliked it but that night it was delicious.

"There was a tiny dance floor packed people dancing in a sexy way I had never seen. Very flamboyant, the women whirling around, the men strong and almost violent. They were all French, no tourists, no military except us. The odor of the sweaty bodies and the Gauloises cigarettes was very strong.

"The more I looked around the more I saw. People were having intercourse on tabletops. I had never seen such a thing. Women with their skirts thrown up, legs kicking in the air. And at some tables, women bending over men as the men smoked and conversed with friends.

"Remember, we had been through years of war. Deprivation, unspeakable emptiness mixed with terror, nightmares of death and destruction, the whole world seeming to be shattered and ruined. And then we were here in this room, surrounded by this uninhibited freedom. I have always been conservative, raised in a respected family, but that night I was swept away."

He sat back exhausted from the memory. But after a sip, he continued.

"So now it's very late, maybe five or six A.M. My two friends have left but I refuse to let the night end. I'm thinking they will soon close and turn me out into the streets.

"Instead, without introduction, a woman singer appeared at the microphone. Tall and slender with short blonde hair. Wearing a cheap green dress. The band was gone now but she had a guitar and she began to sing. The songs were dramatic but soft, mostly in French but some in English. I think today they would be called folk songs. The woman was wonderful and her singing changed the atmosphere of the whole place, from raw to mellow. Waiters brought coffee and fresh bread. When the door to the club was opened, sunrise burst in. I had to be at a meeting at nine A.M. to talk about rebuilding European trade, but I didn't move.

"Perhaps you can guess what comes next," said Drusen. "I gave a waiter a tip and asked him to invite the singer to my table. And she came over and sat down and we talked as if we had known each other for our lifetimes. I have never known such perfect connection. We told each other our stories, our dreams for life in the new world. We embraced, we kissed. She offered to take me back to her flat where we would make love for hours. The catch was that it was a sordid little flat which she shared with other people. I offered to get a hotel room and to be absent from my committee's meetings no matter how much trouble that would put me in. And she said yes to that.

"And then something stupid happened. A man was standing there, a rough-looking French fellow, and he was hostile. Perhaps he also desired this woman or perhaps he was simply drunk and belligerent. He insulted my uniform. He called me this and that. He overturned our coffees and coffee went in her lap and she jumped up shocked with a bad coffee stain. Perhaps it was her only dress.

"Without thinking I rose to fight. I am strong and a good fighter but I was tired and drunk and distracted by falling in love. She screamed and urged me to stop but I could not be restrained. We had an awful battle. The waiters tried to break it up but we would not stop.

"Finally I won. My opponent was on the floor, unable to continue. I turned around for the woman and she was gone. I ran through the club, searching every corner. I came out on a back street, blinded by morning sun, and looked in all directions. No sign of her. I went back inside and begged the waiter to tell me where she'd gone, where she lived. I threatened him, I offered money, but he didn't know. I demanded to know her name. He knew only her first name. Can anyone guess?"

Elvire said, "Sandrine?"

"Close," he said. "Sandra."

That silenced everyone.

"But Sandrine is a diminutive of Sandra. So a girl named Sandra might be called Sandrine."

Drusen finished his drink. "It took me forever to find my way to my quarters. Somehow I went to my meeting but I was obviously in no condition and I lost favor with my superiors. I was ordered home and was never again given international assignments. But all I cared about that day was finding Sandra. I knew that I loved her and would never love anyone else. I would have taken her home to Amsterdam and married her the next day.

"That night, my last night in Paris, I went back to Montmartre and looked for the fellow who had led us to *La Vierge Antilope*. I didn't see him but I asked other fellows and despite my offers of money, they could not take me there. They said they had never heard of it.

"I walked around that whole night searching for it, getting very lost, asking many people if they could direct me to it. I hailed a taxi and paid the driver to drive around and help me search for it. The driver had an old directory listing every establishment in the city, but the name was not to be found.

"Later, from Amsterdam, I continued the search, with inquiries to French government and police officials. I located the two Dutch officers who had been with me. They could not tell me anything useful.

"A few months later I hired the best Parisian detective agency to find her, but with no luck. Sandra was gone. There was no trace of her since then. No hope for my search."

Then he turned to me.

"Until two weeks ago when I read Chick's column."

* * *

IT WAS awkward being dropped back into the present after that excursion to the past. I think we were floored by the romance and mystery of the story even though Elvire, Dee, and I (but not Frieda or the thugs) knew that Drusen's Sandra could not be Sandrine because there was no Sandrine.

Elvire asked the question that was probably on all of our minds: "Do you think this could have been a dream? Dreams can seem very real."

"No!" said Drusen, pounding the table. "It happened, for sure. I had bruises from the fight. My knuckles were scraped from punching this guy."

"Maybe you punched some other guy," said Frieda.

"Maybe you were drunk and fantasized the whole thing," I said. "Maybe it was the absinthe. They say it causes hallucinations."

"Not hallucinations," said Dee. "Just extreme drunkenness."

Frieda asked, "Did this Sandra tell you where she was from?"

"We talked a bit about her childhood and her family. She did not name a place, but several of her songs were about the south of France. D'Avignon would make sense as a name for her."

Yes, Avignon is in the south. But she wasn't from Avignon because she wasn't from anywhere except my imagination.

Elvire said, "It is a lovely story. But if you did find your Sandra, what would you do?"

He seemed surprised. "I would cherish her."

"But what would you *do*?"

"What do you mean, what would I do?"

"Get married? Buy a house? Have babies? And it's likely she has found someone else in all this time. What would you do about that?"

"We had a perfect love. She would come with me." But he seemed befuddled by the question. Was it possible his thinking had never gone beyond his magical memory of finding her?

Frieda asked, "What did you think when you read Chick's column?"

"I thought, 'She is found! My angel has returned.'"

One of the thugs snickered at this. Drusen gave him a murderous look. Then he turned back to the rest of us.

"Do you doubt my story?" he asked, searching our faces. "This is the central story of my life. It is true. Look, I am a smart man. I run an international business, I'm a former military officer, a father of three. I am no deluded idiot. I am insulted by your reaction."

"How old would she be now?" Frieda asked, perhaps not sensing his rising temper. Before he replied she turned to me and asked, "Chick, how old is Sandrine?"

"Twenty-eight, more or less," I said, though I'd never really thought about it.

"So twelve years ago Sandra was sixteen? Or fifteen? Or younger? Was she that young, Mr. Drusen? Did you fall in love with a girl, a teenager?"

"Don't be silly."

"Then explain."

"I can't explain. When you are falling in love do you ask for a person's birth certificate? Did I demand to inspect her identity card? She was not sixteen."

Frieda was about to repeat the arithmetic of twenty-eight minus twelve but Drusen saw it coming and his scowl changed her mind.

He slammed his empty glass on the table. "I have spent my life waiting for her. Now I am close to her, I know it. I will watch this Ed Sullivan show and then you, Mr. Lopritz, will take me to her."

With that he stood, swept the table with ferocious eye contact, and stalked out, Mutt and Jeff following.

"TSBL," whispered Elvire.

* * *

THERE WAS a long silence at the table, a mix of relief and puzzlement.

Frieda said, "It was a fascinating story, very romantic, but I don't know, he seems a bit wacko, yes?"

"Things don't have to square with the facts to be true," said Dee. "I have two teenage granddaughters. Their truth never squares with my facts."

Frieda said, "Young love doesn't care about logic or facts. He is a well-to-do and educated man, a man of substance. Could everything else about him be solid except this one great fantasy?"

"Solid citizens don't hire thugs," I said.

I didn't know what to make of Drusen's story, except that he was obsessed and obsession made him dangerous. But I agreed with Frieda that young love was more powerful than logical. I thought back to the summer when I was fifteen. My family spent a week at the beach, Far Rockaway in Queens. We stayed in a rented cottage with a tiny lawn where I was sitting one day when a girl about my age walked by. She was wearing a gray dress and smoking a cigarette, which was very brash in those days. She had dark and very sophisticated eyebrows that seemed to promise something inter-esting—more interesting than anything about me—but most striking of all was her limp. It seemed to come from some flaw in her hip. It wasn't a big limp but it added character and I was enchanted by it: She was damaged in a way that touched my heart. I fell in love with her, a girl I saw just once and for only half a minute and never forgot. I still think of her. So don't

STEVE ZOUSMER

tell me love is logical. And don't tell me imagination can't seem real: I had imagined Sandrine and she seemed very real.

No one knew what to say. I shrugged. The others seemed to take it as a signal to disperse.

I'd forgotten about my task of informing Frieda about her role as Sandrine, probably because I didn't look forward to sharing the Sandrine experience with her. But Frieda hadn't forgotten and she was not letting me wiggle away. She took my arm firmly as we said good nights and headed out.

Elvire noticed this linkage and I could read her mind. She was aware of something going on between me and Frieda and didn't like it.

CHAPTER 20

I took Frieda to a bar called Lilly's where I planned to present her with the Sandrine role and explain what it would entail.

The first part went well. She may or may not have seen the offer coming but she was overjoyed when it arrived—it was probably one of the great moments of her not-so-easy life. The second part was harder because by this point the bar's male customers had taken a gander at Frieda in her revealing dress and cascading blonde tresses and they were drawn toward our table like moths who'd never seen such an irresistible flame.

I had sat in bars with beautiful movie stars and watched men stare but they kept their distance because the star's fame was a barrier that kept them at bay—the typical bar wolf would never make a play for a Rita Hayworth or Ava Gardner because he knew she was out of their league, an embarrassing rebuff was guaranteed, and witnesses would jeer at his pathetic disgrace. But Frieda had no fame shield to block the droolers. They kept circling in.

Going to another bar and having the same experience made no sense but Frieda solved the problem by saying bluntly, "We go to your apartment, okay?" so we did. And when we got there she won many points by: 1) not telling me what a loser's nest it was, and 2) heading to the bedroom while shedding her clothes.

A minute later we were doing what naked people do when they find themselves in bed together. Technically we'd already had sex but I would dismiss that awkward event and call this our first time. I found myself traversing her body with a fascination that was not solely erotic. I was more like an explorer who'd wandered into a magical mountain paradise filled with breathtaking views and fabulous wonders.

It obviously entered my mind that what I was getting from Frieda was gratitude sex, my reward for giving her a much-desired opportunity. Frieda was far from naive and surely knew that sex could be a reward, but what we were doing seemed like more than that and much better. Maybe it was her true joy and excitement at getting a chance to be a star. She seemed to reach a gratification I didn't expect as an average guy having sex with the likes of her. You figure a goddess has probably screwed the best of the gods and you are humdrum by contrast, but maybe that's not the way the goddess looked at it.

We didn't pretend to be in love but it wasn't as if there was nothing between us. Sandrine was between us. We'd just entered a partnership and the stakes were high. Both of our lives would be altered by how this played out. If Frieda felt gratitude, fine. Gratitude is an admirable emotion. If she was just going through the sexual motions or faking it, she was a hell of an actress but to the contrary, I believed that she had no acting talent whatsoever. She was forthright with no pretenses and no capacity for being anything but herself. Fakery was not in her tool kit. This was a serious drawback because I would need her to *act*, to play Sandrine and *be* Sandrine.

Lying in bed after the main event, we talked for a while and I led into a lecture course, Introduction to Sandrine. Frieda was an earnest student; she had read my Sandrine columns and promised to study them, but one thing I observed about her was that she was savvy about the things she was savvy about (sex and show business) but surprisingly unaware about everything else. She knew nothing about the news, she didn't read books or watch television. She seemed to have a good mind but there was a lot of empty space in it.

Above all, she didn't *get* Sandrine. She and Sandrine were too different and from two different worlds.

Sandrine was a poet and artist; Frieda's body was a work of art but that's where the art ended.

Sandrine's life was about purity and pursuit of purity; Frieda had not had the luxury of purity, having survived God-knows-what during and after the war and then in Sin City with a boyfriend who sounded like a fringe player in the Vegas underworld.

Sandrine downplayed her physical beauty; Frieda was more than willing to display it.

Sandrine's romantic life was mysterious; Frieda's was straightforward.

Sandrine was elusive, not needing a permanent man; Frieda, though seemingly formidable, had always depended on men to protect and guide her, though men had not always treated her well.

It would be a struggle for Frieda to embody so many things that didn't come naturally. But she would try. I could write lines for her and she would say them. I could coach her on evading difficult questions—I'd interviewed many champion evaders and knew how it was done. I could warn her away from touchy topics; specifically I stressed that she should *never mention Las Vegas* because it had sinful connotations for most Americans and *never mention Germany*, which remained at or near the top of America's shit list.

What I couldn't teach her was how to inhabit Sandrine's character the way a real actress could. A Kate Hepburn could put on Sandrine's character as easily as putting on a hat, and once in character she would have a compass to guide every word and gesture: She would instinctively say what Sandrine would say and do what Sandrine would do. This wouldn't happen with Frieda. I worried that this would be the cause of screw-ups large enough to tilt or even overturn the entire Sandrine applecart.

Meanwhile, more personally, since she could not act the role of Sandrine, she could not be anything close to the Sandrine I was hazily in love with. Could I transfer my emotional attachment to the Frieda version of Sandrine? Not very likely.

I did think Frieda had a good heart. She promised to do her best. She pleaded with me to be near her at all times, prompting her. She still believed there was a real Sandrine and begged me to introduce them so she could absorb Sandrine's character face-to-face.

"Why can't I meet her? Why is she hiding?"

"This is the way it has to be," I said.

Maybe I was wrong. Maybe I owed her the truth about Sandrine. But I'd learned that it's difficult to live with a lie and living with a lie while embodying it in public would be even more difficult, maybe a challenge she could not handle, a possible time bomb.

Dawn phoned to tell me the McAdoos had decided to host a gala reception for Sandrine after her Sullivan appearance. The guest list would include VIPs, celebrities, and idiot society friends of the Anus Brothers.

I told Frieda about this and, far from being daunted, she lit up. She loved the spotlight. She said she was good at parties and would be delighted to meet the important people.

"Just keep moving," I advised. "Never get trapped into a real conversation."

We lay still, thinking our own thoughts. She asked what to wear on Sullivan. I said something modest, like a black turtleneck and a simple dark skirt.

She asked if I had anything to drink and I told her there were a few cans of beer in the ice box.

She got up to get the beers and walked across my bedroom. I looked at her naked body and thought: 1) what an astonishing beauty she was, and 2) I actually liked her, and 3) had I done something terrible to this woman?

* * *

ARRIVING AT the theater on Sunday night I led Frieda backstage for a pre-show courtesy visit with Ed but we never got near him because of a brawl between two acts that were slated to appear on the show, a Brazilian bossa nova group and a Hungarian juggling troupe. I didn't see the fight but it was described to me as utter slapstick, with the instruments and props of both groups being used as weapons and a deafening volume of non-English cursing and shouting.

The Brazilians got the worst of it, suffering a smashed guitar, an apparently broken nose that splattered blood on white costumes, and the utter devastation of the girl singer's elaborate hairdo. As the fighting ended, the Hungarians played it smarter, apologizing profusely to Ed while the humiliated Brazilians carried on in a Latin fury, even insulting Ed and waving fists at him.

Ed was a stern boss and took no guff; security guards dragged the Brazilians out of the theater and into show business oblivion. The Hungarians were allowed to remain, but the show minus the Brazilian act was now four minutes and forty seconds light. Ed asked the other acts to stretch their performances but their acts were too finely calibrated to allow much improvising.

So there would be extra time to fill. A producer alerted me that Sandrine might be asked to come up on stage and chat briefly with Ed, as would the other celebrity guests in the studio audience.

This struck double fear into me. Frieda taking a bow from the audience was fine but making her first outing as Sandrine in a national TV interview with Ed Sullivan was alarming (though exciting to her). And the thought of other guests was an unexpected element, which worried me. I tried to get the producer to tell me who the guests were but the anxiety level among the production staff was stratospheric and he hurried off without a reply.

We had two seats in the fourth row, on the aisle. I gave Frieda the aisle seat so she wouldn't have to climb over me en route to the stage. She was doing her best to play Sandrine. She wore a dark turtleneck and dark skirt, as requested, and her hair was in a ponytail, tied with a red rubber band, and she wore no make-up. "I feel stupid in this costume," she whispered. "This is what I look like when I take out the garbage." She'd also applied two small Band-Aids on her cheeks which, she explained, were to cover the last scrape wounds from Sandrine's motorcycle accident.

I was far more nervous than she was. I told her Ed would probably ask softball questions about her experiences in New York: the accident, falling in love with Manhattan, and how she felt about becoming an overnight sensation.

During the first commercial she asked me if I thought she should upgrade her outfit, given that she would appear on stage. During the next commercial she told me she'd brought a different outfit to wear to the McAdoo reception after the show. Why didn't she just slip into it now and look so much better?

I said no, no, no but predictably, the woman who lived by her looks could not bear to be seen in her big TV moment looking like a drab bohemian folksinger. Sometime after the half-hour mark she said she would be right back and everything would be fine and before I could restrain her, she darted up the aisle.

She returned during the Hungarian juggling act. The Hungarians looked ragged from their pre-show dustup. They were dropping things and recovering ungracefully, exchanging dirty looks. They were further distracted by a murmur sweeping the audience which, I knew without even looking, was a reaction to Frieda in her new outfit, which was everything I should have expected: a crimson silk blouse with a scoop neckline and vast acreage of exposed bosom, a tight black slit skirt, tall heels, and blonde hair released from the chaste discipline of the rubber band. The Band-Aids were gone; makeup and lipstick were perfect. If Cleopatra had walked into that theater it couldn't have had more of an impact.

The juggling act ended—"crumbled" might be a better word—and the show went to commercial. Frieda stood up and waved to Ed who looked back with his undertaker's face responding as if a cadaver had just leaped out of a coffin and done a cartwheel. I don't know if he realized she was Sandrine; he had not met her and she bore no resemblance to the Sandrine profile.

It hit me that he would be thrown for a major loop when this sexpot arrived on his stage. Ed's unflagging devotion to on-air wholesomeness was

well-established; he considered himself a guardian of American moral sensi-
tivities, duty-bound to protect his audience from affronts to their sensibilities.

Frieda sat down and whispered, "Isn't this much better?"

* * *

THE PRODUCER rushed by us and said, "Ed will intro her and then call her
up onstage. We've got to eat up two minutes and forty-five seconds."

The commercial ended and Ed was speaking to the audience. "Ladies
and gentlemen, I know you're eager to meet some of the guests in our
studio audience exclusively tonight."

Frieda squeezed my hand.

"As you know, the Soviet Union beat us in the race to put satellites into
orbit around the earth with Sputniks 1 and 2."

"What the hell is he talking about?" Sandrine said." Does he think I'm
an astronaut?"

"But on January 31st, the United States caught up, with the spectacularly successful launch of Explorer 1. We all feel sure that the US will now
proceed to lengthen our lead in the space race, thanks in large part to three
brilliant scientists who are with us tonight. So let me introduce Dr. William
H. Pickering, Dr. James A. Van Allen, and Dr. Wernher von Braun. Let's
give them a very big and very patriotic round of applause."

Three husky men in dark business suits stood up right in front of us,
blocking our view of the stage, and waved to the audience.

Ed said, "What say we bring these heroes up on stage for a special
salute?"

The audience applauded again as the three men made their way to
the stage and shook hands with Ed and then did a lot of waving. I had no
stopwatch but I could feel the seconds ticking off.

"Also in our audience is a very attractive young lady whose story you
may have followed, the French singer Sandrine D'Avignon."

There was an anticipatory tingle in the audience. Frieda squeezed my
hand.

"Sandrine has created excitement and a lot of mystery in New York.
Within one day of coming to America for the first time, she made a fabulous
singing debut followed by a tragic motorcycle accident that left her near
death. Since then newspaper accounts of her brave recovery and romance
with New York have captivated readers in our city and across the nation."

Unless I missed it, Ed had not mentioned my name in connection with those captivating newspaper accounts. Thanks a lot, Ed.

"Until tonight this woman has not been seen by her public. Very few people know what she looks like—but you're about to find out, and remember that you saw her here for the very first time. So without further ado, let me introduce Sandrine D'Avignon. Stand up and take a bow, Sandrine!"

CHAPTER 21

Frieda, after so many years as a background player, knew exactly how to play a star.

She stood, stretched to her full height, rotated twice while waving both arms and displaying her figure. Then, in a few strides, she reached the stairs to the stage, ascended gracefully, turned and waved, and smiled dazzlingly. And then she played her best card: *the showgirl walk*, years of unheralded performances walking around naked in front of strangers now paying off in a vision of elegance as she crossed the stage, erect, unhurried, self-confident, radiant.

The audience, taken aback at first, rose up in a standing ovation. Why? Well, the Sandrine mystique, of course, including the thrill of finally seeing her and of course the showgirl walk, but I think there was also a liberating feeling to Frieda looking so *happy* while looking so sexy. The audience responded by giving her permission to briefly stretch the usual boundaries of sexiness and by giving themselves brief permission to enjoy it before puritanical rectitude returned.

The three space scientists, standing awkwardly on the stage—their suits buttoned tightly, not knowing what to do with their hands—were at first stiffly restrained but as they watched her approaching, the sheer pleasure of seeing her caused them to drop restraint and clap delightedly. Only stone-faced Ed held back.

Each space guy got a Sandrine embrace—their big meaty faces blushing red in black and white. Then she went for Ed who was, of course, the final arbiter, the culture judge who would declare her guilty or innocent, sensational or scarlet.

Ed seemed frozen as she approached but she handled it charmingly, unfolding his arms, which were clasped defensively across the chest, and kissing his hands, and then kissing him on the cheek. Then, instinctively, she bowed, and if she was cleanly taller than Ed at the start of the bow she had lowered herself into a worshipful looking-up position by the end of it. The gesture melted the old codger's wariness and caused him to release a small smile which spread unstoppably into an ear-to-ear grin, an amazing sight which Americans had never seen. That smile bestowed his blessing. Sandrine was triumphant without saying a word.

That would have been a great place to stop.

Ed found his voice and shouted over the din, "I guess we know how people feel about Sandrine D'Avignon!"

That brought another wave of applause. Frieda mouthed "Thank you, thank you." Then she made a show of sharing her applause with the space guys, a generous and patriotic gesture that must have softened Ed even more because he was applauding heartily. Then she made it even better by stepping between Pickering and von Braun and hooking their arms in hers.

The stage manager gave Ed a raised-finger one-minute signal and a hand mike. Ed had clearly planned to kill the last minute chatting importantly about America's space future but Frieda had clearly stolen the show. Before Ed could frame his first question, Frieda gently tilted the mike toward herself and said, "I'm so proud to be standing here with these great American heroes and of course the great Ed Sullivan."

The heroes beamed. Ed beamed.

"Ask me something," Frieda said, laughing as she released the mike to Ed.

Ed grasped for something to say and what he came up with was, "Sandrine, we hear you love motorcycles. Which is your favorite?"

Frieda knew nothing about motorcycles but turned it into a victory: "The big ones that go *vroom, vroom, vroom.*" This got a huge laugh as the giddiness level of the moment soared even higher.

"We've all been reading about your experience in New York. Tell us about it."

"Every minute has been like making love," she said, forgetting her nearly fatal accident. "New York is the place to start a new life, especially after nine years in Vegas," she said, forgetting my advice about not mentioning Las Vegas.

Ed was perplexed. I'd written that Sandrine performed at Chez Dee's on her first night in America, so what were these nine years in Vegas?

Never a gifted improviser, Ed hesitated while trying to think up another question. Only a second or two went by but the silence hung heavily between them. Without a question to reply to, Frieda must have felt abandoned, forced to ad lib in her first time on national television.

A flutter of desperation crossed her face—I'm not sure viewers caught it, but I did. All of her preparation for the Sandrine role seemed forgotten; somehow the single thing that stuck in her mind was my advice about not mentioning Las Vegas or Germany, and having already mentioned Vegas she strained so hard to *not* mention Germany that it had to come out.

"I'm not from Germany," she blurted.

Ed had no response. Frieda knew she'd said the wrong thing and tried to charm her way out of trouble. With a big smile she squeezed von Braun's arm, pressing a creamy breast against his shoulder, saying, "But this handsome man, Dr. von Braun, *is* German, I think. A great scientist from Germany."

Then it got even worse: she spoke German to him. Just a sentence. I don't know what she said and it was probably harmless but von Braun recoiled. His American identity was built on a polite conspiracy to forget that he'd been a Nazi. He'd come over to the American side after the war when the US and Soviets competed to grab up Germany's best rocket scientists. Von Braun was the prize catch, the mastermind behind Hitler's V-2 guided missiles.

But he was now an *American* mastermind and speaking German on national television was the last thing he needed. He looked stricken. Ed was speechless. I was stunned, thinking, "This is going to come back *at me*, and fast."

But, to my astonishment, the studio audience didn't react. Maybe von Braun's story was not widely known. Maybe Frieda/Sandrine was being forgiven for not knowing she was cozying up to a man whose missiles killed thousands of people in London and Holland. But some people would catch it and there'd be hell to pay. All I could think about was the fancy writing I'd have to do to explain it away in my next column.

The moment, painful as it was, came and went quickly, as if the momentum of Sandrine's much-awaited appearance simply rolled over a blip of minor turbulence. The camera pulled back for a wide shot of the stage, showing the audience rising in a standing ovation that continued as the last seconds ticked away. Frieda smiled winningly, waved in all directions, and seemed to bob up and down with pleasure. Ed regained his poise and waved until the red "On the Air" sign blinked off.

* * *

THE SULLIVAN show, usually so straitlaced, had exploded in a last-minute release of unprecedented titillation and the audience loved it. The scene backstage was jubilant. I'd never seen Ed Sullivan so jazzed up. The three scientists were grinning as if they'd just landed a spaceship on Jupiter. Frieda was ecstatic.

A stagehand showed us a back way out of the theater where I hailed a cab and we jumped in. "To your place," she cried. "I'm going to fuck your brains out."

"We're due at the reception," I said. "You're the guest of honor."

"No, I need to fuck your brains out. Right now. Do you say no? I've never had to ask anyone twice."

The cab driver was laughing so hard he could barely drive.

* * *

SHE HAD an orgasm so loud I thought I'd lose my lease.

My brains were completely fucked out. It didn't last long but when it ended we collapsed and dozed for a while, until my doorbell rang. It was a deliveryman bringing a flower arrangement. The card said,

Bravo!
Not what we expected but spectacular.
Have a ball.
Spencer and Kate

"Who are Spencer and Kate?" asked Frieda.

"A nice couple I met in church," I said.

"Come on, let's go to the party," she said.

CHAPTER 22

The McAdoos were cheapskates when it came to salaries or putting money into journalism but they threw open the vault when it came to showing off to their carriage trade friends. I worked the gaudy arena of Broadway and show business and rarely sniffed the same rarefied air as those people, the powers-that-be of New York's business and social worlds. But there they were, in their finery. The men were tuxedoed silver foxes. Their wives were gowned and jeweled to the nines.

Ed Sullivan was there, beaming as he accepted never-ending congratulatory back pats. The space guys were there, reveling in their celebrity and hitting the free bar with flyboy exuberance. I'd insisted on adding two names to the guest list, Dee and Elvire, and Elvire sneaked in her boyfriend, Martin. Alida was unable to attend but I knew she'd watched the Sullivan show so I phoned her. She said, "That Sandrine gal looks a helluva lot like Frieda but don't tell Frieda or she'll get a fat head."

The party was held in a gorgeous rooftop restaurant with the Manhattan skyline glittering below. A quartet played the New York songbook. About a hundred guests shared a common objective: getting a close-up look or touch or word with the magnetic Frieda/Sandrine. They clearly preferred Frieda's sexy version of Sandrine to the soulful and chaste version I'd had in mind from the beginning.

Frieda was in heaven, vibrant and comfortable as if she'd spent her life as the toast of the town. I introduced her first to the McAdoos, who seemed flustered by her. They started a reception line on which guests buzzed with excitement as their handshake with Sandrine approached. I moved away briefly to get champagne.

My instinct was to conceal the erotic fireworks between Frieda and me but the sexual blush must have been present on our cheeks. It rattled me that before the party was minutes old, three people—Sid, Dee, and Dawn—had asked me variations on the same amazed question: "You're screwing her, aren't you?" Elvire seemed to know it too, though she was too proper to mention it, and the McAdoos treated me with newfound respect due to the man who was reaping carnal knowledge of the woman who'd just electrified an entire nation. I'd never tasted the experience of being a sexual high achiever but I seemed to be exuding a charisma that people sensed, maybe figuring that Sandrine had to be screwing *somebody* and I, her chronicler, was the best guess. Two things I knew about sex gossip: it travels fast and it doesn't have to be accurate.

Of course Ed Sullivan's radar picked up on it too. We shared a mutually congratulatory hug as flashbulbs popped. The photo caption would be: "Rival Columnists Make Nice At Sandrine Fete." I tried to whisper an apology for Frieda's blunder with von Braun but he shrugged it off, pulling me closer and warning, "Ride it out, Chick, but be careful. This babe might be too hot for America—and too much for you."

One person was not having a good time: Sid. He was halfway through a Manhattan and might also have downed a Brooklyn and a Queens. He pulled me aside and I could see it wasn't going to be a fun exchange.

"This whole thing was bullshit from the get-go, wasn't it?"

I didn't confirm it, which would have put him in a bad spot as my boss, but I didn't deny it.

"Let me review your transgressions," Sid said in a rising and slurring voice. "First you made up a phony story. Then you compounded it over and over again, making your newspaper complicit in it. Then you found a stacked German blonde to play the role you made up. Then she flirted with the Nazi. Then you compromised your integrity again by screwing her. Is there *any* canon of professionalism you haven't shat on? And the joke is that your job is more secure now than it ever was and the morons who run our paper can't wait for more of your shenanigans."

I wanted to protest, but he was right on every point.

"You've moved into a whole new ball game, Chick." He seemed to have more to say but saying it was too unpleasant. He shook his head and walked away.

The McAdoos tapped the mike and the crowd quieted down. Duffy led a toast to Sandrine. Kingsley babbled about the paper's rocketing circulation since the Sandrine story began. Ed Sullivan, asked to say a few words, compared Sandrine's instant impact on his TV audience to Elvis Presley's legendary appearance a year and a half earlier. He invited Sandrine to perform on his show when her singing voice returned. "We'll see if you can top Elvis's 'Don't Be Cruel' and 'Hound Dog.'"

The quartet launched into dance music and its leader called for Frieda as the guest of honor to lead things off, with me as her partner. I'm no Fred Astaire (not even Fred Astaire with a sprained ankle) but Frieda was a pretty fair Ginger Rogers so I just hung on and we whirled around the floor with everyone looking at her and no one looking at me.

Dee and Elvire had met Frieda as Frieda. Now I introduced her to them as Sandrine. It was awkward but they got through it with good humor. Dee said, "We're happy for you, Chick."

Then Dawn was at my side, tugging my elbow.

She said, "Guess who just crashed the party?"

* * *

SINATRA CAME in solo and smiling, clearly sensing the rippling excitement in the room. The Anus Brothers shoved guests aside to get to him and when they did, they made instant fools of themselves by bowing and scraping. Frank disregarded them, surveying the crowd that formed around him, and with outstretched arms proclaimed, "I gotta meet her."

In a moment Frieda was offered up to him, emerging through the crowd. He put his arms around her, hugged and kissed her without overdoing it. "Is she fantastic, or what?" he said to the crowd.

Frieda was poised and graceful in his grasp; I supposed she'd been grasped by more than one big star in Las Vegas.

"Where's Chick?" demanded Frank.

Then I was pushed forward, into a handshake and shoulder clasp. Photogs snapped front page-destined shots of Sinatra, Frieda, and me. Then Frank pulled me aside.

"You're a big surprise, Chicklet," he said, flashing the great Sinatra grin. "You really put the puck in the net."

"Frank, the last time we talked you called me a Mesopotamian dung beetle or something like that."

"Forget it. Bygones are bygones. We've entered the Sandrine era. I'll tell ya though"—his voice dropping to a whisper—"I've read your columns and this is not the Sandrine I pictured."

"What do you mean?"

"I didn't think she'd make my bird flap its wings."

Frank had heard the clinker: Frieda's Sandrine was not the Sandrine of my columns. But she was *better* than the Sandrine of my columns.

Lowering his voice again, he said, "I saw that finish to Ed's show and wondered if she's as dynamific in the sack as she is on the stage. But how, pray tell, would a humble pilgrim attain the promised land?"

Lust shined in his eyes and I realized: 1) that he hadn't caught on to the chemistry between me and Sandrine, and 2) that Frank Sinatra of all people was out to snake my woman, and 3) that he was asking me to help him.

Before I could say anything, Duffy McAdoo pushed in and sheepishly asked if Frank would do a song to mark this great event in journalistic history. (A total fraud does one minute on TV and that qualifies as journalistic history?)

To my astonishment, Frank put his thumb and forefinger around Duffy's lapel and said, "Young man, if you will provide me with a drinking glass containing four cubes of ice, two fingers of Jack Daniels Tennessee Whiskey, and a splash of H2O, I will sing a special song in honor of the occasion."

Wow. Sending a newspaper publisher to fetch a drink. In the meantime, I had nothing to lose so I told Frank that a promising young singer named Elvire Coutansais was in the room and would be thrilled to meet him.

He asked me to point her out. "What a doll," he said.

I caught her eye and waved her over.

Elvire approached shyly. She was looking cuter than ever. Martin the boyfriend tried to approach too but Dee put a hand on his chest to hold him back.

"Elvire, say hello to Frank Sinatra."

"Hey, it'd be a gas if you'd join me in a song," Frank said. "What kind of music do you do, sweetheart?"

"French," she said.

"Hey, très bien. Teach me some français."

He put an arm around her shoulders and they went off to confer with the quartet's leader as Duffy hurried back with Frank's friend, Jack Daniels.

The room went silent as Frank took the mike.

"Good evening everybody. Tonight is Sandrine's night but first I'd like you to meet a young lady with a difficult name—"

"Elvire Coutansais," she said.

"Now appearing at—"

"Chez Dee in the Village."

Frank said, "I don't ordinarily work from the Gallic songbook, but one great tune comes to mind. Benny Goodman recorded it ten years back with the one and only Peggy Lee on the vocal. It's called 'La Mer.'"

"'The Sea,'" said Elvire. "Written by a man on a train riding along France's Mediterranean coast."

"The young lady's gonna sing it in French and I'll be faking it in the background. Maestro."

So Elvire got to sing with Frank Sinatra. She did the lyrics in her soft but tuneful voice, and crowd was enchanted. Frank hummed along with her for a moment, then took a few backward steps, giving her the spotlight as he sipped his drink and smiled in approval.

When she was done, Frank stepped back in, giving her a hug. The applause was warm and full. Elvire stepped down, glowing.

"Good things come in small packages, huh? Wasn't she great?" asked Frank. "Next time I'll be singing with Sandrine. But before I rush off into the night let me give you a song of my own, the title number from my new Capitol Records album. It's called 'Come Fly With Me.'"

Like him or not, hearing Old Blues Eyes sing live is as good as it gets. The song was upbeat and romantic, raising spirits to the high heavens and beyond. As applause shook the room, Frank waved and made his way out, handshaking his way toward the exits where Frieda intercepted him, with me close behind.

"It was so good of you to come," she said. "It's been a wonderful night."

"It doesn't have to end, Sandrine," Frank said. "I'm heading over to the Waldorf. Cole Porter's throwing one of his incomparable soirées, if you'd like to be my guest."

Without doubt the invitation went beyond chitchat with Cole Porter. It seemed to confirm my explanation of Frank's presence here: he'd seen her on Sullivan and challenged himself to bed her before the rooster crowed at dawn.

I figured Frank's offer would be irresistible to the ambitious Frieda and assumed she'd drop me at hot-potato speed to mix with the glitterati at Cole Porter's and top it off with a wee small hours bounce on the bedsprings with the Chairman of the Board. But to my amazement, she didn't take the bait. She cheek-kissed him and said, "Thanks so much for coming, Frank. But I have other plans." Then she stepped back and took my arm.

Frank got the picture and took it graciously. "As the wise man once said, 'Nothing gentured, nothing vained.'" Then he looked me up and down in a pantomime of admiration and said, "You ain't the Mesopotamian dung walrus I took you for, Chicklet. *Attaboy*!"

We realized at that moment that Duffy McAdoo had hurried over, either to thank Frank or make *his* move on Sandrine. But Duffy stepped on the brakes, dumbstruck as he realized that if Sandrine had rebuffed Sinatra, Duffy had no chance at all.

Frank was amused.

"Thanks for the hooch, kid," he said, snickering at Duffy, shooting him with an imaginary pistol.

CHAPTER 23

Sex, absent from my life for so long, had roared back and by the time Frieda and I returned to my apartment I was as revved as she was for another round of FMBO—Fuck My Brains Out.

In a way this sudden glorious appearance of sex felt like an unexpected inheritance from a relative I'd never heard of: a bonanza I hadn't sought or deserved and didn't know how to handle. Also, I knew (the lesson was hammered in every week on the TV series *The Millionaire*) that miraculous windfalls could bring out unfortunate behavior. Sleeping with Frieda was like sleeping with Venus, a fantasy few men are prepared to encounter. There was a risk of intoxication, addiction, bad judgment, or even head-over-heels emotional attachment. Strange as it seemed, this was beginning. I was feeling it.

Two other sex thoughts:

First, Alida. As she had deteriorated, she seemed baffled by sex, then angered by it, then revolted. So it ended. But it nagged at me that having stupendous sex with Frieda while Alida suffered her heartbreaking fate was unfair and unkind, a breach of faithfulness even though the faithfulness contract had expired with her desire and our divorce. There was nowhere to go with the thought, but it was a weight on my shoulders.

Second, absurd as it sounded, sex with Frieda was not like the sex I'd imagined with Sandrine. Obviously I'd never had sex with the imaginary Sandrine but in my dreams, Sandrine was luxurious, mysterious, and sensitive in bed while Frieda was straightforward, enthusiastic, and athletic. Sandrine was more to my taste. It was hard to believe I was straight-facedly contrasting sex with a real woman to sex with an imaginary woman but that kind of thinking went with the situation I'd created.

The sex we had after the Sullivan/Sinatra party was great but it didn't exhaust our adrenaline. It was late but we were still wide awake. So we went to the window. I put on a robe; Frieda pulled my suit jacket around her bare shoulders.

"I think I've discovered your secret spot," she said. At first I thought she meant some pleasure button on my body but what she meant was the window. "New Yorkers love to look out windows, don't they?"

"In my neighborhood they did, when I was a kid. It was mainly the moms, sitting there for hours looking down at the action, keeping an eye on their kids but also following all the little dramas playing out below. They'd know which parent dominated the conversations on the wooden benches in the playground. They'd see how the other wives envied the elegant Mrs. Coleman, who dressed so well. They'd know which boys were the natural leaders and which girls were flirts and who the bad apples were and they'd know whose dads came home looking like winners while other dads slumped home brooding and defeated and maybe looking to vent some anger on their families. Whenever I went to someone's apartment for the first time I couldn't stop myself from beelining for the window. I needed to see the view and know what was cooking outside. Alida was the same way. We did a lot of looking out windows together. I'd sip a beer, she'd smoke. She was a keen observer."

"She still looks out the window," Frieda said. "It calms her. She says, 'Frieda, let's catch the show,' and I bundle her up in hat and coat and she watches and watches until she puts her head on the sill and goes to sleep."

"Last summer there was a hooker who saw clients in an old Nash Rambler parked right down there," I said, pointing. "I never got more than a glimpse of her but there was a steady flow of johns and always a few standing around in the shadows, smoking and waiting their turns. A good show on a dull night."

"Well, now you get the show in your own apartment," she laughed, putting an arm around me.

"Chick, I shouldn't have spoken German to the German guy, I know that. It just came out. Where was my brain?"

"I guess you didn't know he was a famous Nazi rocket scientist who bombed London."

"You're joking? My God." She was shocked for a moment until a smile started spreading on her face. "I'll tell you one thing about him: He has very strong hands."

"Strong hands? How do you know that?"

"Guess."

"Don't tell me he grabbed your ass."

"Yes, at the party. He was loaded and I was afraid I was going to have a problem with him but this girl of yours, Dawn, rushes in and asked for his autograph at just the right time. And his autographing hand is his ass-squeezing hand. And while he is signing, I make a run."

We laughed at that.

"What do we do now, Chick?"

The streets were empty. Lots of frigid air was coming in. I closed the window.

"Go back to bed?"

"Yes, of course, but I mean what's going to happen with Sandrine? And what will happen with us?"

"I haven't thought beyond the Sullivan show. Can you believe the whole country saw you on that stage, charming everyone?"

"And I did it with clothes on."

"Just barely. That outfit might have been a shocker to the God-fearing American audience. On the other hand, nobody seems bothered by the Vegas and Germany mentions. So maybe we just barrel ahead. I'll try to find a way to put everything right in my Tuesday column."

"What do you mean by 'barrel ahead'?"

"Move forward and see what happens. Que será, será, as Doris Day once said. Whatever will be, will be."

Then we were back in bed.

She said, "Can I move in with you? I don't want to be alone with all this happening. I want to be with you."

It felt suddenly like a movie scene. I was Fred MacMurray and she was Marilyn Monroe pleading for shelter from the cold cruel world.

"Okay, let's try it," I said. "But we have to keep you out of sight till we have a plan."

"Why out of sight? Isn't this the time to do something big? Get more famous? Make money? I can't just hide here and look out your window all day."

She was right. When the iron is hot, you're supposed to strike. But I had no ideas and no instinct for producing Sandrine's career. I was no impresario and didn't want to be one. And in terms of fakery, I was only a half-hearted amateur. Bigger stuff was beyond me.

I said, "For now, go back to work with Alida. Wear your dowdy coat and hat and those horrible black glasses you wore the day I met you. Blend in. This is how Greta Garbo does it. I've spotted her on the East Side. She was the most famous woman in the world but she manages to be invisible. You can do it too. Until we figure out what to do."

"If you say so. But not for long, okay?"

"I'll show you how to get in and out of my apartment without going in the front door, in case Drusen is surveilling us. You just go up the stairs to the top floor, go out on the roof, and from there you can walk to the next roof, then down the stairs and out. The other building's door is around the corner. Take the same route when you come back in. No one will spot you even if they're in front of my building watching."

"Okay, but Chick, this is my moment. I'm scared it will go away if we wait too long."

I tried to convince her not to worry. As I rambled on, she drifted into sleep.

I woke at first light and watched her sleeping. I thought she was right, the flame-out would come fast. The world would get wise. And when that happened, what could she do? She couldn't sing or act. She wouldn't be the first no-talent babe to break into the big-time and for a while she could be a classic celebrity, famous just for being famous, but where would that take her? She saw nothing but fame and fortune but I knew things would go bad as our luck inevitably ran out.

* * *

IN THE morning we taxied to the East Side where she packed her things and moved out of the apartment she'd shared with a bunch of TWA stewardesses. We taxied back to my place to move her in. Then I walked her to Alida's apartment and went on to my office.

Applause and friendly hooting greeted me as I entered the newsroom. A wire photo of me and Frieda/Sandrine and Ed Sullivan was taped to my door along with Dawn's autograph from Wernher von Braun. My desk was covered with messages.

"It was a helluva party," said Dawn. "Sinatra and Sandrine in the same room, making show business history."

I guess she was teasing but I had no comeback. I asked about Sid.

"Brutal hangover right now," she said. "He's pissed at you. But everyone else thinks you're cool."

"What's in these messages?"

"Well, talent agents are calling. They all want to represent her and create events for her and so on. A couple modeling agencies called. Lots of news media and generally a higher class of reporters than the usual hyenas. Harrison Salisbury of the *Times*. Murray Kempton. Also a woman writer around my age who took me out for tea, which is a new one for me but I liked her. Joanne Didion. No, Joan Didion. Oh, and a space official from the government. I guess von Braun and the other two were so hot for Sandrine they got her invited as a celebrity guest at the opening of NASA next October."

"NASA is what?"

"The space agency. National Aeronautics and Space Administration."

"What does Sandrine have to do with space?"

"Chick, she's a dish. They just want to ogle her. Maybe she can attract press, I don't know."

Did I invent Sandrine to create a model who stood around smiling and flashing her curves at publicity events?

"Another call was interesting because the guy didn't want to speak to you—he said he was trying to locate a Frieda Waldschneider. I told him you don't know anyone by that name. He said you do and you'd know where she is. Anything you want to explain to your loyal assistant?"

"Frieda Waldschneider is Sandrine, Dawn. In real life she's Alida's nurse."

"You chose Alida's nurse to be Sandrine? Geez. Did Sinatra really make a play for her?"

"Yes. Did this caller leave a name?"

"No, but he left a phone number and said she'd recognize it. Area code 702. I looked it up: Las Vegas. And he said he's flying East. To my cultured ear he sounded like a wiseguy."

"A wiseguy of the criminal variety? A mobster?"

"I could be wrong. Either that or a senator or some other kind of low life."

It made sense. Frieda had lived in Vegas for years and knew people, including unsavory people, and they would have recognized her on Sullivan. But I didn't like her getting calls from men in Las Vegas. Was this the old boyfriend she'd told me about? Was I jealous already? I picked up the phone and called Frieda at Alida's. Alberta told me she was out taking Alida for a walk. I gave her the message and left the guy's number.

It was time to crank out a column. I sat down at my trusty Royal, hoping for inspiration. I thought about asking for reader suggestions on what Sandrine should do next. Or making up something dramatic about her a seeing doctors and learning she'd never sing again, because having heard Frieda singing in my shower, I knew she'd never sing as Sandrine.

Dawn came in. "The Anuses want to see you upstairs, toot sweet."

When I got there Kingsley McAdoo was waiting at the conference room door, looking excited. "There's someone we want you to meet. This could be highly lucrative for the paper. So I wanted to tell you: don't fuck the dog. I'm warning you, okay?"

"I can't fuck the dog? That's disappointing."

"I'm warning you," he said.

I entered the room and my eyes beheld none other than Hendrik Drusen. He was sitting in a big leather chair and looking regal, in contrast to Sid who looked like a gastrointestinal disaster area. Also on hand: the house counsel, MacAndrew Warren Tisdale, and Tilden Ames, the manager of the paper's business side.

"So glad you could join us, Chip," Duffy said insincerely. "Shake hands with Hank Drusen, who's come to us with a very attractive concept."

"Hank" Drusen, eh? He'd always be Rick to me.

We pretended we hadn't met. Hank was wearing a million-dollar pin-striped suit. He gave me a sly smile and a crunching handshake. He was obviously delighted to surprise me and I'm sure he enjoyed getting the drop on me on my home turf.

Duffy said, "Hank, maybe you'd like to sketch out your proposal for Chuck."

Drusen said, "Of course, Duff, and it's a pleasure to meet you, Chick. Let me keep this simple because it would be premature to get into specific numbers or planning matters. I am the chief executive of a precious metals trading company which does high-volume business in many countries around the world. You haven't heard of us because we keep a discreet profile befitting a prestigious company with an elite client base. Discretion has been our model since my grandfather founded the company. We provided valuable hard asset and currency services to the Allied cause during both world wars and we continue to provide services to Free World governments in the fight against Communism."

The bullshit lights were blinking frantically but I gave him credit for stylish delivery.

Just to be stupid, I asked, "Is Sandrine a Commie?"

"Not at all, you misunderstand," he said, smiling. "I'm only trying to explain the significance of my company in the context of world affairs. If you need confirmation of what I'm saying I could put in a call right now to John Foster Dulles at State or Allen Dulles at CIA."

"Great," I said, calling his bluff. "Let's give 'em a ring. They look like fun guys."

"That won't be necessary," interrupted Kingsley. "Mr. Drusen has brought us an attractive proposal and it has nothing to do with the Cold War."

"Times are changing," said Drusen. "Discretion is a less viable strategy than it used to be and it's not a growth strategy. In our judgment we should now be putting a human face on our company, getting away from stodginess and embracing an image that engenders more retail appeal in today's world."

Somehow this was going to be about Drusen getting to Sandrine, I knew that. He was laying a big con on the Anuses.

"We believe Sandrine showed great magnetism on Mr. Sullivan's program and, I'm told, at the party afterward. We believe she might be just right to become our global spokeswoman, perhaps paired with a distinguished older man of equal charm. We're having conversations with David Niven."

"Loved him in *Around the World in 80 Days*," said Tilden Ames. "Very urbane. Great pairing with the younger woman, Sandrine."

"We think so," Drusen continued. "There aren't that many women in this role so Sandrine would be a trailblazer, something to be proud of. Ideally she'd travel the world, sometimes with Niven and sometimes on her own, visiting our offices, meeting local business leaders and employees, taking part in promotional activities and answering questions from reporters who would undoubtedly be captivated by her."

"She knows zero about business."

"The rudiments are simple. We could teach her easily. She'd be fine."

It wasn't the dumbest idea in the world. Frieda wouldn't have to sing or act. She could learn what to say. Then all she had to do was be sexy and charming while making money, traveling the world, having fun.

Everything she wanted.

But it was not a real offer. It was bogus. It was hot steaming horseshit.

Kingsley stepped in. "Mr. Drusen proposes a unique partnership between his company and Sandrine *and* the paper. There'd be a very substantial and exclusive advertising campaign in our paper to build awareness of Hank's company, and the star of the ads would be Sandrine. Meanwhile we'd build her identity based on the columns you write about her, and some of those columns would report on Hank's company and its contribution to our global communities."

"That is total crap," said Sid, erupting. Dawn was right: He was so hung over he'd forgotten to play ball with the McAdoos. "Writing columns giving publicity and praise to this guy's company while the company runs big ads on our pages? Do we have any fucking journalistic ethics left?"

"Sid, there's no threat to our ethics, trust me," said Duffy.

Sid looked away.

MacAndrew Warren Tisdale cleared his throat and entered the conversation. "Mr. Drusen would be investing considerable capital in this project, Chick, and he concurs with us that everything must be above board and top drawer, befitting the prestige of our two companies. Meanwhile, in consideration of your involvement, he has offered to provide you with honoraria equal to your current annual salary with the paper, in effect doubling your income. And Sandrine would be in line for a six-figure contract over the course of a five-year contract."

I thought of the hooker who turned tricks in the Nash Rambler under my window. That would be me, journalistically. On the other hand, I wasn't exactly Mr. Journalistic Purity.

Drusen said, "By chance I'm about to kick off a tour of many of our overseas offices and I'd like Sandrine to accompany me as a sort of test run. She could meet our people and they could react to her in the spokeswoman role. They're tradition-bound and might resist at first but we've seen the power of her personality. I'm leaving Thursday, starting in Paris, then on to Rotterdam, Bonn, and Zurich, possibly Tel Aviv and Johannesburg."

"How about Amsterdam?" I asked.

"Not on this trip."

"Because your wife and family live in Amsterdam and you don't want them catching you with Sandrine?"

"I have no idea what you mean. For one thing, I'm divorced. But my family is not relevant to this."

Now I saw the whole thing.

"I know what he's up to," I announced to the room. "This deal's not for real. He just wants to pork Sandrine."

Kingsley's eyes widened. "Pork?"

"He means fuck," said Duffy.

"He wants to get his mitts on her. He wants to get her to Paris and take her to Montmartre to relive some old fantasy. But this time he won't let her get away."

Jaws dropped around the room. Sid smirked and I was probably smirking too.

"What has gotten into you, Mr. Lopritz?" said Tisdale.

Kingsley pointed at me angrily as he searched for words. "Chick, I warned you not to fuck the dog but now you've explicitly fucked the dog, knowing that this deal could help put us solidly in the black again. It could save the paper."

"The deal is a sham," I said. "He's bullshitting you."

Drusen said, "Perhaps the next step would be for me to discuss the deal face-to-face with Miss D'Avignon, who might see things more positively than Mr. Lopritz. Perhaps you should instruct Mr. Lopritz to expedite this meeting."

"I'll give you a one-word answer to that," I said. "Go fuck yourself."

"We need this deal, Lopritz," said Kingsley. "But you walk in and obstruct it and insult this fine gentleman. Well, we don't give a rat's rectum where you stand. We're doing this. You'd better rethink your thinking if you think you can be the asshole in this shit storm, buster. Now get out of here because we have to discuss firing you."

CHAPTER 24

I was telling Dawn what happened upstairs when Drusen came striding across the newsroom with Sid scurrying behind him. I could lip-read Drusen saying over his shoulder, "I'll talk to him alone."

Sid dropped back as Drusen marched into my office, slamming the door behind him and looking around in disgust. "I can't believe you have such a shitty office," he said. He'd clearly dropped the affable global businessman act and was back to dangerous.

"I've got you now, Lopritz. You will produce Sandrine for me or I will tell them that unless you're fired I'm walking away, dropping the entire ad campaign."

"But there is no ad campaign, Hank or Rick. You're trying to make them force me to give her up to you. You have no intention of buying ads. You're not going to change your company's image and you're not going to hire Sandrine for anything."

He looked around to make sure we were alone. Then, proud of himself and grinning, he said, "But they did fall for it, didn't they? Without a moment's skepticism. Even the arrogant lawyer. What idiots. And as we say in metals trading, the only idiot bigger than a sex-hungry idiot is a money-hungry idiot."

I said, "You know who's a bigger idiot than a money-hungry idiot? A clinically deluded idiot. Like you, Drusen. Someone who walks around for twelve years thinking he fell in love with a woman who didn't exist in a nightclub that didn't exist and who your investigators couldn't find because she never existed. You don't love her. You love the delusion. It keeps you warm at night."

Here I was, Sigmund Freud Lopritz. How did I know what the reality of that Paris night might have been? A complex delusion or simple drunkenness? An embellishment of something that did happen or a total fabrication by an insane mind? Or just a sweet little dream that grew into an obsession?

"No," he said. "It is the truth. You have written about her and I have seen her. You seated me next to her at Chez Dee's. How cruel that was. You let me tell my story in front of her. Our knees touched and I thought nothing of it because I didn't know that the woman I've searched for was there next to me."

"You weren't supposed to meet her. Remember that you'd hijacked me on the subway. That wasn't part of the plan either."

He wasn't listening to me. "Then I look at this Ed Sullivan show and there she is," he said. "*There she is!* I've found her."

"She's a little different though, huh?"

"Yes, not exactly as I remember her, I admit that. Taller. A fuller figure. I don't remember her as so glamorous and outgoing but people change over time."

"And German. When you met her in Paris she was French."

"She said on TV that she wasn't German."

"But she told you at Chez Dee's that she was from Munich. And her accent is clearly German."

"I'm sure these things can be explained. I need to talk to her. You must connect me to her. What will this take? Money? I will give you money. If not money, what?"

"Are you really divorced?" I asked.

"Yes, I was married almost ten years. But there was always the other woman."

"The other woman being Sandrine?"

"Sandra. Yes. She haunted our marriage. My wife was not the woman I wanted and she knew it. She couldn't live with it and neither could I."

For a moment I started to soften about this guy. He might be a deluded psycho and I didn't know whether the woman he remembered was real or a fantasy but he loved her and he'd filled his life with pain over her. Unless he was lying, which I'd seen him do. I'd also seen him furious and violent. He was a threat to Frieda and a threat to my employment. So forget about changing my tune.

The phone rang. I picked it up and—could it be anyone else?—it was Frieda.

"I'm sorry to bother you," she said.

Drusen's face changed. Somehow he intuited that I was talking to the woman he was so desperate to find.

Frieda said, "I've made a dinner date for us tomorrow. A couple old friends and a superstar you might know—"

"You're talking to Sandrine?" cried Drusen, jumping up.

"—Lana Turner."

Drusen seized the phone and wrenched out of my hand, shouting "Sandrine, is that you? This is Hendrik." But I'd pressed the button, disconnecting him. He was enraged.

"That was her? And you hung up? I don't believe it."

He raised the telephone over his shoulder. The next move would be bringing it down on my skull, bashing it into a thousand fragments of bone and brain.

"No, it wasn't her," I shouted, my hands up defensively. "It was a source calling in a gossip tip. Something about Mickey Rooney."

Dawn rushed in yelling and waving a pair of scissors which she apparently planned to use as a weapon against Drusen. Drusen glared at me and then her and then me and then threw the phone at me. He missed. Then he turned and pushed past Dawn as he charged out.

"What the hell did you say to him?" asked Dawn. "He looked deranged."

I sat there begging my heart to slow down. She disappeared for a moment and returned with a coffee cup full of warm vodka. "Drink," she ordered.

I took a good slug of it.

"Chick, don't you want me to do something about this guy? Sooner or later he won't be able to restrain himself. He'll kill you. You'll die over a fake woman."

I was vulnerable, yes, but so was Drusen. I had a weapon I could use against him. I whirled around to my trusty Royal.

AN URGENT MESSAGE TO SANDRINE:
BEWARE THE DUTCHMAN
CHICK'S CLICKS, BY COLUMNIST CHICK LOPRITZ

Be careful, darling.

You were spectacular on Sullivan. Sinatra sang to you at the party afterward. The night was *fabbo del tutti fabbo*.

Yes, there were surprises—I'd never pictured you as the zesty and chesty type and that neckline and tight skirt combo was perhaps more sexsational than you intended, not aware of the discomfort your natural beauty might cause to wholesome Americans. Maybe, in your inexperience, you thought a daring outfit was required for your first big-time TV appearance.

Your fans love you and will forgive you.

Also, I didn't know you were German-born, though only a toddler when your French parents rushed you out of Deutschland and back to La Belle France in flight from Hitler's horrors.

Another thing I didn't know was the size of your heart—a heart big enough to chat graciously with Wernher von Braun, the fuehrer's top rocket genius. Many Americans will not forgive von Braun but I say he's a key player on our team now so let's cut him some slack.

Now let's get very serious.

Here's what gives me the shivers and quivers.

That pure and radiant soul of yours will inevitably attract people who are neither pure nor radiant. Every star has encountered dangerous nut jobs whose obscene obsessions and demonic desires cannot be detailed in a family newspaper.

They're not always easy to spot. For every foaming, drooling wild-eyed psychopath, there's another who comes on as an upstanding citizen. He's prosperous, well-dressed, well-spoken. Seemingly well-intentioned. The Perfect Gentleman. He claims a love for you as unsullied as the snows of Kilimanjaro.

One member of this loathsome tribe stood in my office yesterday. Your appearance on the Sullivan show revealed, he thought, a love lost years ago and painfully pined for ever since.

I call him The Dutchman.

The Dutchman is a legitimate international businessman— but also a very sick man.

His life, he says, has been a wretched search for a woman he thinks he met on a drunken Paris night years ago when she sang chansons d'amour as dawn broke over the City of Light.

He lost her, then searched for her fervidly, but to no avail. He married another woman but could not love her because she was not the woman he calls Sandra.

Sandrine, the Dutchman believes *you* are Sandra.

He believes this—based on columns by Yours Truly—with a passion that leaps across the line into madness.

Yesterday he wormed his way into an audience with the esteemed leaders of this newspaper and tempted them with a blatantly bogus partnership in which you, Sandrine, would become the living emblem of his company. The first step would entail whisking you off on a European tour starting guess where?

Paris, bien sure.

My very shrewd bosses saw through this fraud and showed him the door. But he found his way to another door, mine, where I refused to surrender you despite his threat to crush my skull with a telephone receiver.

He backed off, but this maniac's quest will not end until he has what he wants and needs: you.

Naturally I've notified the police. Our esteemed Commissioner Stephen Kennedy and New York's Finest are on the case.

Tomorrow, a possible bad-news medical bulletin regarding Sandrine's quest to sing again.

"Scolding Sandrine on her revealing outfit?" asked Dawn. "That's kind of a cringer for me, Chick. Frankly everybody ate up her outfit. I never saw anything that sexy on TV."

"Mr. and Mrs. America may have been thrilled by it once, but the next time they'll have their Judeo-Christian guard up," I said. "They'll slap her with the hussy label. And that would put a fatal kibosh on the whole saga because Americans don't love hussies."

Dawn started out, to carry the copy to the desk.

"Hey, Dawn, before you turn it in, run it by Sid, okay? Duffy and Kingsley and those other schmucks think they're swinging a big deal with Drusen but I'm wrecking their deal and announcing it in print. This might not initially go over well."

Dawn took the column to Sid and came back ten minutes later with a smile on her face.

"Sid loved it. He says go with it. Fuck the Anuses and fuck Drusen."

CHAPTER 25

March 18, 1958

The next morning I asked Frieda to fill me in on our dinner with Lana Turner.

"She'll be there but it's really about you meeting Danny. Danny Chone. He's the guy who got me out of Europe, took me to LA and then Vegas. We were together a long time. Funny thing: I met him in Paris just after the war, about the time Drusen was there having his Sandra adventure."

"Please tell me you're not saying you could have been Sandra."

"Of course not. I never sang anywhere, I never set foot in Montmartre, and I never met Drusen. I was a showgirl at the Lido. Danny was a US Army sergeant, a supply sergeant. On the side he was involved with the black market, which was very big because Parisians had nothing in those days. No stockings, no soap, no butter, no decent clothes. Danny could get American goods. There was a lot of Mafia involvement in the black market. The money Danny made paid our way for a long time."

"He was with the Mafia?"

"No, he's not a tough guy. But he dealt with them. And later, when we came back to LA, he did shady things but nothing criminal, I know that. The thing about Danny is that he's always got big dreams. Vegas was just being created when we moved there and he tried very hard to get a foothold but nothing panned out. But he's not a bad guy. I owe him a lot."

"How does Lana Turner fit into this?"

"Danny has a friend, Johnny. A small-time hoodlum. Used to be in the Mickey Cohen gang in LA. Ex-marine. Good looking. Snappy dresser."

"So?"

"Johnny's a ladies man. They say he has a gigantic schnitzel."

"You mean a dick?"

"Yeah, a dick. They call him 'Oscar' because his dick is supposedly the size of the Academy Award statuette. They also say he pads his basket."

"Which means what?"

"He stuffs socks or something down his pants to make a big bulge."

"Gee, I never tried that. Does it work? Do you know about the schnitzel from personal experience?"

"Oh, God no. I was only with Danny. I would never be with Johnny. He is not a nice guy. He beats Lana. Everybody knows it."

"He's with Lana Turner? She's a movie star. What's she doing with a small-time thug?"

"He had the hots for her and chased her for years and I guess she finally gave in. Things are not going well for her. One marriage after another kaput and her career's on the skids. Her last few movies were duds. MGM cut her loose."

"So she needs big strong Johnny to lean on?"

"I guess so. Plus the schnitzel."

I asked, "Do you know her?"

"I've met her. She's not a happy woman. You don't see a smile with her."

"What brings these people to New York?"

"I don't know. They're probably up to something."

"Danny saw you on Sullivan. I know because he phoned my office."

"Yeah. Have you ever met Lana?"

"No. She opened a movie here six weeks ago, *The Lady Takes A Flyer*. A real turkey. There was a PR bash but I skipped it. Nobody went."

* * *

WE WALKED to Alida's place.

While Frieda and Alberta were in the kitchen Alida motioned me to her and made me lean over so she could whisper in my ear.

"You're playing footsie with Frieda, aren't you?" she said.

I straightened up and looked at her, not sure what to say.

Alida raised her right forefinger and wagged it in my face in a warning gesture but then Frieda and Alida came into the room. Alida had more to say but didn't get to say it.

I said I had to go.

Frieda whispered, "See you tonight."

* * *

"Dᴉᴅ ʏᴏᴜ see the Al Percy story?" Dawn asked as I walked into the office.

I hadn't. I'd fallen behind on newspaper reading since Frieda moved in, disrupting my domestic routine. The headline was:

SANDRINE A HOAX?
SUSPICION GROWS

"Al's been dying to write this," I said. "When it's all over he doesn't want people looking back and saying he whiffed on the story. Has he got anything new?"

"Maybe the use of the word 'hoax' is new."

I sat down and read it. It amazed me that the Sandrine story had held up so long and that readers still believed in Sandrine. But Percy's piece would hurt. Dawn was right that he had made the jump from attacking unverified facts to suggesting that the whole story was false. He didn't have enough to call it an outright hoax but he did have enough for a "*suspicion grows*" angle.

* * *

Dᴇᴇ ᴄᴀʟʟᴇᴅ.

"Elvire is upset. Could you come down and talk to her? I've tried but nothing I say is working. She's talking about moving back to Ohio."

"After that huge success with Sinatra? That should have been a dream come true. A young singer getting a moment like that—she ought to be ecstatic."

"It doesn't seem to work that way. Plus her boyfriend dropped her."

"Martin the grad student? Why?"

"After Sinatra they had a scene of some sort and he wouldn't talk to her for a while and then he dropped the bomb. By phone."

I didn't get it.

"Talk to her. It might help. She seems to think you're a fine person who understands life."

"I definitely do not understand life but I'll talk to her tomorrow."

As I said goodbye, Sid walked in. He was fretting about the Dutchman.

"I'm having second thoughts, Chico. Maybe it's time to back off. You had this sweet little Sandrine story and now you're mixing in a guy who sounds like a dangerous pervert. It's a little sick and scary, especially for all the teenage girls who follow Sandrine. It's not exactly TSBL. Sooner or later his identity will come out and he'll sue us, and certain owners of this newspaper will go berserk."

I didn't see it that way. "I say we stick with it for a while. Every great story needs a villain. It could develop into a running feud and be juicy, the kind of pizzazz the Brothers like. And how do I stand with them lately?"

"They had a big bone for Drusen's deal but Drusen apparently had a tantrum after talking to you and demanded that you be fired but then they couldn't get him to commit any advertising money and the whole deal started to wobble. And then you torpedoed it in your column but praised the business acumen they didn't show so they decided you might be right about how he just wanted to get to Sandrine. So you get off scot-free on this one. You're safe till you screw up again. Just saying this reminds me that we hate Drusen now so what the hell, keep him in the column."

"Are you okay, Sid? Is this Sandrine thing driving you crazy?"

"I'm okay. Not sure what to do, but right now I'm working on regaining my sense of humor. That seems to be the key to dealing with this thing."

* * *

THE LANA Turner dinner was at a snazzy East Side joint called Fiori. I reserved a private room upstairs figuring that even in a sophisticated restaurant the impact of Lana Turner *and* Sandrine D'Avignon walking in would resemble a comet hitting the earth, causing out-of-control ogling behavior and unwelcome interruptions.

And forgetting who I was, I found myself dreading that the goddamn gossip columnists would come buzzing around. I'd never been on the celebrity end of celebrity versus gossip hound.

Frieda and I were on time but Lana, Johnny, and Danny were late. A heavy snow was falling; we figured they'd run into transportation trouble.

I drummed the table impatiently. "What do they *want*?" I kept asking, but Frieda was mum.

At last they swept in. Introductions were made: Frieda and me, Danny Chone, Lana Turner, and Johnny Stompanato.

Stompanato had more charisma than the movie star herself. Lana was subdued in a conservative gray suit that hid her famous hour-glass curves and a hat that concealed most of her famous platinum hair. Johnny had the dapper gangster look down pat. He wore a sports jacket with a loud West Coast pattern, black pleated slacks with a big silver belt buckle, and a silver bracelet engraved with "LANITA." His black silk shirt was open a few buttons displaying a hairy chest. He was strapping, with dark hooded eyes, curly hair, and a Hollywood-quality air of menace.

I couldn't tell if his basket was padded and didn't want to get caught looking.

Frieda had warned me Johnny wasn't a talker, but he was eager to explain why they were late. They had stopped off at the Park Sheraton Hotel so Johnny could get a trim in the barbershop where the mob boss Albert Anastasia was murdered in a hail of bullets back in October in a Mafia rub-out that made national headlines.

Johnny was delighted. "I sat in the same chair Albert was in when he got smoked. They say he got his gun out but was so panicked he fired at the mirror instead of the hitters. Funny, huh? I don't know if that's true or not but so they say."

He laughed.

I said, "It's nice that you honor the historical figures of your chosen profession, getting a haircut in the same shop and same chair."

I meant it as a harmless wisecrack but hoodlums are touchy about being ribbed. His face darkened and Frieda put a cautionary hand on my arm: don't tease Johnny Stomp.

Danny, quiet until now, must have recognized that I'd skated onto thin ice because he jumped in to retrack the conversation. "Johnny, they ever nab the shooters in that thing?"

"Nah," Johnny said, without taking his eyes off me. "They say it was a Profaci hit but the triggers was imported from out of town. Like, for instance, Montreal. But I wouldn't know."

That put an end to the Anastasia topic and left an uncomfortable silence. Danny cleared his throat and I sensed that we were about to leave small talk about assassinations behind and move on toward the strategic objective of the evening.

This was Danny's role; he was the idea guy, the talker. He reminded me of Willy Loman or Van Johnson: husky and conventionally good-looking, a backslapping salesman type, once confident but now fading, still looking to get lucky.

"So Chick," he said, "tell us how Frieda came into your life."

"We met by accident," Frieda said, before I could answer and give away too much.

"It sure worked out good," said Danny. "I almost fell on the floor when I saw you on Sullivan. And then I had to find out about this story—what's the name, *Sandrine*? So Chick, you turned Frieda into Sandrine, right? What a great con."

I didn't like the word "con" and I wasn't happy that these people had so effortlessly seen through the Sandrine story. Then again, they knew Frieda and seeing her introduced on TV as Sandrine D'Avignon was a good clue that something fishy was going on. And of course Danny was evidently something of a professional con man himself so he would recognize a con when he saw one. And because he was a professional he saw what I didn't see: The original con was just a first step on the ladder toward a bigger con, leading to a pot of gold.

I started getting wise to what was happening. Danny wanted in on Sandrine. He wanted to turn it into a moneymaker. Hence the trip to New York.

Danny was the con man.

Johnny was the intimidator.

Lana was the bait.

I was the target.

Danny knew he could pull the wool over Frieda's eyes and that left me as his only obstacle. He'd had at least one phone conversation with Frieda and she might have complained that I didn't know what I was doing, had no big plans for her, and hadn't earned a cent for her. Therefore he probably pegged me as a chump and a pushover.

"I would have asked Lana to play Sandrine but she wasn't available," I said, joking but also emphasizing my role as master of the Sandrine deception. I had to show that I wasn't an amateur.

"I might have taken it; I'm a lot more available than I used to be," said Lana, acid in her voice. The way she held her cigarette, with her elbow cocked and the V of her upraised fingers pointing elegantly upward, reminded me of countless smoking scenes in her 1940s movies. The smoking went with "smoldering," the adjective that was always pinned to her name. I never bought the smoldering concept. To me she was tense and charmless on the screen and not much different across a table.

"I thought you were *glorious* on Sullivan," Lana said to Frieda. "But can I offer some advice? Nix on the cheesecake."

"She means don't flash the tits," Johnny said.

Lana glared at him. "Yeah, that's Johnny's way of putting it. But what I'm saying is if you flaunt it too much the church ladies will come after you like a pack of wolves. When I was sixteen I did this movie called *They Won't Forget* and nobody forgot the sight of me in a tight sweater and the 'sweater girl' label stuck with me and I hated it but couldn't shake it. Yeah, it gave my career a boost but it hurt me, too, you know. And you saw all the censorship crap Otto Preminger had to put up with over *The Moon Is Blue* a few years ago? The Legion of Decency and so on?"

"Couples sleeping in twin beds with pajamas buttoned up to their necks," snickered Johnny. "Some day Americans will find out that people fuck."

"Americans are such prudes," said Lana. "The French aren't like that, right, Frieda? You're French, aren't you?"

"Frieda is German. Sandrine is French," said Danny, with a smile. Danny said everything with a smile.

We ordered food and it came and we ate and talked. I know the celebrity table rhythms and this conversation was not smooth. The two men were on edge. Frieda was quiet and Lana, puffing on cigarettes even as she ate, would not put a lid on her tales of woe, professional and private.

"You know what's good about unhappiness?" Lana asked.

"It's better than lung cancer?" cracked Johnny.

"As if you would know anything," Lana said. "No, the good thing is that unhappiness makes you grow. You don't grow when you're happy."

"Eat any more of that dessert and you'll grow," said Johnny. "Have you checked out your hips lately?"

Frieda said, "I've had plenty of unhappiness and it's only made me grow older."

"You weren't unhappy with me, were you?" asked Danny.

"Lanita wakes up unhappy," said Johnny. "Four guys have divorced her. I wonder why."

"I wonder why you don't go fuck yourself," she said.

Johnny clouded over on that one. He looked like he was about to give her a whack across the face but Lana made a quick move, standing up and inviting Frieda to join her in the little girls' room. The two women left the table. Some strange-looking liqueurs arrived.

Danny said, "So Chick, while the girls are powdering their noses, let's talk a little."

I said, "It sounds like I'm gonna hear a pitch."

"No, no. No pitch," he said, but then he pitched me. "Frieda's built for stardom, don't you think? You've given her this Sandrine thing and that—"

"She's built but I don't know about stardom," said Johnny.

"Johnny's always joking, he don't mean no harm," said Danny, smiling again. "So I was saying, you've created this great Sandrine scam. How about if we come in and help push it up to the big stage and the big bucks. You don't know my background but I'm a major player in Vegas. I know the ropes and I know the dopes."

"Get to the fucking point," said Johnny.

"Yeah, sure. I see starting with a major casino revue starring Frieda as Sandrine. We call it SANDRINE—THE NAKED TRUTH. She's the hottest thing around, can you imagine what people would pay to see her nude? To see her riding a motorcycle across the stage in her birthday suit? We'd dress it up with music and dance numbers and a lot of babes walking around naked, acting out Sandrine's life story: hard times in Germany, sexy times in Paris, the Sullivan show and so on. With my connections I could set this in motion right away. I'm thinking about the Desert Inn, the Sahara, maybe the Trop."

Johnny said, "Back up the money truck, baby."

"And Chick, you're in for a nice slice of this pie," Danny went on. "You have the exclusive writing rights or whatever they call it. Nobody else gets in, just you."

"Writing rights? Writing rights to what?"

"To anything. Any writing that gets done, you own it and we're behind you. You could move out there and do a daily Vegas column or you could stay back here in NYC churning out columns about Sandrine's life in Vegas. Either way, you're in for a fat weekly envelope from the casino."

"Sound good, Chick?" asked Johnny. Then he answered for me, "Sure it does."

Danny said, "And don't worry about me getting between you and Frieda romantically. Frieda and me are splitsville. Just friends. She's all yours. You'd have a great life together in Vegas."

"Drink, fuck, and fly," said Johnny. Apparently that was his motto. "Hey, I hear Frank sang at your party."

"Gents," I said. "I appreciate the offer. Frieda and I are entertaining a lot of ideas and the key is to latch on to something that's just right for Frieda and, secondarily, right for me too. But the Sandrine idea, which has worked so well, is not a tits-based thing. It's not about her walking around naked. It's more long-term than that. We'll give your proposal serious thought but I'm not sure the tone of it is right for her at this moment."

"Of course it's right for her," said Johnny, not smiling.

Danny said. "What you don't understand, Chick, is that I can get this thing rolling very fast and speed is the whole thing here. Right now you'd get audiences kicking each other in the chops to see Sandrine naked. A month from now, she's just another bimbo and nobody gives a shit. She loses the chance of her life. Can you hurt her like that, just to keep your column story going?"

"Or bad things could happen," said Johnny. "You got a great scam going but any day, somebody could walk in and drop the A-bomb on you. Expose you and everything you've done. Tell the truth about your lying in the newspaper. Talk about some of the things Frieda's done—and she's never been a Girl Scout. Talk about how she's fucking you as part of the deal. All this could come out, from people who'd rather be on your side than against you. You know what I mean?"

Sure I knew what he meant: *blackmail*.

Lana and Frieda returned. Without sitting down, Lana said firmly, "The party's over," and everyone was ready for a quick exit. Johnny gave me a punch on the shoulder and said, "You don't look so good, Chick. Cheer up. We're copacetic, right?"

Lana did final cheek-kissing with Frieda and me as Johnny helped her into her mink coat. "You're a major talent, Chick," she said. "Hollywood writers know how to create characters on the screen but you brought her to life *off* the screen. And fabulously."

That said, she forgot me permanently and turned toward the exits. Johnny and Danny fell in behind her as she squared her shoulders, fixed her eyes straight ahead, and did the movie star walk through the restaurant. Every head turned. Her name was whispered around the room.

Then Frieda did *her* walk. Hers was better, technically, and the same heads turned but Lana was the star, Sandrine was something less. And Frieda felt it.

CHAPTER 26

We emerged from the restaurant into a classic Gotham snow scene. Getting a taxi was impossible but Danny offered us a ride in Lana's limo. Danny and I took the little jumper seats, Johnny sat with legs outspread between the two women, arms around their shoulders. Lana was scowling, Frieda had a smirk on her face as her eyes directed my attention to Johnny's bulging basket.

Back at my place, Frieda and I headed straight to my window. I think these window sessions were becoming romantic, a shared pleasure. We gazed out on a proverbial winter wonderland, all the urban grime concealed under a pristine blanket of newly fallen snow.

"So Frieda, tell me what got said in the ladies room."

"She's ditching Johnny. Soon. He's out of the gang and has no job and takes it out on her. The reason she wears that suit—she took off her jacket to show me the black-and-blue marks on her arms and shoulders from where he hits her. One time he threatened to cut her face with a coat hanger. Which would be terrifying because Lana's biggest fear in life is damage to her face."

"Is Danny close to Johnny?"

"They're not lodge brothers but they've worked together. They're a good pair. Danny's the mouth, Johnny's the menace. They must be working together on something now."

"Yeah, and it's you. Don't tell me you didn't know this. They want you to star in a nude revue in Vegas. They're gonna blackmail me if I get in the way."

"Blackmail? That's terrible, Chick," she said, acting horrified but she's not a good actor. Then, after a pause, she asked, "But is starring in a revue such a bad idea? Starring in a Las Vegas revue? If I can sign a contract quickly and start cashing in before the world forgets about me?"

She was reading from Danny's script: Throw together a slapdash show, grab the upfront cash, and skip town when the show nosedives. But she didn't see what came next: Frieda on the junk heap. Sandrine destroyed.

"Frieda, they want to take over Sandrine. And they've got Sandrine all wrong. They might make some fast money but you wouldn't see a dime of it."

"Danny wouldn't do that. I think you're jealous of him. Maybe this is just Sandrine growing into a new stage in her life. You could write a great column about her victory over the heartbreak of losing her singing voice and then going through pain and growing, as Lana says, and then a great scene where she stars in her own revue on a Las Vegas stage."

This was Danny-think at a level Frieda could never have attained on her own. The concept of a singer losing her voice but then "growing" into stardom in a nude revue was farcical and I told her so but she shook her head, refusing to hear me. I told her it was Sandrine's purity that won the hearts of so many Americans. That purity had to be protected. Riding around naked on a motorcycle in front of three hundred screaming drunks was not a good way to protect purity.

"Am I impure because I show my breasts? You don't object when I show them to you. No one in any audience has ever wanted their money back because I'm impure."

"Look, remember how pleased you were when they invited you to be a celebrity guest at the NASA opening? That invitation's gonna be yanked back in a tenth of a second if you do a nude revue. You'll never be invited to anything respectable."

"Aren't you being *Father Knows Best* with me? It's my life, you know."

Our first angry words. Clearly she listened to Danny. I wondered if he had a special gift for putting a spell on her and if he had been her puppeteer during their years in LA and Vegas. Then maybe he'd decided she was used up, so he dropped her. Which caused her move to New York. But now he'd recast his spell, seeing her as a ticket on the gravy train of her fluke stardom.

Was I jealous? *Yes*! I was being shouldered aside by third-rate con men who were going to hijack Sandrine and turn her into a vulgar hee-hawing breast-bouncing slut-on-wheels. My despair must have shown on my face because Frieda got the message and backed off to softer territory. "Chick, if you really hate the Vegas idea, I won't do it," she said.

"I'm just trying to protect you."

"Sure. But it sounded like fun. My name in lights and so on. They'd give us a great suite and comp everything. And imagine the sex we'd have. We'd have a huge bed and a picture window looking out over the desert. Vegas sex is the best."

That was a tempting image but I would not budge on the revue idea. I'd prevailed for now but I sensed the Vegas idea would resurface as soon as Danny got her ear again.

"Bedtime?" she asked, and that ended the Vegas discussion. But as we headed to the bedroom she had something else to slip in: "Oh, by the way, Chick, Danny's mom is on her deathbed in Chicago. Mama Pauline. Lovely lady. I knew her well and she was always nice to me. Danny wants me to fly out with him to say goodbye to her."

"When?"

"Tomorrow. Only for a couple days and then I'll be right back. It's important, Chick. And don't worry, there's nothing going on with me and Danny."

Already. Danny making his move. I knew she'd come back raring to go on the Vegas idea. I told her I would not yield on that. She nodded agreement and I nodded my okay for Chicago. How could I oppose a deathbed visit to Mama Pauline? I didn't like it but maybe I'd smelled enough rats for one night.

I said I'd find a nurse to help Alberta with Alida while she was gone.

"You need some great sex to tide you over," she said.

* * *

I woke up around four A.M., halfway to an idea. I lay there for a while, trying to grasp the other half.

I got up and sat in the living room thinking about what an amazing chain of events had developed from a few paragraphs I dashed off the night I invented Sandrine. Now, almost three weeks later, remarkably few people knew or strongly suspected that Sandrine wasn't real. I grabbed a piece of paper and made a list:

> Dawn Linguino (editorial assistant)
> Dee Harkovic (nightclub proprietor)
> Elvire Coutansais (aspiring songbird)
> Sid Lepanzer (newspaper assistant editor)

Frieda Waldschneider (ex-showgirl, nurse, performer)
Alvin Percy (newspaper reporter)
Spencer Tracy (movie star)
Katharine Hepburn (movie star)
Danny Chone (Las Vegas loser)
Johnny Stompanato (West Coast hoodlum)
Lana Turner (movie star)
Leo Linguino (airport baggage supervisor)
Betty Linguino (Queens housewife)

Something about the list made me laugh. What a story.
That's when the idea came into focus: I would write this book.

* * *

THE NEXT day Alida tried to commit suicide.

It wasn't a wholehearted effort but even attempting suicide is scary.

Alberta was carrying in morning coffee and found Alida on her knees on the window sill with the window wide open. For a moment Alberta thought Alida was just looking at the snow (the storm lasted three days and became known as the Blizzard of 1958) but realized Alida was trying to slide out the window into a five-story fall to the pavement.

Alberta seized her sister and tried to wrestle her back inside. Alida fought for a moment, then gave up. She was hysterical.

Alberta called me immediately. I could hear Alida's loud sobs in the background and it was terrifying. I was awake and dressed because Frieda had just left for Chicago, taking a train because the snow had closed the airport. I shot out the door and ran to the apartment. By the time I arrived, a doctor, who was a neighbor, had come and gone. He'd given Alida a shot and she was out cold.

"Did she say why?" I asked Alberta.

"She muttered something."

"What did she mutter? Tell me, goddamn it."

"She said you were with Frieda now and no longer with her so everything was over," Alberta said. "It's like she just faced up to what had happened to her life."

I felt tears starting to come.

"It's none of my business, Chick. You've been a good guy. You did nothing wrong. You should do what makes you happy. If it's with Frieda, so be it. You deserve a life."

I arranged for the building superintendent to nail the window shut. I figured Alida had turned a corner and needed more vigilant care so I told Alberta to look for a hospital or sanitarium for her.

I would help pay for it, of course. But I didn't know how. Danny Chone and Hendrik Drusen had both tempted me with easy money but crossing that line with either or both of them was a line I would not cross. I'd learned my lesson about crossing uncrossable lines.

We couldn't find a nurse for the day so I decided to babysit Alida myself. I sat at her bedside. She awoke a few times, groggy. I tried to get her talking about the suicide attempt but she insisted she didn't remember it.

I took this quiet time to crank out a column. Alberta didn't own a typewriter so I had to write in longhand, which gave me a headache.

SANDRINE, ARE YOU A HOAX?
CHICK'S CLICKS, BY COLUMNIST CHICK LOPRITZ

My Fourth Estate rival Alvin Percy is serving up a plate of journalistic baloney-on-wry suggesting that Sandrine d'Avignon is nothing but a figment of Yours Truly's imagination.

She doesn't exist?

So who was that beautiful damsel Ed Sullivan introduced on TV? Is Ed's imagination figmenting too?

And who was that gorgeous creature Frank Sinatra serenaded at a party that night, singing his top-of-the-charts hit, "Come Fly With Me"?

Was Frank singing to an imaginary woman?

Did a roomful of metropolitan movers and shakers, the brightest brains of our city, elbow each other out of the way to get within pawing range of a simulated Sandrine?

And why did the American TV audience ooh and ahh at a fictional femme? Because they're gullible dimwits who don't know shellfish from Shinola?

That's what Al thinks.

I mentioned Al's hoax accusation to Sandrine this morning as I put her on a choo-choo to Chicago where she'll undergo medical tests by America's primo voice specialists. The docs will probe for ways to repair the pure-as-a-bell singing voice that was damaged in Sandrine's tragic accident.

We'll know the verdict from the Windy City soon. Be warned: Early indications are not rosy.

The French songbird might never warble again.

How is she taking it? Anger and self-pity? Or brave good humor?

The latter, Al. When I read her your report in a Penn Station waiting area, she burst into laughter so infectious that half the passengers boarding her train wore wide smiles—without even knowing the joke.

It's great when a nonexistent woman gets laughs.

Uncle Miltie would be envious.

Why would Al be so eager to tag Sandrine as a phony?

Well, why does Al take such overweening pride in his self-bestowed nickname?—"No Mercy Percy."

I'd say Al's living in a fantasyland that tops Disney's. He sees himself as a hard-bitten trench-coated Camel-smoking investigator who digs out truths other reporters miss. And he exposes these truths with no compromise, no fear, and no mercy.

But Yours Truly suspects Al doesn't even do his own legwork. Instead, he gets his info hand-delivered from a source I call The Dutchman, the Sandrine-stalker I identified yesterday.

The Dutchman's highly paid investigators found supposedly discrediting facts about Sandrine and shoveled them to Al, who ran with them in his glory-seeking hoax piece.

Isn't it odd that The Dutchman, a slave to the illusion of a long-lost Sandra, would be the main source insisting that the illusion is not Sandra but the real-life Sandrine?

But I promise to check. The minute Sandrine gets back from Chicago I'll ask her again: Do you really exist? If she says no, I'll treat Al to a steak dinner and maybe a new suit, replacing that shabby brown corduroy thing he's been wearing since the decline of the Roman Empire.

Meet me here tomorrow for more on the saga of Sandrine.

I dictated the column by phone.

Alida was still dozing.

I thought of Elvire. I'd promised Dee I'd have a counseling conversation with Elvire regarding her Sinatra experience and her woes about her lost boyfriend.

I picked up the phone and gave her a buzz. The point of the call was to soothe Elvire but she ended up soothing me, getting me to recount the story of Alida's suicide attempt.

Elvire said, "What's the address? I'm coming right now."

* * *

ELVIRE FOUGHT through the snow and spent the afternoon with me, co-nursing Alida. Elvire's mother nursed at an old folks' home in Ohio and Elvire knew the drill from working there with her.

Elvire was at ease with Alida (as Frieda never was). She brought a guitar and sang songs to her and even *with* her—sitting in the other room I heard them singing "Frère Jacques." Somehow Alida reached through the fog and remembered the lyrics and was delighted to be singing. I noticed later that she'd barely smoked during the day.

We bundled Alida up and took her for a short walk in the snow and that went well too. As we arrived back in the apartment, Alberta was returning from shopping so she took over the Alida watch. Elvire and I decided on another snow walk but instead of going downstairs, I had a better idea: the roof.

I'd always liked New York rooftops. No one has much reason to go there so they're virtually private and you have a big outdoor platform to yourself. Street noise hardly reaches you and the view is great.

It was even better in a blizzard. The snow was above my knees. We trudged across it, leaving deep footprints, and leaned on a wall, looking out at a city dressed in white. The street below was a mix of snow and slush. Cars and pedestrians were snow-topped. Except for occasional honking horns or the rumble and scrape of snowplows, it was very close to a silent movie.

"It's beautiful," she said. "I'll always remember this view."

Conversation came easily. I filled her in on what had happened on the Sandrine front since the night Drusen told the tale of his love for Sandra. Then I brought up the ex-boyfriend, Martin. Why had he left her?

"It was my singing with Sinatra," she said. "It was the thrill of my life, of course, but it disturbed him. It was too big for him. He said he didn't want to be involved with someone in show business. He was afraid I'd become a star and not be his little French girl. The fact that I'm not French and am no longer a girl didn't matter. I mean, did he think I was going to become a big star and he'd just be a left-behind nobody? Because, Chick—I know this will sound strange—singing with Sinatra made me realize that I'll never be a star. Standing next to someone like him you realize how small your talent is. It's like a boy thinking he can be a famous baseball player and then he sees Willie Mays or Mickey Mantle hitting balls or doing things he'll never be able to do so he might as well stop dreaming about baseball and get back to reality. And that's how I feel. How can I ever be anything more than a singer in a little club? So I think I should go back to Ohio where I belong."

"Maybe this is just because you feel hurt by Martin."

"No. I just feel that instead of spending two or three years finding out that I'll never make it and feeling like a failure, I found it out in the time it took to sing 'La Mer.' And I wasn't a failure, I was a winner. I sang with Frank Sinatra. Thanks to you."

"I hope you don't go."

She smiled. "Let me tell you how it ended. Martin broke it off in a call from a pay phone. The operator came on and asked for another dime and maybe he didn't have any change or maybe he was just—"

"Just what? A loser?"

"He just hung up. I waited for him to borrow a dime and call back but he never did."

"What does Dee think about Martin?"

"She didn't want to say but I kept asking her and finally she said, 'Well, I think he's sort of a wet noodle.'"

"So look at the upside," I said. "You could have become Mrs. Wet Noodle. But you got lucky and escaped."

"This has been a great adventure in New York. I'll look back on it happily. But of course it's painful when someone doesn't want to be with you anymore."

I said, "It's the kind of experience musicians write songs about, isn't it?"

"Do you think writing the songs makes the musicians feel better?"

"It probably hurts while you're writing it but later it's kind of out of your system."

"Okay. Maybe I'll try that."

"Let's do it now. Let's write the song."

"Write the song?" she looked at me bright-eyed. "Now?"

I thought for a moment and sang,

Martin
I'm not sorry we're partin'

She thought for a moment and added,
And I think Martin farted
She blushed but we laughed.

Then me,

So I'm not brokenhearted

She sang,

Martin

**I guess I'll never take part in
Any family you're startin'**

Then me,

**You belong in kindergarten
La-de-dah de-dah de-dee**

We'd run out of rhymes but hummed along a bit. Then she made a snowball and threw it at me and I threw one back. We ended up chasing each other around the roof having a snowball fight and playing like puppies.

The scene was movie-like. It seemed to require a sudden spontaneous Hollywood embrace as the lovers realize their feelings for each other and music wells up. The couple kisses and the helicopter-mounted camera zooms out, widening on a Manhattan panorama as giant snowflakes fall and closing titles roll.

But we were too timid to go that far. We cut the scene short, ran down the stairs, and exploded into Alida's apartment, snow flying off us in all directions.

"You two are certainly having a grand time," said Alberta, who was sitting in the living room having coffee with Alida.

We sat and joined them. The snowball fight and the Martin song had cheered us up. Elvire was relaxed, confident, funny. She talked about her childhood and her experiences at Chez Dee's. I told some funny old-days stories, including stories about great times Alida and I enjoyed in that very living room. Alberta chipped in a few anecdotes.

Alida sat smiling peacefully—and it was how many hours since she'd attempted to jump out a window?

The afternoon flew by. Evening came and Elvire had to leave for Dee's. She kissed Alida goodbye and Alida started to cry so Elvire picked up the guitar and played a boisterous "*Frère Jacques*," and then asked Alida if she could come back the next day.

Alida nodded, overjoyed. Elvire was in the other room getting into her coat and boots, leaving Alida and me with a private moment. Alida said, "Chick, this is why I got the divo."

Divo: gossip column lingo meaning divorce.

I was slow on the uptake. Alida looked up at me with watery eyes. She seemed to be willing me to understand something she couldn't say.

We heard Elvire and Alberta laughing. Alida glanced in their direction, then reeled me in. We shared a goodbye hug and she whispered, "The big one's okay but the little one is right for you."

She couldn't remember their names.

When Elvire saw my face she asked if something was wrong. I said no, but that was the moment I understood why Alida wanted the divorce.

To set me free.

She wanted me to enjoy life again. With Elvire.

CHAPTER 27

A surprising notion was taking shape in my mind: there were *three* Sandrines.

The first was the fantasy Sandrine.

The second was Frieda, who physically embodied the fantasy.

The third was Elvire, who made the fantasy a reality.

They'd come to me in a progression, *a circle of Sandrines*, incarnations of the same woman as I wandered in a wilderness toward a life after Alida.

I'm wrong to say Elvire was third. She was first. She inspired the fantasy. She'd given me the idea of the fresh, aspiring young singer coming to New York. She'd given me the innocence and purity and TSBL. I'd glamorized her to make her a sexier sell in my column but it was still Elvire underneath. The Sandrine qualities that won the hearts of readers (and me) were Elvire qualities.

And then this thought: Would Elvire, having begun the circle, now complete it? Until this point I hadn't had a seriously amorous thought about her but she'd affected me from the start. What elevated my awareness was our merriment on the snowy rooftop capped off by Alida's signal about "the little one." Despite Alida's tragic confusion, she'd seen what I'd been slow to see.

* * *

THERE WERE no cabs because of the snow so I walked home. As I approached my building, I noticed lights on in my apartment.

Frieda. I'd expected her to be away longer but perhaps Danny's Mama Pauline had passed the point of needing bedside visitors. I would have to adjust my mood to be properly sympathetic. On the other hand Frieda's return was good news—I was glad to have her company again and of course her return would initiate a mini-Olympics of welcome-home sex.

But then my momentum toward Elvire came back to me—my God, nobody had a love life quite like mine. I climbed the stairs and opened the door in a state of highly conflicted emotions.

It wasn't Frieda. It was Drusen, sitting in the chair by the window. Crying.

He glanced up at me and then turned away, trying to hide his tears. Then he gave up on concealment and openly dabbed his eyes with a handkerchief.

It was a stunning sight. I asked myself these questions: Had I done real damage to this guy, laying it on too thick in my columns and pushing him over the edge? Had he finally experienced the shattering of his Sandrine illusion and started going to pieces, in my living room? Was his emotional pain about to become my physical pain? Was he going to throw me out the window?

I waited for him to speak but words didn't come. I opened the ice box and pulled out two bottles of Schlitz. I opened them and placed one before him on the window sill. The crying tailed off and stopped.

"I hate American beer," he said, head down.

"Oh sorry, I'll run out for a Heineken."

"I'm going to ask you for the thousandth time, *where is she?*" he asked in a quavering voice. "I thought she lived here. My people told me a woman was seen with you in this window. So I came here tonight to find her."

"She doesn't live here," I lied.

"But she keeps her clothes in your closet?"

"They're not her clothes. They're mine. Sometimes I just feel like wearing a dress to work. Or sometimes a nice blouse and skirt ensemble."

"You see me in pain and you make stupid jokes."

"Look Rick, or Hank. I'm tired of you. This obsession of yours is becoming a bore."

"Yes, it bores me too," he cried, finally looking up at me. "You think I enjoy this? I have seen psychiatrists and Gypsy fortune-tellers and all kinds of charlatans trying to get rid of this pain. My marriage broke down, my children are poisoned against me, my colleagues have figured out that your 'Dutchman' character is me. And I was starting to do better, living with it better. And then I read your goddamn column and it came back again."

"My column had nothing to do with your Sandra. I tell you that with total assurance."

"You owe me," he said.

"Why would I owe you?"

"You owe me decency because you're a decent man. Not perfect but decent. I've studied you. You know I'm in pain. I don't know what keeps you from helping me."

"I tend not to help stalkers who get me beaten up or break into my apartment. People who push over a sick woman's wheelchair. People who insult my country's beer. People who are huge pains in my ass."

I said these words but his saying I was a decent man rang in my ears. I was raised to be a decent man. I'd disgraced my profession, yes, but it was just a nutty thing that happened and there'd been no ill intent. My professionalism was besmirched but my decency was still intact, I felt. Drusen was not suffering because of me. He was suffering because he had mistaken *my* fantasy woman for *his* fantasy woman.

I suddenly knew how to release him from his pain. By telling him the whole fucking truth. And then maybe he'd not kill me and leave me alone.

What the hell.

"Okay Drusen, listen to me now. Those women's clothes in the bedroom aren't actually mine. They belong to Frieda Waldschneider. You met her at Chez Dee's. She's the beautiful blonde who plays Sandrine. She's acting. Because there is no Sandrine. I made her up. She doesn't exist. I can't tell you where she is because *she isn't anywhere*."

"She isn't anywhere? That's so stupid I don't know what to say," he said. "It's bullshit."

"It's not bullshit. Well, I suppose you could say that Sandrine is bullshit but the fact that she doesn't exist is not bullshit."

"My head spins listening to your craziness. And you insult me, thinking I would believe this crazy double talk."

We stared at each other.

"I regret calling you a decent man. I take that back," he said. "You are a vile man and a liar."

He stood up and dropped a business card on the coffee table. "Call me at my office if you ever decide to do the right thing. And don't think you're done with me."

* * *

I spent the next morning at Alida's. Elvire arrived around lunchtime, bringing Chinese food, which we all enjoyed. Elvire sang with Alida, who then napped. Alberta went out. Elvire and I sat and talked until it was time for her to leave for Dee's.

I walked her to the subway and then stopped off at Saint Malachy's. Tracy and Hepburn weren't there and there were no luminaries to sit down with me but I left the church feeling as good as possible, given the conflict of falling in love with Elvire while looking forward to Frieda's return.

I rode the subway downtown to the office thinking about Elvire and Frieda and wondering why Frieda hadn't called. With my mind on Chicago, I sat down and drafted a column about accompanying Sandrine on her visit to consult with eminent Chicago voice doctors. The verdict, as I'd already signaled, was that Sandrine would never sing again.

Dawn and I were sorting through Sandrine's fan mail, organizing another SANDRINE ANSWERS YOUR QUESTIONS column, when Sid came in, laughing his ass off, which was something I hadn't seen in a while.

"This is funny," he said. "Kingsley McAdoo just stopped me in the corridor. He said he'd had a dream which revealed to him the perfect next move for Sandrine. Are you ready for this? Take a guess."

We couldn't guess.

"Here it is: She goes to work for Eleanor Roosevelt. She becomes part of Mrs. Roosevelt's all-woman team that does high-minded good deeds for mankind."

The next sentence or two was lost in another burst of Sid's laughter but I think he said that Kingsley's senile father, Chester, had met Mrs. Roosevelt a few times at journalistic events—she has a syndicated newspaper column—and could lever this connection to persuade Mrs. R to add Sandrine to her circle. Kingsley had seized the initiative and placed a call to Mrs. R's office, attempting to set up a conversation between her and Chester.

"I'm supposed to deliver this great vision to you," Sid said. "Consider it delivered. I plan on never mentioning it again and I expect it to go away, though I would pay big bucks to hear the conversation between Chester McAdoo and Eleanor Roosevelt."

* * *

Two MORE days passed and still no word from Frieda. Traveling was a mess because of the blizzard and I told myself that was the reason, but I was becoming concerned.

Then came a late afternoon call from Al Percy.

"Al, you're not going to tell me Sandrine is a hoax? Please, please, please, not that again."

"I didn't like your wisecrack about my suit, Lopritz, but I'll take the steak and I want it big and expensive. How about Keens Chophouse?"

"Always a delight to chat with you, Al, but can we skip to the punch line?"

"Sure. I'm obliged to give you a chance to comment."

"On what?"

"You know what. Don't give me the dummy act."

"Give me a clue. Or I could guess: Colonel Mustard with the candlestick in the billiard room."

"I'll take that as a 'No comment.'"

"Take it and shove it."

He hung up.

I was worried. Was something happening that I was missing? But I'd be damned if I was going to call Percy back and give him the pleasure of the upper hand.

* * *

An hour later Dawn told me to pick up another call. "This guy says it's very important for you to talk to him."

"Not likely," I said, but I picked up.

"Mr. Lopritz, my name is Roy Jervis. I'm a broker at E.F. Hutton here in the city."

"Working stiffs like me don't buy stocks, Jervis, so if this is a cold call you're wasting your breath."

"No, I'm not selling anything. I'm calling for my wife. We live in Port Washington, out on Long Island. I'm guessing you don't get out this way."

"You're right, my passport's no good for travel outside Manhattan."

"We've been reading your columns and we're interested in this person you call the Dutchman."

"Yeah, lots of calls on him."

"I don't suppose you would give me his real name?"

"No, not a chance. It's Top Secret."

"Would his name be Hendrik Drusen?"

That shocked me right out of my wiseass patter. I went speechless and he took my silence as confirmation.

"I'd like to invite you and Mr. Drusen to visit tomorrow. Come to the Port Washington high school around four. Go to the principal's office and ask for Mrs. Jervis."

"Maybe I have better things to do," I said.

"You don't," he said, hanging up.

CHAPTER 28

Frieda, after a five-day absence and not a single call, burst in around eight Monday night. She was glowing, ecstatic, as if she'd won the Oscar. I deduced that she had not been anywhere near a deathbed.

"Chick, my life is taking off," she said breathlessly "I'm so happy. And I owe so much to you. We'll be so happy together."

She held a large manila envelope. "They gave me copies. Let's go into the bedroom where I can lay them out on the bed."

I followed her into the bedroom where she speedily arranged a layout of about two dozen eight-by-ten glossy photos. Nude photos of herself. I was stunned not just by the nudity but the ultra professional quality of the photography.

"They're great, aren't they? This guy Ted is America's foremost glamour photographer. And a really nice guy. He had a crew of ten or twelve people. We worked really hard but it went great. And we drove to someplace outside Chicago for the exteriors, a place that looks kind of like France. Start with this one."

It showed Frieda on a giant motorcycle, seen from over the handlebars as if she were driving toward you. She wore a tight pink T-shirt with nipples perking through. Blonde hair whipped by the wind. Fabulous smile.

"This will be the cover shot."

"The cover of what?"

"*Playboy*! What else? Can you believe it? I'm on the *cover.*"

"You're the Playmate? Miss March? Or April? Whatever."

"No. Better than that. It's a special feature, SANDRINE UNVEILED. Six pages of shots of me plus everything about my life story, like riding the motorcycle in France and writing songs. All the info is taken from your columns and I insisted you get credit in the text."

I was not enraged. I was dumbfounded. Incredulous. Her beauty didn't surprise me but I couldn't believe how completely her enthusiasm overrode any reality about how I'd react or how America would react.

There were shots in a luxurious bedroom and shots of her standing naked as she contemplated a sunset over supposedly French farmland. The poses were natural and graceful—the camera loved her. Her legs were sleek and silky, her breasts were mountainous fantasies. There was a series of shots showing her sitting in a large wicker chair, wearing only wire-rimmed glasses and holding a strategically placed pad and pencil.

"That's me writing a song," she gushed.

"You write music naked? Well, Beethoven and Mozart always wrote nude, why not you?"

She gave me a playful poke.

I could understand the thrill of seeing yourself looking so good in such brilliant photos. Frieda was a perfect nude without any lighting, editing, retouching, or air-brushing, but in these photos, she was *beyond* perfect, almost supernatural. Almost—am I being unfair?—cartoonish.

"Ted said he took more than two thousand shots over three days of shooting. These are the winners. Hef makes the final selections."

"Hef meaning Hugh Hefner?"

"Yes, he was so nice."

"You met him?"

"Sure. He stopped in at one of the photo sessions. He said he'd thrown out his plans for the next issue as soon as he found out I was gettable. He said it was a titanic scoop for *Playboy*. They were going to run a pictorial on Bardot but they bumped it back a month because I'm so hot now. There's going to be a big publicity campaign. Press releases have gone out already. I'll have to make appearances all over the country. The wheels are already turning."

Publicity wheels. Some of those wheels must have run over Al Percy. This must be what he wanted me to comment about. He had the story: Sandrine Goes Nude. It would be played out with an enormous lack of subtlety.

"You know what Hef said? He said he'd read all your columns about Sandrine and was dying to do a photo spread on me but didn't know how to reach me until I did Sullivan and then Danny called to offer me for a pictorial."

"Danny is connected to Hugh Hefner?"

"Yeah, they're very close. Danny is Hef's man in Vegas. When Hef needs something Danny is his Number One call."

"What about Danny's mother?"

"I haven't seen her for a few years."

"She's not dying?"

"No, that was a fib. I'm sorry, Chick. Danny made it up because he said you'd get in the way or slow down the *Playboy* thing and we had to act fast. I'm making real money for this, Chick. Thousands of dollars. "

"What's Danny getting?"

"He gets a fee, of course. He deserves it."

"What's his fee?"

"He asked for fifty percent but I told him I absolutely won't go above thirty-five."

"Thirty-five is quite a cut. And thirty-five of what?"

"That's still being negotiated but it'll be big. And the *Playboy* exposure will boost my price way up and I'll make a ton more when we sign for the Vegas revue."

"I thought we agreed not to do the Vegas revue."

"But the timing is so perfect. *Playboy*, then Vegas, then maybe Hollywood. I've never had money. I think of the things I had to do in Germany just to eat. Now I'm going to be rich. My dreams are coming true. Which is your favorite shot, Chick?"

I felt some sort of inner trembling as the shock of this set in. I couldn't come to grips with the contrast between her unabashed pleasure and the disaster she'd created.

She said, "I like this one, with me wearing a beret. Very French and artistic, yes?"

Of course the beret was the only thing she was wearing. It was an outdoor shot, a side view of her strumming a guitar as she sat cross-legged on an old stone wall.

"It was really cold, sitting there naked. No problem getting erect nipples."

I was supposed to laugh but I couldn't.

"What's wrong, Chick?" she said, staring into my face, clutching my arm. "Don't you like it? Maybe you like the indoor shots better. Do they excite you?"

She grabbed and stroked me, looking for proof that I was aroused. She didn't find what she was looking for.

"Aren't you happy for me? Tell me you're happy for me."

"I'm happy for you."

That's what I said but not what I meant. What I should have said was, "I'm happy for you, *Frieda*, I'm not happy for you, *Sandrine*. Because you've pretty much demolished Sandrine."

"Then what's wrong?"

She didn't get it. It never occurred to her how appalled I was at what she'd done.

I felt my temper rising. I didn't want her to get hurt when the explosion came.

"Gotta run out for a while," I said.

* * *

I WANDERED around and ended up in Smith's Bar.

No one was sitting at the far end of the bar so that's where I plopped down. I ordered a double scotch. I looked up at the TV and caught a news story about Elvis Presley entering the army. As I sat at the bar focused on whether my life had been ruined, poor Elvis also faced adversity: He was being led to an army barbershop to have his famous hair shaved off.

The Elvis story was a brief distraction but no match for the foulness of my mood as I assessed my recent stupidity. Of course I should have seen this coming. Frieda could not resist a cunning conniver like Danny Chone. Neither she nor Danny saw Sandrine as anything but a big bucks opportunity.

I tried to direct some fury at Frieda but fury wasn't coming. Asking her to be a virtuous Sandrine was like asking the dog to refuse the biscuit—she just couldn't do it. With show business nightlife in Los Angeles and Las Vegas as her only exposure to American culture, she never learned how fiercely Americans reacted against all but the most sanitized sexual expression. She had no inkling of how Americans would regard a woman who smiled so wholesomely while flaunting her tits in a magazine many regarded as pornographic.

My scotch arrived. I took a big slug and looked down the bar to where I'd sat with Dawn the day she confronted Drusen. How would Drusen feel turning the pages of the next *Playboy*?

I forgave Frieda for screwing herself. I even forgave her for screwing me. What I couldn't forgive her for was the same thing I couldn't forgive myself for: screwing the readers who trusted my column and swallowed my fictions about Sandrine, who wrote worshipful letters to her and wore TSBL buttons, and perhaps cherished fantasies of personally knowing her, exchanging gentle intimacies with her. We'd done a bad thing to those people.

Frieda also screwed the McAdoos. I had no affection for the Anus Brothers but there'd be no more Sandrine columns to sell papers and circulation would drop. The paper would be tremendously embarrassed and its future would become even more tenuous, which I didn't like because I was a pro-newspaper guy. Sid, just because he was my boss, was probably a goner. Dawn would be thrown out with the trash—the trash being me. That stung more than anything. What would I say to her mom and dad?

As for myself, I had no defense. I was guilty of everything. There'd be no mercy from Al Percy, who would lead a chorus of guffaws at my humiliation. Rival columnists, who'd envied my Sandrine glory, would join in. A righteous public would revel in my downfall. Proper women would glare and scold. Cabbies would lean out their windows waving fists or giving me the finger.

I hoped it could be kept from Alida. That would entail more lying. The lying would never end.

I called Dawn. "Where have you been?" she said. "I've been trying to reach you. Everybody here's gone crazy."

I asked if we'd received a press release from *Playboy*.

"Yes, that's what I've been trying to call about. I have it right in front of me. Chick, this is atrocious. How could she do this?"

"She had to do it. It's who she is."

"How about you? How are you?"

"I'm fucked, Dawn. You're fucked too. Sid's fucked. The Anus boys are fucked."

"I saw this coming from the first night," she said. Then she added, "Sorry, I shouldn't say that."

"I'll get in early tomorrow. Have the firing squad ready."

"It'll be ready. Count on it."

I slurped down the last of the scotch and grabbed a cab to Chez Dee.

* * *

IT's A movie scene or maybe a Sinatra album cover: I'm speeding downtown on a bitter cold night, my woman's done me wrong, my career's in the toilet, and I've had the first of many drinks. There's some serious self-pity ahead, some solitary brooding and maudlin moping at the bar. The most I can hope for is some cool and consoling music in a relaxed saloon.

And I got it, from Elvire. I marveled once again at how far she'd come in a short time. The voice was braver. Her songs were worldly and deeply felt. She was still petite but no longer seemed lightweight. She was singing when I walked in and waved to me as I sat down.

Dee joined me, reading me in a glance, knowing something grim had happened. I didn't mouse around, jumping right into the story of the Danny, Johnny Stomp, and Lana Turner dinner leading up to the *Playboy* bombshell.

"A painless way out was never in the cards," Dee said. "I'm sorry, Chick. I know it hurts."

"The *Playboy* story's going to hit with tomorrow's headlines. It'll spread like the clap."

Elvire finished her set. Dee rose and intercepted her on the way to my table and whispered to her for a moment. Elvire sat down with me and we kissed, which surprised both of us. It was our first kiss, spontaneous and long-lasting because neither of us backed off.

I stayed around until closing time. By then I'd told Elvire I was finished with Frieda, though Frieda was probably asleep in my bed. I couldn't face joining her.

"Why don't you let Dee drive us back to her house in Jersey. She's got plenty of beds. Or you could sleep in mine."

CHAPTER 29

I was fired as expected but there were a few twists along the way.

The papers went hog-wild with the *Playboy* story and Al Percy was the wildest hog in the pigpen. The photo of Sandrine on the motorcycle was blown up to cover the whole front page of his paper's early edition. A censor's puritanical black tape made Xs over her nipples.

The word **SHOCKING!** was plastered across the top of the photo and beneath it was this:

DREAM GIRL GOES DIRTY
SANDRINE STARK NUDE IN *PLAYBOY*

Al led the way in florid fulmination. He called Sandrine "the goddess who became an exhibitionist, the songbird who went naked as a jaybird, the princess who traded adoration for remuneration."

On and on like that. He would have included my comment, if I'd given one, but I'm glad I didn't because I would have looked defensive and pathetic. Al treated himself to a field day until—in my view, anyway—he ran into a logical complication, his own earlier story that Sandrine was a hoax. If Sandrine was a hoax, she didn't qualify as a goddess, songbird, or princess. Her nudity was no more than ordinary cheesecake. Al tried to play it both ways.

I made this point in a phone call with Dawn who told me *Playboy* had noted the hoax allegation in its press release but, obviously not wanting to undercut the thrill value of its Sandrine pictorial, tried to brush it off as "journalistic penis envy" by other tabloids.

Then the story changed.

The effort by *Playboy* to sidestep the hoax issue blew up in Hugh Hefner's face. My guess was that his Las Vegas amigos who knew and recognized Frieda were calling reporters or Hefner himself to tell him he'd been hoodwinked: Far from unveiling a superstar, his Sandrine was only an aging former daffodil whose nudity had been devalued by hundreds of naked nights on Vegas stages. She was not worthy of an exclusive splash in *Playboy*.

It was highly embarrassing to the magazine, and newspaper coverage pounced on that with great relish in later editions. The impact of Sandrine's nudity receded as the story became Hugh Hefner's humiliation.

PLAYBOY DUPED BY SANDRINE HOAX
SHE CONNED US—AND HEFNER TOO

VEGAS BIMBO PLAYED SANDRINE

That was the cruel end of Sandrine D'Avignon.

It was also the end of Frieda's dreams of glory because *Playboy* identified her by name. She was disgraced. So was my newspaper. So was I. Mea fucking culpa.

* * *

THE SANDRINE flame-out was an irresistible story. I saw readers lined up at newsstands to buy papers as I headed downtown to attend my execution.

What I noticed entering the newsroom was that everyone reached for the closest telephone, urging colleagues to hurry if they wanted to observe the spectacle of my beheading. It occurred to me that I'd been in that situation before and escaped. This time there'd be no reprieve.

MacAndrew Warren Tisdale stepped out of the elevator on the newsroom floor and looked around as if he were inhaling the odor of a men's public toilet in Istanbul. His presence was greeted by the hush that falls over a place when the lord high executioner arrives. The immaculate Tisdale was an incongruous sight striding through the slobs of the newsroom in his lawyer-gray pinstripes, his gleaming black shoes, and his razor haircut.

I had never witnessed a big-time firing; I was curious to see how it was done.

Tisdale entered my office, followed by Sid.

Glaring at me he said, "Get the fuck out of here."

"I was afraid you'd sugarcoat it," I said.

"I'll give you five minutes. Then burly guards will hurl you out on the street and your meager belongings will be thrown out after you. Your column is finished. Sandrine is finished. You are finished. Your career in journalism is finished."

"Why is everything Finnish? What about Swedish?"

Dawn laughed but Tisdale was slow to get the joke, which caused him to redden in furious chagrin.

I asked, "Do I need to see the Anus Brothers?"

"Who? No. They're busy in meetings about saving this newspaper. And we don't tolerate that repulsive nickname. If there's an anus here, it's you, asshole."

It was not a dignified exit line for a Yale man but he had nothing else in the tank. He did an about-face and marched out, flashing a you-could-be-next glower at everyone in the newsroom who dared eye contact.

Well. That was a succinct career ending.

Sid said, "Tell ya what: I'll take you to lunch. At a restaurant where no one will know us. We can get blotto."

He noticed Dawn sitting there looking miserable. and said, "You too, Dawn. Join us. Our last lunch."

* * *

SID AND Dawn were confident they'd be fired too. Sid said the newsroom's over/under betting number for him was four days, but he'd put fifty dollars on the under, wagering that he wouldn't last twenty-four hours.

There'd been no betting on the low-ranking Dawn. There was a chance the Anuses would *forget* to fire her. But Sid guessed that my successor would get rid of her quickly to erase every trace of Chick Lopritz and the Sandrine debacle. Did she have any chance of getting another newspaper job? Not really: she was still female and now she had the additional blemish of her association with me.

We ate at a dingy place in Chinatown. Sid drank a few Bloody Marys, claiming that nobody makes Bloody Marys better than Asian bartenders. I didn't drink because I had to make the late afternoon drive to Port Washington with Drusen and I wanted to have my wits about me. Dawn didn't feel like drinking. So we didn't get blotto but Sid gets credit for a classy gesture. Some other time we'll meet and hit the booze and have cathartic laughs about the Sandrine episode.

But one good thing happened at lunch. I asked Sid if there'd been any talk of who might take over my column. He said there were no candidates so far and the pickings were slim.

Without thinking I said, "How about Dawn?"

Dawn and Sid were surprised and I was surprised too. I'd never given a serious thought to anyone replacing me.

"That's flattering, Chick," said Dawn. "But we know it's not going to happen."

"You've learned everything about writing a gossip column and you'd be great," I said.

"I agree," said Sid. "And look, no offense but the Anus Brothers have no idea who you are, Dawn. If I told them we had a great candidate, they might bite, just to have a quick solution and they wouldn't care whether it's male, female, or snapping turtle. We could call the column 'Dawn At Midnight' or something like that."

He said he'd take the idea upstairs, shop it around, and try to sell it before he got axed.

We all felt good about that.

* * *

I HAD time before meeting Drusen so I dropped by Alida's. She was unaware of the Sandrine outcome but as she knitted and smoked, Frieda and I wandered into the living room to talk.

"Everything was going so well," Frieda said.

"You went with your instincts," I said.

"My instincts are no good. They never were."

"Mine weren't so great either. I didn't give you much guidance. It wasn't my kind of thing."

"It was Danny's kind of thing, but his thing always has a bad ending. I'm done with him now. I'll never see a penny for the *Playboy* shoot. And now my pictures are in every newspaper and I'm a bimbo and the papers are calling me 'Frieda the floozy' or 'Slutty Sandrine.'"

"Got any plans yet?"

"No. For now I will stay with Alida. I may go back to Europe where nobody will recognize me or know about Sandrine."

We had a good hug and that was it.

* * *

I STOOD on the designated street corner until Drusen rolled up in his black Mercedes-Benz and we headed for Long Island.

I hadn't told him much about what was ahead because I didn't know much myself. Roy Jervis had gotten me interested but said there'd be no further discussion until Drusen and I showed up at the high school in Port Washington.

We barely talked during the drive. I couldn't blame Drusen for being pissed at me, even hating me. I apologized. I also told him I'd been fired. He glanced at me with apparent sympathy but said nothing.

We were wounded survivors of the Sandrine saga. It wasn't clear if we were still enemies or more like former combatants who meet long after the battle and discover a surprising bond.

Port Washington is a nice commuter town, not quite an hour from Manhattan. We followed Roy Jervis's directions to the high school.

School had been out for an hour but plenty of students were milling around. We parked and went in, finding our way to the principal's office. "Yes, we're expecting you," said a woman in the outer office. "Mr. Hendrickson, our principal, isn't here right now but you can use his office for your meeting with Mrs. Jervis. I'll let her know you're here."

A minute later Mrs. Jervis breezed in, a slender pleasant-looking woman carrying a shopping bag. She was in her late thirties with cropped blondish hair and wire-rimmed glasses.

"I'm Sandie Jervis," she said offering her hand, which we shook while saying our names.

"I teach French and music here," she said, with a faint trace of accent. "Please sit down."

She studied Drusen intently and said, "So you're the Dutchman?"

"Yes. Mr. Lopritz has given me that name."

She said, "It is nice to see you again."

The word "again" hung in the air.

My heart leaped as I caught on. Drusen caught on faster.

"You are Sandra?"

"Yes. I'm Sandra. *C'est moi, vraiment.* Sandra from August 14, 1946."

"My God."

It hit him slowly. I watched his face crumple as tears welled in his eyes.

"Actually I was called Sandrine briefly as a girl but Sandra as I became older. But the funny thing, since Mr. Lopritz's Sandrine became famous, I hear my students calling me Sandrine. Behind my back, of course."

The woman lived in the present. Drusen was fighting to break out of the past.

"By the way I read the Sandrine columns with fascination, even before the Dutchman started appearing. It's been an interesting experience."

She said some more about the column. She was a chatterer, or maybe she was just nervous and pretending to be lighthearted. I could not imagine what was going on in Drusen's head and heart.

"I wasn't a good singer but I needed the money. I got up very early and went around to clubs in Montmartre that stayed open all night and they let me sing a bit around dawn, for tips. You gave me a very nice tip. Do you remember that?"

"No," he said, in a choked voice.

"I needed the money to get through student life. And later in New York, when I was going to City College, I tried to sing in clubs again but never got hired. Here's an amazing coincidence: one place I tried was Chez Dee. The woman there was very nice but I knew I wasn't good enough. But when I read about Chez Dee in your column I just about had a cow. What a coincidence."

"I searched for you," Drusen said.

"But how could you possibly find me? You didn't even know my last name, which is Tessier. The people in the clubs knew me only by my first name so no one could have helped you find me."

"I came back the next night. That is, I tried to. I couldn't find the club."

"Sure, it was hard to find. The streets are a puzzle. I was there waiting for you the next morning. But you didn't come and I decided you were just another soldier in Paris, getting drunk and falling in love for a few hours. I was hurt when you didn't show up. It was important at the time but I put it behind me and went on with life."

"I hired detectives to look for you. When I got out of the army I went back to Paris and had investigators looking everywhere, including the south of France."

"Why the south? I'm from Paris."

"I thought you said you were from Provence."

"No. I've never set foot there. Memory can play funny tricks, can't it?"

"I've thought about you every day for twelve years."

I could see that emotion was starting to hit her as she comprehended how much effort and heartache Drusen had poured into searching for her.

"Your investigators wouldn't have found me. I left France in 1947 and came to New York. My aunts and uncles here took me in and helped me. I finished my education. I became an American citizen. I found a wonderful husband. We have a six-year-old son, Richard, who we call Ricky."

"Ricky after me?"

She smiled slyly. "Do you have children, Hendrik?"

"Three. Boys."

"Are they as good-looking as their father?" she asked. "Time has treated you well."

"You're being kind. But you are just as beautiful as before."

"No, no. I am a suburban mom and busy schoolteacher. I don't look at all like I did then. I was twenty-four, now I'm thirty-six. I am certainly no Sandrine."

"You were to me. You always will be. Tell me—and this is what I've needed to know—was it real, that night?"

"It was magical, Hendrik."

"Would you have married me?"

"Yes. I think so. Yes."

The door opened and the principal came in.

"Clifford Hendrickson," he said offering his hand. "Am I interrupting? I understand that Sandie is involved with you both in a rather extraordinary story."

"More extraordinary than I thought," she said.

"I'm glad you've had a chance to talk," he said, "but let's try to keep it from the students. Who knows what they'd do with it."

He said this with a smile. We gave him back his office and Sandie walked us to Drusen's car, carrying her shopping bag.

"What are you going to do now, Hendrik?" she asked him.

"I don't know," he said. "It will take some time to get used to this but I think tomorrow I will wake up without the terrible feeling that you are lost and I can't find you."

"I have something for you," she said, reaching into the shopping bag. At first it appeared to be a squashed brown rag but I realized it was a military cap, battered and shapeless, its gold insignia tarnished by time and dirt.

She handed it to him. He looked inside it and found a name tag where he had written his name long ago in blue ink that was now close to faded: H. K. Drusen.

"You left it in the bar. I saved it for you. When you didn't come back I started wearing it myself because they say young women look cute in military hats. My son, Ricky, has worn it too. Take it. A souvenir of our night."

Drusen said, "Sandie, thank you for getting in touch with me. It's been very important for me."

"My husband said I had to do it or I'd always regret not doing it. I was too nervous to make the call but he just picked up the phone and did it. I'm glad he did."

We stood there in the parking lot, with me trying to be invisible as they gazed at each other for the last time.

He fit the shrunken cap onto his head, smiling because he knew he looked silly, and they kissed. Not a big kiss but a good one, maybe the best of his life.

In the car I asked if he'd recognized her.

"Perhaps not at first," he said. "But it was her. The cap proves it. Thank you, Chick."

Then I asked, "Are you disappointed?"

"Oh no, not at all. The opposite. A burden has been lifted."

CHAPTER 30

It already seems like long ago, but it was only two months.

I'm now sitting on the front porch of an old white house on Oxford Street in Worthington, Ohio. The house belongs to Elvire's lovely parents who are letting us stay here while we decide what to do next. Marriage is a possibility.

We've been together since that night in New Jersey. I wondered that night, sleeping with Elvire, if I had become a promiscuous dog. Frieda was in my bed at home, waiting for me. The imaginary Sandrine still had a place in my heart. And here I was crawling into the sack with Elvire. I told myself I was not an immoral sex pig: I had felt love for three women (one of them fictional) but in my mind they were all Sandrine. Therefore I was monogamous. This argument would not stand up under examination but to me it was the truth.

As I see it now, I committed a major sin journalistically and I will never grant myself clemency for that, but I've done a few good things that, to some degree, even the score.

One: Sid sold my idea about Dawn taking over my column, so I feel I did right by her. Dawn was very happy. Her parents, Leo and Betty, were even happier.

Two: I brazenly suggested to Elvire that Alida be moved to Worthington where she would become a patient at the nursing home where Elvire's mother is a senior nurse. Elvire's parents said yes to this without hesitation. Alida stays in the spare bedroom here on weekends and in the nursing home on weekdays. The change of scene seems to have helped her. She is in good spirits most of the time though she continues to decline.

I now find myself among very warm and wonderful people. They're aware of my role in the Sandrine story but it means little to them and nobody blames me or asks about it. Elvire's dad tries to teach me to fish, though I still prefer my fish on a plate in a Manhattan restaurant rather than swimming in the muddy waters of the Olentangy River.

Three: My columns led to Drusen finally finding the woman of his dreams and that was a great thing for him. Then I did some sensational matchmaking: Drusen and Frieda. Frieda got a stable and prosperous man who needed her; Drusen got a beautiful woman who was not Sandrine or Sandra but had briefly worn that identity and that was good enough. They were married in late April in Amsterdam. We received an invitation but we were too busy with the transition to Ohio to make the trip. Drusen sent wedding photographs showing a very happy couple. We have been invited to visit them in Amsterdam or New York whenever it's convenient.

Elvire retired without regret from her brief singing career. We had a great last night in New York, a party at Chez Dee.

Elvire is glad to be home again. She talks about pursuing a degree at Ohio University, which she'd attended for two years before New York, or getting pregnant. I'm fine with both or either. In the meantime she drives one of her father's two taxis and, guess what, I drive the other. I'm learning my way around Worthington and it's a terrific little All-American town, the kind I read about in the *Saturday Evening Post* but never really laid eyes on during my New York days. The spring weather is beautiful but they tell me the winters are rough.

I hear from Sid now and then. He was fired (in less than twenty-four hours) but the newsroom rose up in protest and he was rehired almost instantly when they couldn't function without him as a leader. His standing in the paper's hierarchy is diminished but he says he doesn't care, he's easing out. The paper has no future anyway, he says.

I'm not worried about Duffy and Kingsley.

Danny Chone—who knows what he's doing and who cares? I figure Frieda is safe from him now, out of his reach and under Drusen's protection.

Eleanor Roosevelt never called.

Alberta moved back to Pennsylvania.

Johnny Stompanato is dead. At our dinner in March, Lana Turner told Frieda she was going to break up with him and on April 4th she tried to do just that, but some things don't go smoothly. Johnny went violent and Lana's teenage daughter intervened to protect her mother, fatally stabbing Johnny with a butcher knife. It was like a movie scene and it made national headlines. Lana testified at a coroner's inquest the next week. News photos showed her wearing the same gray suit she wore to our dinner.

That's about it. My own life is no longer hectic. I'm no longer out till all hours and I haven't seen a celebrity in two months. I hope to never see one again. Sometimes I think about volunteering my services at the Worthington newspaper but I hold back because it might lead to a stirring-up of the Sandrine story and cause embarrassment.

But I do write. When I'm not driving the cab or sitting on the porch watching the high school kids race by on their Schwinn bikes, I work on my book. I knew a few literary agents and publishers from my columnist days and when I called them to pitch a book on the Sandrine affair, they jumped at it, because so many people had followed Sandrine's adventures and there was a big appetite to read the full story. I haven't signed a contract yet but if you're reading this, the deal must have gone through.

Now and then I get a hankering for city life and when this happens I take a day off and travel down to Columbus, thirteen miles away. It's no New York but I enjoy walking around smelling city smells, buying peanuts from street vendors, window-shopping outside the Lazarus department store.

I always check out the newsstands and I've found an out-of-town stand that sells the New York papers, only a day or two old. I buy them all and read them over a beer, always turning first to the gossip columns, always starting with Dawn's column. She's doing great. I think she has a hell of a future.

ABOUT THE AUTHOR

STEVE ZOUSMER grew up in the time and place described in this book—the journalism world of New York in the 1950s. His parents were journalists and most of their friends were journalists. His father was a writer and producer for Edward R. Murrow.

Steve graduated from Stanford and the Columbia University Graduate School of Journalism. He was a reporter for the Providence *Journal* and San Francisco *Chronicle* and served as a Navy information officer in Vietnam. Moving to television at ABC News, he was chief writer of *Good Morning America* and *20/20* and senior producer of *Nightline*. Then he spent eighteen years as a speechwriter for several dozen CEOs.

The Phantom Songbird of New York is his seventh book, following a comic novel, *Falling into the Mob*. An earlier novel, *"FAMOUS,"* was co-authored with Richard Liebmann-Smith. Steve has also written how-to books about TV newswriting, speechwriting and memoir writing. As a change of pace he co-wrote a book about the Galapagos with paleontologist Dr. David Steadman.

www.ingramcontent.com/pod-product-compliance
Lightning Source LLC
Chambersburg PA
CBHW020422180626
46812CB00003B/1107